CW00357912

WESTERN ISLES LIB

Readers are requested to take great care
possession, and to point out any defects that they may no
them to the Librarian.
This item should be returned on or bef
below, but an extension of the peri
desired.

DATE OF

. . .

. . .

. . .

. .

. .

.

34134 00148971 2

Leabharlainn nan Eilean Siar

The Fetch

The Fetch

Jack Gerson

WESTERN ISLES
LIBRARIES
F3982
WITHDRAWN

PIATKUS

Copyright © 1993 by Jack Gerson

First published in Great Britain in 1993 by
Judy Piatkus (Publishers) Ltd of
5 Windmill Street, London W1P 1HF

**The moral right of the author
has been asserted**

*A catalogue record for this book is available
from the British Library*

ISBN 0-7499-0163-2

Phototypeset in 11/12pt Linotron Times by
Computerset, Harmondsworth, Middlesex
Printed and bound in Great Britain

For my good friend Bill Craig
with much thanks over
the years
for many things

Fetch: n. the apparition, double or wraith of a living person.

Prologue

It was an afternoon in May when Alistair Matheson first came face to face with himself in Oxford Street. It was two years later when this incident came to the attention of David Sutherland.

Of course Sutherland had been in the United States for five years. He had been Visiting Professor of Economics at Harvard, had followed this up with a lecture tour of the States and then spent some time in New England writing a book on and entitled *A New Theory of the Principle and Practice of Modern Economics*, his theory concluding, at the end of three hundred pages of diverse arguments, that economics was such an inexact science as to allow for a multitude of theories, none of which was proven to be anything but unreliable.

It was after he had finished this work and was taking a vacation in New York that he was summoned back to London at the earnest request of the Prime Minister to fill the position of economic adviser to the government. It was a job he was loath to take, recalling the fate of other economic advisers to previous governments, unfortunate souls who had found themselves the centre of controversy, accused either of being interfering egotists or grey eminences behind imagined thrones. There was a large enticing carrot placed in front of him, however; he was assured that, after a short period, on the retirement of the present incumbent he would be offered the governorship of the Bank of England. He returned to England.

A few weeks later in the smoke-room of Black's Club in St James's he encountered an old acquaintance, Edgar St John

1

Clement. They had been at Rugby together, indeed Sutherland had been Clement's fag those many years ago. Since schooldays Sutherland had never liked the man. But Clement, who was now director of a Merchant Bank, had been a junior member of a Tory administration which engendered a certain false affability and an assumed knowledge of all that went on behind the seats of the great, the good and the not so good. And when he encountered an old school fellow, especially one heavily rumoured to be on the way up, Clement saw no reason not to cultivate an acquaintance. For his part, Sutherland did not feel able to be ungracious and perhaps hoped the man would fill him in on a political scene he had been detached from for five years. He accepted Clement's invitation to dine.

'Of course I shall go to the Lords,' Clement said expansively over the brandy. 'In the next Honours List. Not that it means much these days. Makes head waiters jump to it and all that. And the title on the odd board of directors is always welcome. Worth a few bob, eh?'

Sutherland suppressed a smile. 'Always.'

'And one does hear all the gossip in the Lords,' Clement went on, hands fluttering. He was that type, 'Always first with what's worth hearing.'

'I'm a little behind with the gossip,' Sutherland replied. 'I would appreciate a summing up of the political situation.'

'Oh, you needn't bother about all that. Gossip's the thing. You'll be up on all the New York stuff – must fill me in there, haven't been across the pond for a couple of years. And of course I can tell you most of what's been going on here. Let me see . . . did you hear about Cecil? Of course you probably did. Be in the New York papers, I'm sure. And then Norman and the . . . the Lady. Then there's Matheson . . . now *that* you wouldn't have heard about. Didn't get into the papers. Hushed up, it was.'

'Matheson? I don't think I know . . .'

'A Scot. Civil service type. It was a bit of mystery at the time. Was in the Scottish Office. Then the Ministry of . . .'

'Wait a minute. A Scot? Matheson? Alistair Matheson? I did know him slightly.'

'Of course you did, dear boy. And I suppose one might have expected it from a Scot . . .'

2

Sutherland frowned. 'I'm a Scot.'

'Oh, yes, but you haven't been in Scotland for years. Rather obviates your Scottishness, don't you think? This all happened not long after Matheson came to London. You did know him then?'

'Yes, slightly.'

'A pretty humourless type. Typical Presbyterian, Mouth and morals a tight straight line. Accounts for his story, I suppose,' Clement considered his remark before going on. 'Yes, only a Scot could tell a story like that. Fantastic. Weird. Of course I heard it secondhand but the fellow who told me . . . Aidan Mansell, the QC . . . swore it was true. Made me promise not to pass it on. Not that he was serious. Not that the story could hurt Matheson now.'

'What story?' Sutherland was beginning to feel impatient.

'I mean, he's beyond it, isn't he?'

'Edgar, I haven't the faintest idea what you're talking about. Do you mean he's dead?'

'No, no! But . . . you did know him, didn't you?'

'I said so. He was, as you say, a very serious, rather pompous soul.'

'Not now. Or perhaps more so!'

'What happened to him, Edgar?'

Clement waved the waiter over. 'Two more brandies, John.'

The waiter moved away. Clement turned back to Sutherland, leaning forward discreetly. 'Of course it's all insane. Obviously the man had cracked. But this is the story Matheson told Aidan Mansell who told it to me . . .'

3

Chapter One

It was one afternoon in May three months after he had first settled in London that Alistair Matheson saw himself across Oxford Street.

He was strolling leisurely along the south side of this packed thoroughfare when his eye was caught by the familiar figure walking in the opposite direction on the north side of the street.

He stopped with the most extraordinary feeling of recognition. Not the kind of recognition where one sees an old friend and comes to a stop with perhaps a raising of the hand in greeting. No, this was a sudden shock as if there, on the opposite pavement, was the vision he was accustomed to seeing in the mirror in his bedroom every morning. But here, there being no mirror, was some kind of image freed from the confines of frame and glass and taking on a life of its own. It was almost as if he himself was split in two and walking in opposite directions at the same time.

After the initial shock, with its attendant *frisson*, he made to cross the road, filled at once with an overwhelming, if nervous curiosity. Later he was to ask himself what else he could have been expected to feel? Certainly one does not expect to glimpse one's *doppelganger* in the centre of London on a busy street on a greying spring Saturday. His attempted crossing of the street brought the irate honking of a taxi's horn, and Matheson, suddenly flushed and damp with perspiration, jumped back on to the kerb.

He waited for a gap in the moving columns of red buses and dark taxis. As he waited his eyes scanned the far side of the street looking for the all too familiar figure now seemingly lost in the bustling crowd of shoppers. As if, his vision diverted for a moment, the familiar image had disappeared. His eyes then fastened on the back of a sports jacket not unlike one hanging in a wardrobe back in his apartment. It was a jacket he rarely wore, preferring as he often told himself the elegance of his dark business suits.

Matheson found a clearing in the traffic and finally crossed the street, switching direction and moving after the sports jacket. He moved quickly, pushing his way through the stream of would-be shoppers and possible sightseers until he was only a few feet behind the sports jacket. And here he could see that although similar to his own, it was of a different pattern (although he noted the tweed was of equally good quality).

His quarry stopped to stare into a window of Selfridges which displayed a selection of summer wear for men. Matheson took the opportunity to circle around the figure and stand, ostensibly staring into the next window of the store but in fact eyeing the wearer of the sports jacket covertly. And now he had an excellent view of a familiar profile. His own.

The man then turned as did Matheson and they were facing each other, eye to eye. The resemblance, so very precise, caused Matheson to flinch, visibly he was sure. He could confirm to himself the face was exactly the image he saw every morning in the mirror.

At the same time the man he was facing gave no sign of recognition, but simply stepped to one side and walked on in the direction of Marble Arch.

Matheson stood unmoving. Indeed for the second time he was shocked, this from the simple fact that the man had stared directly at him and showed not one sign of recognition.

It was a long moment before he stirred, but now no longer to follow his double. Without mutual recognition it seemed pointless. The man could not have failed to see him, yet had chosen to ignore the resemblance. Matheson had no notion of intruding on a stranger's privacy. He therefore proceeded in his original direction towards Oxford Circus and beyond.

Questioning himself as he went.

Had he been mistaken? Was there no real resemblance, only perhaps a superficial likeness? The day was dull and his

6

eye might have been tricked into presuming a much greater similarity than there was. The man himself would surely have been startled and perforce would have had to acknowledge his surprise. Yet Matheson could not, he knew, dismiss the incident so easily.

Of course he was determined to try.

He straightened up and began to retrace his steps, heading as was his original intent towards Charing Cross Road and Zwemmer's book shop where he intended to browse among books on the cinema, his longtime hobby.

While the impression in his mind of the encounter with his lookalike should diminish into a trivial and uncertain memory, something perhaps to be talked about amusingly over his morning tea in his office on Monday, he was still uneasy.

Alistair Matheson was forty-two. He was a Civil Servant. (The capitals were his own and underlined his vision of his profession. He was in the higher reaches of the Service.) He was tallish, six feet, with dark hair, greying rather neatly at the temples and thinning at the forehead, creating the impression of a high, almost domed brow. He was mildly vain of his looks, believing they were appropriate to his profession and the prospects of a career that had progressed well.

His forty-two years had commenced in a terraced house in Edinburgh's new town. (The 'new' was a misnomer. The buildings were Regency and the newness related only to the original Edinburgh around the Castle and the Royal Mile which were much older.) His father was a merchant with interests in a number of at first speculative ventures, all of which prospered. His mother had tenuous family links with minor Scottish nobility, her family distinctly a cut above her husband's, a fact she never let Archibald Matheson forget. Alistair was educated at George Heriot's Academy and from there, ignoring Edinburgh's own university, had gone up to Oxford. There he read Philosophy and Political Economy and secured a double first. He sat the Civil Service Examinations, came in the top ten and should have gone into the Foreign Office. But his mother, sickly and demanding, wished him back in Edinburgh and using whatever influence she had, obtained for him a position in the Scottish Office. Two years later she died, of what no one was quite sure,

7

although those members of the family without medical knowledge referred to her illness as 'melancholia', their Victorian euphemism really attributing her death to marrying beneath her. Even in these later years of the twentieth century there were those in the minor Scottish aristocracy who still held such notions to be valid.

Two years later Archibald Matheson followed his wife to the grave, weighted down by a considerable bank balance and a particularly virulent stomach ulcer which exploded with fatal side effects.

While at work in the Scottish Office, Alistair Matheson inherited a substantial fortune.

This he made sure did not disturb the tenor of his life. He climbed the Civil Service ladder with determination and a considerable enthusiasm for the job. His now substantial inheritance removed all financial worries, allowing him to concentrate on his progression. At the age of thirty-seven, if not through talent alone, then certainly through the aforesaid determination, he became Assistant Permanent Secretary of State. And was duly noted as promising by the Tory Secretary of State, a narrow man in all but his ability to do what he was told by the Prime Minister and who respected those who implemented his orders. Promoted to Secretary of State for Defence, he had requested that Matheson among a very few others follow him to London and the Ministry of Defence.

Matheson grasped the opportunity. With perseverance and ever present determination, the highest ranks in the Civil Service now looked to be possible. Three months before the encounter in Oxford Street, he moved to London and took up his new duties. His personal wealth expedited his removal from Edinburgh. He purchased a comfortable apartment in Chelsea with large living room, dining room, library and small study. He had two large bedrooms, one for guests (of whom he expected few), an equally large bathroom with sunken bath (a rather decadent luxury to his Presbyterian upbringing), an ample kitchen with its own small bedroom off which was to be used by a servant. To this end he employed a manservant, William Dobson, in his late twenties, a onetime footman at Buckingham Palace, who felt he had achieved his professional ambition to be manservant or butler to a gentleman of means.

Thus did Matheson with Dobson's help create a gentleman's establishment out of time with this day and age.

Also from this it may be gathered that Matheson was unmarried.

Which might indeed have caused some gossip at a time when single men, living alone but for a male servant, are open to all kinds of gossip.

It would have been ill-founded. Alistair Matheson liked women. He liked their company and, in a gentlemanly and restrained manner, their bodies.

He had for a time in his early thirties been engaged to a young Edinburgh lady seemingly ideal to become the wife of an up-and-coming civil servant. The engagement had lasted five months and, while Matheson himself was deciding they should marry shortly, the lady had unexpectedly proved her unsuitability by eloping with a dental surgeon from Stockton-on-Tees. Matheson had from this time on been nervous of personal intimacy with other suitable candidates. He had, he told himself, retired from such a competitive field to nurse obvious wounds. This of course had not ruled out impersonal intimacy on occasion with the more expensive professional ladies. These occasion were arranged and occurred with meticulous discretion. Not a word of scandal could be allowed to taint a senior Civil Servant.

Such activities, which Matheson told himself might be not unenjoyable, were also necessary to preserve his general health. While at university he had first indulged in this manner of liaison and found it adequate for his needs. Of course socially he met other unattached young women at official functions but, after the disastrous outcome of his engagement, leaving him stranded among the emotional wreckage, he became perhaps excessively polite and was careful to exhibit little other emotion. He would not permit himself to be so wounded again.

This then was Alistair Matheson. Until the extraordinary encounter in Oxford Street.

He proceeded on his original path along Oxford Street, down Charing Cross Road and into Zwemmer's. There he browsed, seeking volume one of the *Aurum Film Encyclopedia*, devoted to the Western film. Indeed the Aurum volumes, of which he possessed volumes two and three, were the most complete guide to the cinema under various subject headings ever published. The search for what he knew to be a large book temporarily drove from his mind the encounter on Oxford Street. He was lost in this preoccupation. Unable to find the book he was looking for, he turned to one of the sales assistants who disappeared to make enquiries while Matheson flicked through a thick volume of *The Memos of David Selznick*.

The assistant returned. 'I'm sorry, sir, but volume one is not in stock. In fact it is out of print just now. We may be able to find you a second-hand copy but it will take some weeks.'

Matheson replaced the Selznick book. 'I should certainly be interested in a good second hand copy.'

'If you'll leave us your address . . .'

Matheson did so, and eventually purchasing an American paperback edition of *Thalberg: Life and Legend* by Bob Thomas, left Zwemmer's to find the dull clouds had darkened and rain was falling. He flagged down a taxi to take him home. Not that he had no transportation of his own. He took delight in his Aston Martin, telling himself it had been, when purchased, his one unnecessary self-indulgence, justifiable only in terms of his sheer enjoyment of the style and power of the vehicle. Not that he used it in Central London – a car was no longer an asset in the Cities of London or Westminster. It was a car for the countryside at weekends when he would, on occasion, drive north-west to the Chilterns or to Oxford.

It was four o'clock when he let himself into the Chelsea apartment. He was greeted in the hall by Dobson dressed in a long raincoat and soft hat.

'You're back, sir,' the manservant stated the obvious.

'And you are about to go out, Willie.' Matheson always referred to Dobson as Willie. It was a mild informal indulgence which pleased Matheson and to which Dobson did not object.

'You did give me the rest of the day off,' the manservant replied.

'Of course, of course. Go now!'

Dobson hesitated. 'You are dining tonight at Mr and Mrs Groves' home, sir. I have laid out your grey lounge suit. A dinner jacket is not, I believe, called for.'

'Quite right. No messages from the Ministry?'

'None, sir. I believe young Mr Makepeace is duty officer for the weekend.'

Matheson nodded. Makepeace would never call on his superiors unless war broke out. And it would have to be a major war of consequence.

'May I get you anything before I go, sir?' Dobson added.

'I don't think so. I can make myself a cup of tea . . .'

Dobson, who had read Wodehouse avidly from cover to cover, was as always determined to play the perfect manservant. 'Allow me, sir. Pointless to keep a dog and bark yourself.'

The tea arrived in the living room seven minutes later on a tray with a plate of plain biscuits by its side.

'Will there be anything else, sir?'

'No, no, Willie. Go out and enjoy yourself.'

'Thank you, sir.'

Dobson was at the door when Matheson spoke again. 'Oh, Willie . . .'

'Sir?'

The memory had come back to him.

'Oxford Street, this afternoon . . . I had rather a strange experience.'

'Sir?'

'Have you ever . . .? No, of course you haven't. And anyway I must have been mistaken.'

Dobson said nothing now. He stood waiting for some elucidation.

'I was walking along Oxford Street and I saw this man on the other side of the street. He looked exactly like me.'

A small silence while Dobson, uncertain of what was expected of him, cleared his throat. 'I believe, sir, that basically there are only about five facial types in the world. When we see one of those similar to ourself, I suppose there may be a moment of recognition.'

'But this fellow wasn't just similar. He was identical.'

Another silence while the manservant absorbed this. 'They do say, sir, that somewhere in the world we all have a double. I suppose you may have been fortunate enough to come face to face with yours.'

11

Matheson frowned. 'I would hardly describe the experience as fortunate. Still, I expect you're right. But it is rather disconcerting to come face to face with . . . with yourself. All right, Dobson, get off and enjoy yourself.'

Left alone, having recalled the incident in Oxford Street, Matheson could not get it out of his mind. He tried to concentrate on the morning's *Times* but found himself merely staring at the print without taking in its meaning. When eventually he turned to drink the tea Dobson had left, he found it was cold.

After a time he dozed off and found himself dreaming over and over again of his double sitting facing him while he served cold tea. He was about to ask the double who he was when the dream seemed to revert to its beginning and he again sat facing his own image. He found himself unable to ask the question which seemed of overwhelming importance.

When he awoke it was after six o'clock, time to dress for dinner. And, in the dream, the question was still unasked.

Chapter Two

The dinner party.

Charlie Grove as host sat at the head of the table. Matheson had first met him at Oxford when they were both undergraduates. They had become friends, to the surprise of their fellows. They were such opposite types. Charlie Grove was an extrovert – loud, occasionally amusing, a woman chaser and a drinker, indulging heavily in spirits. Alistair Matheson was the quiet studious type, a moderate drinker and would-be connoisseur of good wine. Though not uninterested in women, he was hesitant, even timid, in showing his interest. It was the attraction of opposites. After University they had gone their own way, Charlie apprenticed to a merchant banker in the City of London while Matheson had returned to Edinburgh and the Scottish Office. They had kept up a desultory connection over the years, Matheson occasionally having a drink with Grove when in London on Scottish Office business, Grove calling in on him when in Edinburgh. But now, with Matheson permanently in London, he had been grateful for the dinner invitations from the Groves, returning them by taking Charlie and Nan Grove out for dinner frequently. Charlie was amused by Matheson's solemnity, impressed though he would never admit it, with his rank in the civil service.

Nan, the present Mrs Grove, was George's second wife. The first had slipped quietly into obscurity with substantial alimony, having divorced George for his adultery with Nan Massard, daughter of the senior partner in Massard, Grivas Frères, merchant bankers, London and Paris. George had needed little prompting then to marry Nan, literally the boss's daughter. He was now, not surprisingly, a partner in the firm. Nan was a pleasing, doting wife, ensnared still by her husband's aggressive sexual prowess. She now sat facing him at the opposite end of the dining table, indulging herself in playing hostess to a small number of prominent and successful guests. This she at once enjoyed and believed to be the principal purposes of her existence. In this she was out of her time; she should have been born in the late Victorian era.

Her guests consisted of two other couples, a single lady and Alistair Matheson. The Snodgrasses: Samuel, an industrialist beholden to the bank for a large loan, and Susan, a platinum blonde whose main hobby, interest and purpose in life was clothes. The Gosforths: Sir Herbert, was a tall, thin figure in his early sixties, emaciated probably by the many trials of managing his own considerable wealth obtained on the property market. He had recently been knighted by a grateful Prime Minister, ostensibly for services to the nation, in fact for a large donation to Conservative Party funds. Lady Alice Gosforth, equally emaciated and as tall as her husband, had few interests beyond the furtherance of her husband's career and the accumulation of wealth. From an old but impoverished county family, she intended to make sure her previous penury would never be likely to recur. Although she would never admit it, she considered that, in dining with such as the Groves, she was demeaning her social standing and was content to do so to assist her husband in his business activities. It will be seen that Lady Gosforth was a snob. But Herbert Gosforth banked with Massard, Grivas and transacted all his property dealings through the merchant bankers. It therefore behoved Alice Gosforth to mix socially on occasion.

The other guest, invited to make up the numbers and provide a partner for Alistair Matheson, was a not unattractive woman, tall with a good figure. Margaret Mower was a woman novelist, an acquaintance of Nan Grove's. She was a well-respected novelist who had once been nominated for (but had not won) the Booker Prize. A writer of some renown. Nan and Susan Snodgrass had both attempted to read her novels but had given up and returned to their staple literary diet of Mills and Boone and *Woman's Own*. Alice Gosforth never read books.

14

The Groves' guests had, with one exception, met before and therefore, despite their diverse interests and preoccupations, could relax, enjoy the meal and indulge in casual small talk. Alistair Matheson, while a fairly recent addition to the Groves' table, had met all of the other guests several times. The one exception was Margaret Mower. Nan Grove always provided an extra lady at these little affairs as a partner for Alistair. She could not resist playing matchmaker. But since so far nothing had come of these encounters, she was determined to shuffle the deck of her guest lists until something came to the fore. On this occasion it was Margaret Mower. A mass of red hair framed a face liberally endowed with freckles, this making the texture of the skin more like a child's than a mature woman. Yet certainly Alistair was more interested than he had been in previous dinner partners. In the first place he had heard of the woman. He had read and enjoyed two of her novels, *The Hotel at Montpellier* and *Summer Dead and Gone*; it followed therefore that he was attracted by her mind, or so he told himself. There were other obvious attractions. He considered she must be intelligent. Not that the conversation so far had been anything but trivial, small talk interspersed with occasional muttered business asides between the host, Sir Herbert and Sam Snodgrass. Nevertheless, he knew an intelligent mind had written *The Hotel at Montpellier*.

They had finished the coffee and the men were selecting cigars, with the exception of Matheson who didn't smoke. The conversation was momentarily flagging when he decided to relate to the company his experience of that afternoon.

'I had a strange encounter on Oxford Street today,' he announced to nobody in particular.

Nan Grove, the ideal hostess, leaned forward. 'Tell us, Alistair.'

'Sounds like one of those, "A funny thing happened to me on the way to the theatre" stories,' Snodgrass said with an inane grin.

'You said strange, Mr Matheson?' Margaret Mower did not yet feel she was on first name terms with Alistair. 'Not "Funny"?'

'I said strange advisedly.'

15

'Tell us,' she went on.

'It's very simple. I was walking up Oxford Street and came face to face with my exact double.'

A small silence while his fellow guests absorbed this odd piece of information.

'You mean, somebody who looked like you?' Charles Grove said, lighting a cigar.

'No! It was more than that. Like looking in a mirror.'

'Never met anyone who looked faintly like me,' Sir Herbert affirmed, frowning at the thought that such a thing could be possible.

Margaret Mower looked thoughtful. 'A mirror image?'

'Yes. Came face to face with him outside Selfridges.'

'Didn't somebody once say everybody has a double somewhere in the world?' Alice Gosforth said.

'If that's so, then I was face to face with mine.'

Charles Grove drew on his cigar. 'If you saw him, face to face, he must have seen you face on. What did he say?'

'Nothing. Oh, he looked straight at me all right, then walked on.'

'No sign of recognition?' asked Margaret Mower.

'No. Couldn't have helped seeing me, but no sign. Not even surprise on his face.'

Sam Snodgrass laughed. 'Didn't recognise himself, eh?'

Matheson shrugged. 'Which was why it seemed even stranger to me. I certainly recognised myself.'

Perhaps embarrassed at the likeness, eh?' Sir Herbert rolled his cigar between large, fleshy fingers before lighting it.

Margaret Mower said quite suddenly, 'A fetch!'

'What?' said Nan Grove.

'A fetch. I think it may be an old Scots word,' she explained. 'According to the dictionary it means an apparition, double or wraith of a living person.'

'Huh!' said Gosforth. 'Rubbish!'

Margaret Mower looked at him coolly across the table. 'Perhaps, Sir Herbert. Nevertheless the superstition exists.'

Matheson felt the chill in the air and sought to dispel it. 'I'm merely telling you what happened. It was . . . curious, that's all.'

16

Sam Snodgrass laughed, further removing the chill. 'Tell you what, if I met myself, I'd probably try and get some further financial backing from him. Me, that is.'

'Wouldn't he be equally likely to do the same to you?' Margaret suggested, smiling.

Further laughter came from the others with the exception of Gosforth who merely glared down at his empty brandy glass. When the laughter died, Matheson, feeling the subject to be exhausted, turned to his host.

'Tell me, Charlie, you still weathering the raised bank rate?'

The conversation plunged into business economics now among the men while the women came together to talk in undertones of the latest gossip in their not too far-reaching social circle.

During the next two hours conversation ran through the bank rate to the latest takeover bid in the City, the imprisonment for fraud of the directors of a large brewery . . . 'Only crime they committed was getting caught', Sir Herbert pronounced . . . and on to the rising crime rate and eventually to the Channel Tunnel now under construction.

'Rocky financial proposition,' said Snodgrass. 'In the short run anyway.'

'It'll pay in the end though,' Charlie Grove added.

'Make it damned easy for foreigners to invade us.' Gosforth glowered at his fellow guests, and particularly at Matheson. As he spoke he spilt cigar ash on the white table cloth. Ignoring this he went on, 'You're in the Ministry of Defence, Matheson. You must surely agree . . .'

'I think we're looking more to the Common Market than the idea that our neighbours might consider invading us,' he replied.

'Huh!' Gosforth pouted. 'If you can't think of that, think of rabies!'

Matheson hadn't thought of rabies and expressed his uncertainty as to its pertinence in relation to the Channel Tunnel.

'Think, man,' Gosforth pressed on. 'Bloody rabid animals coming through from Europe. Rats! Mice, even! Spread it throughout the country. Play havoc with our quarantine laws. An end to fox hunting, mark my words!'

17

The prospect seemed to worry none of the other guests.

Gradually the evening drew to its close. For once Matheson found himself pleased to offer to accompany his partner home. She was, as he had already assured himself, a great deal more interesting than previous females he had met at the Groves' dinner parties. Margaret Mower accepted graciously.

She approved too of the Aston Martin which he had brought out for the evening.

'Very impressive,' she said, settling into the front seat beside him with a small smile. 'I always knew civil servants were overpaid.'

'I have private means,' he replied seriously, switching on the ignition. 'Otherwise this would probably be a Ford Escort.'

Margaret Mower lived at Richmond. They drove in silence for a few minutes. He searched desperately in his mind for a topic with which to break the silence. This was his old failing: uncertainty, lack of confidence with females, resulting in silences. Finally he settled on an opening.

'I'm a fan, you know. Read *The Hotel at Montpellier*. Liked it. And *Summer Dead and Gone*. Very fine.'

'Thank you. I wonder if you'll like the next one. It has a civil service background.'

'I shall read it with interest.'

'And superior knowledge of the milieu?'

'Can hardly avoid it, can I?'

Another pause. She changed the subject.

'I was interested in your experience in Oxford Street. It was too easily dismissed at dinner.'

'That word you said . . .?'

'A fetch.'

He was conscious of giving an involuntary shudder and hoped she had not noticed. 'It's an evocative word.'

'Yes. Origin unknown, I'm afraid. Have you ever read *The Sinner*.'

'I don't think I've heard of it. One of yours?'

She laughed. 'No. A novel by one of your fellow Scots. *Memoirs and Confessions of a Justified Sinner*, by James Hogg. Known as the Ettrick Shepherd. Contemporary of Walter Scott. You should read it.'

'Why?'

'Because it's quite brilliant, before its time, and about a man who meets someone who looks exactly like him.'

'I shall try and get hold of it.'

'I don't know if it's still in print. I can lend you my copy if not. Of course, it's about a deal more than a man simply meeting his double. It's an attack on Calvinism, the belief in the Elect, and if you like a study of schizophrenia a hundred and fifty years before Freud had thought of it. If it was Freud. Anyway, if it wasn't, it, should have been.'

They were driving across Barnes Bridge now.

'And of course the double . . .' she went on '. . . he's called Gil-Martin . . . is really the devil.'

'I hardly think old Nick would appear to one on a Saturday afternoon in Oxford Street,' he said quite seriously.

'Perhaps not to just anyone, Mr Matheson. Maybe you were specially selected for a visitation.' She was smiling broadly now at his granite demeanour.

He tried to smile back at her, but found it difficult. 'Why should I be so honoured?'

'On the lookout for a good Scots Presbyterian to work his wiles upon. Probably thought you were a likely target.'

'I should have thought he would steer clear of practical types like civil servants.'

Margaret shook her head vigorously. 'Quite the contrary. Ideal target. Go where the power is.'

The Aston Martin took Richmond Hill with no effort. Margaret indicated. 'Pull in here. This is it.'

It was a row of Georgian houses long since divided into large flats.

'Would you like to come in for a night-cap?' she said.

'No more drink when I'm driving. Very much frowned on in the Service. Wouldn't mind a coffee though.'

She made coffee while he prowled her sitting room, very large, Georgian and pseudo-Georgian furniture well spaced to give plenty of room, two large, out of place but comfortable armchairs in front of the marble fireplace, walls lined with bookcases. He looked over the books on one shelf; P.D. James next to Muriel Spark, next to the almost complete works of Graham Greene, rubbing covers with Beryl

19

Bainbridge and Jorge Luis Borges, Penelope Lively bringing up the rear. He moved over to the large desk by the window on which stood a large imposing computer, practical but out of place in the surroundings.

'Studying the magic box?' she said, coming into the room with a tray in her hands. She deposited it on a small table in front of a large gas fire.

'I've been promising myself I should buy one of these,' he replied. 'Not that I'd know what to do with it. But it appears to be an item no home should be without today.'

She was pouring the coffee from a copper pot into two large mugs. 'Of course I only use that as a word processor. Invaluable to a writer. But as a computer, it's a mystery to me.'

He joined her by the fireplace and sat perched on the edge of the large deep armchair, fearful of sitting back and disappearing into its all-encompassing embrace.

'I feel I should learn all its functions. Apparently small children learn it easily. I do feel I should do the same.'

She handed him his coffee. 'It's not essential. Or are you just competitive? I hope you don't mind your coffee in a mug?'

'Not in the least.'

He studied her in silence. She was squatting beside the coffee table, ensconced on a pouffe. Her long blue dress had settled in soft folds over the carpet.. It was low-cut but not too much so, enough to indicate well-rounded breasts under the sheen of the material.

He said nervously, 'I must go soon.' It wasn't true. Tomorrow was Sunday, the day was his own, yet his admiration for her made him nervous, afraid he might reveal his timidity.

'As soon as you like,' she said. 'But finish your coffee.'

Another pause.

'It must have been unnerving, coming face to face with your . . . double?'

'Yes, I suppose so.'

'Were you unnerved?'

'Oh, yes, certainly. Strange feeling. Like looking in a mirror. May I phone you again some time? Perhaps we could have dinner one evening?'

20

Her lips twitched though she stopped herself from smiling. His sudden change of thought in mid-paragraph was so sudden, so unexpected.

'Yes, please do. I should like that. You say this man was a mirror image. That would mean he was like you in reverse. But side by side there would be differences. Or would there?' Her own change of thought in mid-paragraph was deliberate, an imitation of him.

'It wasn't simply a likeness then?' she added.

'No. Wouldn't have struck me so forcibly. As you said, unnerving. Do you enjoy writing or do you find it an effort?'

'Both.'

'Where do you get your ideas from?'

She sighed. 'Everybody asks that question. May as well ask where thought comes from.'

'Yes, of course. I see that. Stupid of me. I really must go.'

She finally saw him to the door. He shook hands formally.

'You wanted my phone number?' she said.

'Ah, yes, if you don't mind . . .'

'I don't mind.'

She scribbled the number on a scrap of paper and gave it to him. He folded it carefully and put it in his wallet.

'Goodnight!' he said.

Chapter Three

The next incident.

On a Monday morning in Whitehall Matheson sat behind his large desk in his spacious office. Brown was the dominant decorative motif but the wallpaper was a dull Ministry of Works green. Of an expensive dullness, befitting his station in the Ministry, it was overshadowed by the dark brown varnished wood of its surrounds. A large window looked down on to Horseguards Parade which made the room highly valued as a viewing point during the Trooping of the Colour.

By eleven o'clock, Matheson had completed three hours' work, ploughing through memoranda, proposed army estimates, and reports on the current state of naval establishments. It was now two weeks since his strange encounter on Oxford Street and the memory of it had almost faded from his mind. Indeed, when he did think of it, he could now wonder whether or not it had really occurred; wondered perhaps if he had not been mistaken in his impression of the man and the resemblance to himself; whether the likeness had merely been superficial. It seemed now more like the kind of resemblance that his onetime fiancee had seen in him.

'Robert Donat!' she had said. 'You look quite like Robert Donat. When he was alive, of course. In *Goodbye, Mr Chips*. The earlier part. He died of asthma, you know.'

She had been full of useless information and was sure to collect such facts that she felt might pander to his interest in the cinema. Later, before going off with her dental surgeon, she had applied herself to a brief study of dentistry and could talk with seeming knowledge about the alveolar ridge, impacted wisdom teeth and the various flavours in a new line of dental floss.

However his mind was now far from that Saturday in Oxford Street as he studied naval estimates on proposed reductions in civilian employees in Rosyth Naval Dockyard. Questions would be asked about this one, he told himself. The Permanent Secretary would be asked by the Minister to provide answers. And inevitably it would be his job to dig up the answers. Or instruct his minions to do so.

There was a tap on his office door.

'Come,' he said.

His secretary, Miss Lubovious, pale-faced and efficient, hair prematurely greying, came in. (She was in her early forties and of severe demeanour attributed to her almost certainly being still virginal and accounting for her nickname, Lugubrious.) She had joined the Ministry straight from Girton at the age of twenty-two and pursued a career determinedly up through the secretarial ranks, untroubled by marital prospects, attachments or sexual adventures. Her aim was to be secretary to the Permanent Secretary and she would almost certainly achieve this before retirement. Meanwhile she was content to be Girl Friday to the Assistant Permanent Secretary.

'Excuse me, sir,' she said. 'But I have to remind you that since the P.S. is on leave, the Minister is expecting you in the House. He goes before the Defence Committee in half an hour.'

'I have not forgotten, Miss Lubovious. You have the requisite documents for me?'

She placed a folder on his desk. He opened it and slipped the document he had been studying in with the other papers.

'The Rosyth business,' he explained. 'In case the committee gets inquisitive on that one.'

She nodded and seemed to relax. 'I hope you had a pleasant weekend, sir?'

Matheson gathered up the folder, mildly surprised at her remark. Miss Lubovious rarely commented on his or even her own private life. And what on earth was she talking about?

23

'Oh, very much the same as usual,' he replied, rising from his desk and wincing slightly as he felt a twinge of rheumatic pain in his right leg.

'You . . . you enjoyed your trip to Brighton?' she continued, a vague pleasantry.

He frowned. 'I've never been to Brighton in my life.'

She matched his frown with her own and then seemed flustered. 'Oh, I'm sorry. I . . . I didn't know . . . you never said . . .'

'I never said what?'

'At the hotel . . . when we spoke . . .'

'I haven't the slightest idea what you're talking about, Miss Lubovious.'

The pale face was now scarlet. 'Oh, it's . . . it's all right. Sorry I mentioned it. If you'd only said . . . but then perhaps you couldn't . . .'

She was backing towards the door now, her normal calm deserting her.

'Wait!' he said. She stopped, back to the door, silent.

'You are saying you saw someone like me in Brighton?'

'Not if you don't want . . .'

'You saw me?' Sharper now. Feeling a growing irritation. And something else. A tinge of fear?

'Tell me exactly what you saw, Miss Lubovious.'

'You see, I took my mother down to Brighton for the day. On Sunday. Yesterday . . . I do feel the sea air does her good.' She hesitated, face still flushed. Matheson was vaguely aware she lived with her widowed mother somewhere in Cricklewood.

'Go on.'

'She hasn't really been too well recently, and we always like to go to the Grand. For afternoon tea. They do it rather well with Devonshire cream.' Another pause. 'We were in the foyer. You . . . he . . . the man was at the reception desk . . .'

She stopped again, expecting some comment from him. Or at least a denial. She received nothing and decided to go on.

'You turned just as I noticed you.'

'Not me.'

'No, of course not. He turned just as I noticed him. And then you . . . he . . . he smiled at me. And nodded. I said,

24

"Good afternoon, Mr Matheson". And you . . . he nodded again. He . . . he was with a young lady. But of course she barely glanced at us. He muttered something to her and came over . . .'

'He spoke to you, this man?'

'He said, "Good afternoon".'

'He actually spoke?'

'I said so.'

'Did he sound like me?'

'Yes, I . . . I think so. Of course he did. I mean, I thought it was you.'

Matheson cleared his throat. 'Do you still think it was me?'

'Yes. No. Not if you say it wasn't.'

'I'm telling you it wasn't. What happened next?'

'I introduced him to Mother.'

'He didn't seem surprised at your . . . at a complete stranger . . . introducing her mother to him?'

'No, not really. And I wasn't surprised at his not being surprised. After all, I thought it was you. Are you sure it wasn't?'

'I spent Saturday night having a drink with an old friend, a Mr Charles Grove. We were at The Grenadier. That's a pub not far from my flat. Sunday, apart from a walk on the Embankment, I spent reading *The Sunday Times* and a new novel by Margaret Mower called *The End of Things*. I wasn't at Brighton, and as much as I would like someday to visit that estimable town, I have never yet done so. Certainly not with a young lady.'

'Of course not, sir.' Was it possible that the imperturbable Miss Lubovious was near to tears? He prayed not. He couldn't stand weeping women.

'However,' he continued, 'tell me more about this man who looks like me.'

'Well, that's it, Mr Matheson. He looks like you.'

'Clothes?'

'Yes, of course. I mean, he was wearing a sports jacket, flannels and an open-necked shirt. With one of those silk scarf type things . . .'

'A cravat?'

'Yes, exactly. Very neat, it was.'

25

'What happened next?'

'Nothing. He tipped his cap. He was wearing a checked cap . . .'

'Have you ever seen me wearing a checked cap, Miss Lubovious?'

'No. But then I've never seen you away from work.'

Matheson coughed. He was having trouble with his throat this morning. 'I do not possess a checked cap. I have never worn or possessed a cap of any kind.'

'No, sir.'

'Go on then.'

'He rejoined the young lady who . . . who took his arm and they went out.'

'You didn't see him again?'

'No. But I got the impression . . . probably from the way he was talking to the receptionist . . . that he was resident there for the weekend. Yes, for the weekend. You see, he handed the receptionist a room key. So naturally I thought . . .' She tailed off awkwardly.

'You thought?'

'He . . . you . . . he was staying there for the weekend.'

Matheson took a deep breath. 'Again I assure you it wasn't me.'

'Of course not. No, indeed. I realise now I was mistaken. And . . . and perhaps the resemblance was quite superficial. Yes, quite superficial.'

'You never found out the man's name.'

'He never gave it. Not to me, Mr Matheson.'

'You might have got it from the hotel register.'

'I didn't look. Why should I? I was sure . . . I mean, I thought it was you. There was no reason to look at the register.'

Matheson glowered down at his desk. He knew if he glowered at Miss Lubovious she would certainly burst into tears.

'Very well. If you see this man again, please try and ascertain his name.'

'Oh, yes, indeed. Certainly. Even if I think it is you, I will ask . . . you, I mean. Yes, I will.'

'Thank you, Miss Lubovious.'

26

'Thank you, Mr Matheson.' She now opened the door and was about to step out when again she turned. 'You really should be at the House now, Mr Matheson. The Minister will be expecting you.'

He stood quickly. Must not be late. Not for the Minister. Especially as the Permanent Secretary was ailing and very possibly would take early retirement. A chance for Alistair Matheson. He could be promoted. Permanent Secretary. Top civil service job in the Ministry of Defence. And if he were, he was young enough to go on. And even if he went no further, that job would guarantee his K. Although he would never admit it, it was his long-time ambition. Sir Alistair Matheson would sound good if it meant nothing. Might get him a table in a busy restaurant – always went down well with head waiters. Might get him on to a few boards of directors with concomitant financial benefits. It might even attract an interested female, should he decide to marry. Lady Matheson . . . Impressive. All this if he kept the Minister happy and impressed the Cabinet Secretary. Oh, he was in line if all went smoothly. It might just happen earlier at the Minister's request.

Thus his train of thought as he left the building, gripping his briefcase, and walked smartly up Whitehall, across the road and into the Palace of Westminster. The uniformed policeman on duty recognised him and saluted. That was a good feeling. To be so recently appointed from Scotland and already recognised. He acknowledged the salute with a brisk, 'Good morning.'

The meeting of the Parliamentary Committee on Defence lasted ninety minutes. It went well. Any question the Minister found awkward did not faze Matheson. He had the answers to hand. The Minister allowed himself to look fleetingly relieved as they came from the committee room.

'Thank you, Alistair,' he said 'Now I know I was right to bring you from Scotland.'

He came out of the Palace into a Whitehall darkened by a threatening rain cloud. Swinging his briefcase, he ran across the road and moved swiftly past the Home Office.

It was then that he saw the figure coming towards him. On this occasion dressed exactly as he was dressed: dark grey

27

flannel suit, white shirt, dark blue tie. And carrying a brief-case. As if he was walking towards a mirror and this time was seeing an identical image.

Matheson stopped. The figure advanced on him. And this time, as the man drew parallel, gave Matheson a brief nod of seeming recognition. No surprise at the resemblance but simply the acknowledgement of a passing acquaintance be-fore moving on, leaving Matheson to turn and stare at the back of the receding figure. At Parliament Square the man turned right, away from the Palace of Westminster and out of sight.

Matheson felt nauseous. Phelgm rose at the back of his throat. He moved back towards the square, starting to run, as he did, thinking how unseemly for a senior civil servant. He drew to a halt at the corner, searching for his own receding image. And could not find it on the crowded pavement.

He found himself shivering uncontrollably. His spine was like an icicle. A woman passed, staring at him curiously.

After a long moment, with some considerable physical effort, he seemed to pull himself together, straightening his shoulders. He turned back and retraced his steps along Whitehall.

Before leaving his office, Matheson made two phone calls. The first was to another government office building.

'Gavin Randall?'

'Who is that?'

'Alistair Matheson.'

'Please hold the line.'

The line went dead. He waited some minutes. The line came alive again.

'Alistair, how are you?'

'Gavin. Fine. Yourself?'

'As always. Hearing good things about you. Future P.S., so they say.'

'Yes, well only when the present P.S. retires, I think.'

'So what can I do for you?'

Matheson hesitated. Randall was an old acquaintance, after some trouble in Scotland a few years back at Rosyth Naval dockyard when a man had been charged with sedition. Since then Matheson had met Randall on a few social occasions.

28

'Not quite sure, Gavin.'

'Official business?'

'Again, not quite sure. Might be, might not be.'

'Tell me.'

He told Randall only part of the story; that part related by Miss Lubovious, about her seeing someone looking like himself in Brighton.

'That's it?'

'Yes. Probably nothing.'

'Very probably. Someone who looks like you.'

'Acknowledging my secretary?'

'She acknowledges him first. He's good-mannered. Thinks he may have met her somewhere. He responds politely to her. Nothing more than that.'

Matheson cleared his throat. His hand felt clammy against the bakelite of the telephone receiver. It all sounded so unconvincing. And Randall was obviously not convinced.

'You're probably right,' he replied. 'But once or twice around town I've caught a glimpse of someone who . . . well, who looked rather like me.'

'It happens. To all of us.'

'I thought you . . . your people should know. I mean, if it was deliberate.'

'Someone seeking to take your place? A bit far-fetched, don't you think?'

'Are they not always? Anyway, thought I should report. Thought of you. Don't want to make a fool of myself.'

'Right thing. Better safe than . . . and all that. Tell you what, Alistair, I'll get permission to put somebody on it to sniff around.'

'Not too much trouble?'

'No, no, our job. Let you know, eh?'

'Thank you.'

'Apart from this, you settled in all right?'

'Yes, yes.'

'Must have a drink sometime.'

'Yes, indeed.'

'However, as I said, be in touch. 'Bye!'

Matheson replaced his receiver and at once dialled the second number.

29

Margaret Mower's voice came on the line, brisk and formal.

'This is Alistair. Alistair Matheson. You remember, we met a couple of weeks ago at the Groves'?'

'Of course I remember you, Mr Matheson. What can I do for you?' The formality was still there and mildly off-putting.

'I wonder if you would care to have dinner with me?'

An eternally long moment of silence.

'I did say I would ask you,' he added.

The silence at the other end of the line was broken. 'That would be very pleasant. When?'

'Are you . . . doing anything tonight?'

A second pause.

'You don't give a girl much time.'

He flushed. Not that there was anyone to see him. 'I'm sorry. I've ben rather busy and then . . . I found myself to be free this evening.'

'I was going to wash my hair and do some work,' she replied.

Why were women always about to wash their hair? He said, 'Perhaps another time then?'

'No, wait. You weren't planning on eating anywhere very grand, were you?'

'No, not 'specially.'

'There's a very pleasant little Italian restaurant quite near my place. Why don't you drive out here, pick me up and we'll go there? It's all very informal but the food is rather good. Say here at eight o'clock?'

'That would be fine.'

Chapter Four

The Italian restaurant, low ceilings and walls decorated with Chianti bottles was in a side street off Richmond Hill. It was almost empty, with only one other couple apart from themselves. They sat at a corner table at the rear of the room.

'It's always quiet during the week,' she said, lighting a cigarette. She smoked incessantly between courses. Since he rarely smoked he found this rather objectionable. Yet he had to admit to himself, apart from the chain smoking, she had fewer faults than any other woman he had met in recent years. She had besides obvious charms and these, combined with intelligence and a degree of wit, pleased him.

'Of course you always get these little old ladies who come up to you afterwards.' She was describing lecturing to a literary club. 'They take you aside and tell you they have a marvellous idea for a novel. They then suggest that they tell you this marvellous idea, you can write it and they will go fifty-fifty on any monies earned.'

She was laughing as she related this.

'That is not done, I gather,' he said, unaware of his own natural solemnity.

'Not exactly. They're expecting you to do all the work while they collect half the money! Also they're rather apt to forget you have quite a few ideas of your own. No, I'm afraid it's just one of the occupational hazards of agreeing to lecture.'

'I've often thought I might write a book some day.'

'An awful lot of people think they could write a book. When they say what you've just said, you know they'll never do it.'

31

He frowned. 'I don't see why you should say that. There are lots of stories to be found in the Civil Service. And quite a few writers have come out of it.'

'I can only think of C.P. Snow.'

'There's James Allen Ford.'

'Two, then.'

'Douglas Hurd,' he ventured.

'He doesn't count as a Civil Servant. He's a politician.'

He accepted that. 'All right. What about John Le Carre?'

'Oh, spies, that's another thing. They're always writing books. Anyway, even if there are hundreds of civil service novelists, I still say anybody who says they think they might write a book never gets around to actually doing it. You know, that first blank sheet of paper in front of you can be very intimidating.'

'Yes, I suppose so,' he said, still thinking anyone could write a book if they just had time to get down to it.

They were on the coffee now and had covered various subjects, gossiping about their mutual friends the Groves and the other guests at the dinner party they had both attended.

'Of course, I can't stand Herbert Gosforth,' she'd said. 'So arrogant, and so little to be arrogant about.'

Matheson, who dared not admit he's been rather impressed by the man's knighthood, simply said, 'Yes, I suppose I know what you mean.'

'That man's another reason why I'm a Socialist,' she went on.

He blinked. In view of his presumed neutrality in the matter of politics, he'd always avoided discussing political parties.

'Of course we have to be impartial,' he said. 'Can't have any politics.'

'You must have opinions,' she insisted.

'On political matters I avoid thinking . . .'

'You can't avoid thinking!'

'Can't take sides.'

'You must. Even if it's only inside your head.'

'No. Not expected of you. To be avoided.'

She suddenly giggled. 'I hope you don't succeed in avoiding it.'

32

'Leave it to others, I always think. Like becoming a monk or a priest, joining the Civil Service. Like swearing to be celibate . . .'

The giggle became more pronounced. 'You swear to be celibate too?'

'No, I mean, swear off taking political sides.'

'But surely you advise the politicians?'

'That is our function.'

'Then, in giving them advice, you must advise one particular policy. Therefore you can't be apolitical.'

'We point out alternative policies. The politicians chose the one that suits their particular political philosophy.' He chose his words carefully. Trying to believe them.

'And I suppose you leave your own particular beliefs to this *doppelganger* of yours?' She stubbed out the remains of one cigarette and then almost mechanically lit another.

She had brought the conversation around to the subject he wanted to talk about.

'The man's been seen again, by somebody else. My secretary.'

She was interested. He told her about Miss Lubovious's encounter in Brighton.

'There you are then,' she said, which did not seem to Matheson to be a very bright remark.

'But he . . . he spoke to her. As if he was me. She thought it *was* me.'

Margaret smiled. 'Either it was you on a dubious weekend with a young woman . . .'

'It wasn't, I assure you!'

'. . . or your secretary made a mistake and the poor man, uncertain whether he knew her or not, was merely being polite in acknowledging her.'

Matheson shook his head quite violently. He would not believe it. Or didn't wish to.

'Then I saw him again myself today. In Whitehall!'

'So you saw someone who resembles you.'

'But in Whitehall?'

'Alistair, a great many people have business in Whitehall.'

'But this man . . . he stared straight at me and yet registered nothing.'

33

'His mind may have been elsewhere.'

It was true. The man could just have been preoccupied. But Matheson didn't believe it. The lack of recognition was, he told himself, deliberate. He was staring morosely at the dregs of coffee in his cup. Margaret stated at him, a sympathetic look on her face.

'You're letting this affect you,' she said.

'No, no!' The denial was a reflex reaction and he realised it at once. 'Well, maybe I am. It . . . it is disconcerting.'

'You mustn't dwell on it, you know. After all, what is it? You've seen a man who looks like you. You've seen him twice. And your secretary has seen him once. So what?'

'Maybe it's like that word you used. What was it? A fetch? Something not quite natural about a fetch, isn't there? Something outside nature. I looked it up in the dictionary. "The apparition, double or wraith of a living person". That's it, isn't it?'

'Yes, but that's superstition. There's no such thing.'

'I know. But I keep seeing him.'

They walked back to Margaret's apartment. There was a mist creeping up the hill and the streetlights seemed indistinct, casting pools of yellow light which swam and shivered before the eyes. She invited him in for a final drink.

He demurred. 'I am driving. Wouldn't do if a senior civil servant is picked up driving a car over the limit. End of career and all that. But I will drink another coffee.'

While she made the coffee he wandered again around her living room. The clock on the mantelpiece registered fifteen minutes to midnight. At the windows heavy curtains were drawn, cutting out any glimpse of the night. Abstractly he pulled one of the curtains aside and stared down into the street. The mist outside still swirled around the streetlamps. And under the nearest of these, leaning against the lamppost, was a figure in raincoat and soft hat.

As Matheson looked down, the figure, perhaps observing the shaft of light from the window and the open curtain, looked up.

It seemed then that their eyes met. Matheson recognised the face under the light. He took a step backwards, letting go of the curtain, once again surprised by the sight of his own features staring up at him. More than surprised. A stab of fear ran through him.

Margaret came into the room carrying a tray on which were two mugs of coffee.

'Quick!' he said. 'Come over here!'

She laid the tray on the coffee table. 'What . . .?'

'Come quickly! It's him. Out there.'

She came to his side. He pulled the curtain aside again. Her eyes followed his gaze down to the street.

She said, 'I don't see anything.'

'There, under the lamp.'

There was no one under the lamp. Not now, he told himself. Only mist swirling in the pool of yellow light. He turned away from the window quickly, feeling an even greater stab of fear.

'He was there. Under the lamp.'

She stared at him, her eyes questioning. 'Alistair . . .'

'He was there. I saw him quite distinctly. He looked up at me. The man. Again. My face.'

The questioning look became sympathetic. She let the curtain fall back.

'Come and drink your coffee.'

'He was there! I saw him.'

'Who?'

'He looked up at me.' He followed her over to the coffee table, glancing back towards the window and curtain. 'I saw him in the light. It was . . . my face!'

'Whoever it was, he's gone now. Sit down. You look quite pale.'

He stared at her, his expression verging on anger. 'How should I look? I've just been staring down at myself. Staring back up at me.'

She handed him one of the mugs of coffee. 'Drink this.'

'You don't believe me, do you?'

'I believe you think you saw someone like you. There was nobody there by the time I got to the window.'

'Perhaps he was making sure you didn't see him.'

'Was he? He was successful. It's not exactly the best of nights. That mist is quite damp. Oh, I believe somebody

35

stopped . . . perhaps to get his bearings . . . and then simply moved on.'

'I told you, he was staring up at me. I was staring up at me.'

'You opened the curtains. He merely looked up at the light.'

'But the man had my face.'

'Possibly some slight resemblance. Or perhaps you were looking for your own face. Alistair, it was probably someone who looked a little like you.' She took a sip of coffee, staring down at the carpet.

'What . . . what does that mean? Looking for my own face?'

'You have this on your mind, Alistair. And that mist distorts vision. You thought you saw . . .'

'I saw my own face, I'm telling you!'

She was silent for a moment, eyes still cast downwards. When she did speak, she looked up and stared straight at him.

'Alistair, you must be very careful about this,' she said.

'What is that supposed to mean?' He was trying to control his anger but without much success.

She replied very quietly, 'This thing is getting hold of you. You're getting yourself into a positively paranoid state.'

He was aware then that allowances were being made, tolerance being exercised. But with a degree of strain.

'I'm sorry,' he forced himself to say, while not being in the least sorry. If only she'd seen the face of the man under the lamp.

He stood up. 'Perhaps I should be going.'

'Finish your coffee.'

He hesitated. Then a strange, uneasy sensation came over him. He went over to her and, taking her arm, raised her to her feet.

'What . . .?' she started to say. He silenced her with a shake of his head.

'Don't know why, but he's back. I . . . I feel it. Come to the window again.'

Gently he propelled her to the window and pulled back the curtain. They both stared down at the streetlamp.

The mist had cleared at least around the base of the lamppost. The yellow light spilled across the pavement at the foot of the figure standing once again under the lamp.

Alistair gasped. 'I knew it.'

'How did you . . .?'

'I don't know how. I simply knew he'd come back. Now look at him!

'It's just a man in a raincoat.'

'His face! Look at his face.'

'I can't see his face.' The figure was staring away from them, head turned towards the foot of Richmond Hill.

'Wait, he'll turn towards the light.'

'He's not watching this place,' Margaret said. 'He looks just like a man who's lost his way.'

Just then the man turned his face towards them. And again Matheson felt the shock of recognition.

'There! The face. You can see it now.'

Abruptly, as if he had settled on a direction, the man seemed to make up his mind and strode vigorously away down the hill and into the darkness.

Matheson let the curtain fall back. He turned towards Margaret and grasped her shoulders.

'You saw. You did. You saw the face.'

She nodded. 'I saw his face.' It was said calmly, evenly.

'You saw my face, didn't you?'

'I saw a face. And the man was about your height.'

'But . . . he had my face!'

'Perhaps I didn't see it very well.'

'Margaret, it was my face.'

Another long pause. She stood staring up at him, her eyes wide open.

'It was just a face, Alistair. Not particularly like yours. Not like anyone I know. Nondescript, that's the word. Just a face.'

Somewhere across the river, faintly, a clock chimed midnight.

Chapter Five

That night, in his dreams, a face, *his* face, sitting across a table, stares at him, saying, 'There's a lot of staring going on. Me at you, and you at me.'

Which one is he? The staring or the stared at?

They are in a room. Four walls, ugly furniture. Like no room he has ever been in before. Smooth, light, Swedish-type furniture. To Alistair, so unpleasant, so cold. To both of them. You see, he could say to himself, I know what the Other is thinking. Or was he the Other?

He can see the room from two viewpoints. One, facing the window across a table. The Other, back to the window, facing himself. Either way.

One of them speaks. 'Who are you? What are you?'

'I'm you.'

A conversation inside two heads.

'You dress the same.'

'I could say the same of you.'

'I dress as I am.'

'I also. As I am.'

A long pause. Staring still. Looking for differences and finding none. As if gazing into a mirror. That's been said before. If one is a mirror image, then there are differences. He looks for them. He, Alistair Matheson, has a small scar under his right eye, a boyhood injury caused by a cricket ball. Ah, there's a difference. The other has the same scar but under the left eye.

But which one is in the mirror? And is this all in his imagination. If so, is there a word for it? Is this a form of schizophrenia?

'No!' Loudly. 'I am not mad.'

38

'Neither am I,' the Other, who obviously has a sense of humour, says smiling.

The scene changes. They are in Oxford Street. Outside Selfridges. Only it's a different Oxford Street.

Silence.

No traffic. Empty. No people. Just the two of them facing each other, some yards apart. Like a Western movie. High noon in Oxford Street.

'I am me,' asserting himself again.

'I am you too,' the Other asserts himself. And adds, 'There is nobody else.' Look around. Or he is alone. But for himself. Facing him. Nothing else in the world.

'Bishop Berkeley said nothing exists unless perceived by oneself,' the Other says, a seeming non sequitur. 'There is nothing when we perceive nothing. There is only oneself.'

Alistair can feel his eyes filling with tears. The other, facing him, is weeping.

Madness? Weeping without cause. Or with fear. Of what?

Schizophrenia?

Paranoia?

Struggling against it. Rising to the surface. Climbing out of sleep. Away from a deep, deep fear. Coming from terror.

He wakes.

The sheets cling to him, damp and sticky as are his pyjamas. Yet gratefully he comes into a familiar darkness.

It is morning, for which he is grateful. Pathetically grateful. And mercifully alone.

He was late in getting to the Ministry that morning.

Miss Lubovious, behind her desk, stared at him strangely.

'Are you all right, Mr Matheson?'

'Of course. Why should I not be?'

'You . . . you look very pale.'

In the mirror, shaving two hours earlier, he had seen nothing. Perhaps a slight darkness under the eyes, the result of an uneasy sleep. And he'd had a bad dream although now he could barely remember it. Odd how quickly one forgets dreams. Also he'd been nervous coming to the mirror to shave. Nervous of seeing his own image. Now that was strange. Nervous enough to cut his chin, quite a deep cut, nearly an inch long on his chin. It had bled profusely . . . when things bleed, they always bleed *profusely*. Was that a literary conceit? It had then taken him several applications of a styptic pencil to staunch the flow of profuse bleeding. And of course there was now a small scar across his chin. But he hadn't noticed his complexion as particularly pale.

'I'm quite all right, Miss Lubovious,' he informed her, mildly irritated by the suggestion. Thinking, One can be perfectly well until one meets someone who says, 'You're not looking well.' And at once you feel unwell.

He began to feel he must be positive ashen-faced. He went into his brown and green office and sat behind his desk. After some moments he glanced down at the papers in front of them. Disposition of Forces: BAOR. Proposed reductions in Armoured Divisions . . .

C.I.G.S'. Confidential.

He read the words, almost unaware of their meaning. Thinking of other things. Something about a dream. (What was that dream?) And words. Paranoid? Margaret had called him that last night.

'I am not paranoid!' he said aloud, nervously looking around after he'd uttered the words. As if there might be someone else in the room. The Other?

He was alone. Talking to himself.

Another word came to mind. Schizophrenic!

Again aloud: 'I am not schizophrenic.'

He added, 'No, I don't need a psychiatrist,' as if someone had suggested he did. But no one had. It was entirely his own idea. And he was dismissing it. Still perspiring. Yet it wasn't a warm day.

He looked down at another file on his desk. Costings of the newest naval armament, missile development reports. Below it yet another file. Something or other, he should know, remember what it was. He was expected to write assessments of these documents for the Minister. Work to commence today. God! With the other thing on his mind, how could he function? How ridiculous! Letting some odd incidents, the likeness of himself to some passing stranger, distract him from work of national importance and supreme confidentiality, restricted to only a very few top civil servants and their secretaries.

He pressed a button on his desk. Miss Lubovious came in.

'Sir?'

'These three files. They go to Stanley Crowther.'

Crowther was the deputy assistant to the Permanent Secretary. In fact, Matheson's assistant.

'You wanted to assess them yourself before Mr Crowther . . .'

That's what he had told her last week. But not now.

'I want Mr Crowther's comments first.'

'But you usually . . .'

'On this occasion I wish Mr Crowther's assessments first.' Repeating himself? Or another voice? The professional reasserted himself. 'With particular attention to finance and the options of the Treasury which are amended.'

Miss Lubovious and the files left the office.

He lifted the phone and dialled Gavin Randall's number. As usual it took some moments before he was connected.

'Gavin, Alistair here.'

'You don't waste much time, old man.'

'Because your people don't. Anything for me.'

'Not much yet. I did have the hotel in Brighton checked.'

'And?'

'Ninety-three couples there at the weekend. Moderately busy. None of them seemed to resemble you.'

'How did you manage that?'

'We have our methods, Watson. Actually one of my people took our latest file photograph of you down and showed it to the hotel staff. No one remembered anyone like you. Of course it doesn't mean anything. Negative results don't mean too much in our business. Character might have got by without any resemblance being noted. Or, of course, our information was wrong.'

'It wasn't.'

'Well, we'll keep at it. But don't ring me. I'll contact you if we get anything. Be talking to you, old man.'

The receiver was replaced.

Matheson sat alone, thinking about his other self.

A week went by. He gradually forced himself back into a work routine. Assessments were written, opinions put in print. After work he went home, watched television, read and went to bed

41

early. He meant to telephone Margaret Mower but kept putting it off. He wanted to see her, was definitely attracted, but so very unsure of himself. He was afraid she would laugh at him, would bring up the subject he wanted to avoid, the subject that was slowly ebbing away from his memory and consciousness.

During that week there was no recurrence either in dreams or reality, no sign of the double, for which he thanked a God he didn't quite believe in. One week without a sighting or a visitation. In time, he began to tell himself, he would be able to dismiss it as some momentary aberration.

In time.

On the eighth day he'd risen early and in his rush to get to his office, shaved in such a hurry that he'd reopened the previous cut on his chin. At the office he'd completed his assessment of one of the longer documents in a hard morning session and decided to give himself a decent lunch at a trattoria off Victoria Street. He enjoyed lunching alone. It happened all too infrequently; more often than not he had working lunches with the Permanent Secretary or with other senior members of the secretariat. But alone he could consider his options, form his opinions, even relax and read a chapter or so of the latest detective story he had borrowed from the Chelsea lending library.

The table he preferred was at the rear of the restaurant, in a corner, against the wall. Today he ordered lamb chops with mint sauce, new potatoes and broccoli. With a small glass of white wine. Waiting, he studied the morning's *Times*.

Having read the editorial and glanced through the obituaries, he looked up.

The Other was there, sitting two tables away, eating lamb chops, with broccoli and new potatoes.

Alistair started to shiver.

Strangely the aroma of lamb chops came to him, as if his lunch had already been served. Which it hadn't. Then the taste of grilled lamb was in his mouth.

Still shaking (he was sure it must be visible to all in the restaurant) he studied the profile facing him. His profile? The thin nose, the lines under the eyes, the pale complexion (which hadn't been noticeable in Oxford Street on that first occasion); it seemed too as if the man himself might be shivering almost imperceptibly.

42

Taking a deep breath, Matheson rose, brushing past the waiter who was hovering, and crossed to the other table.

He took a second deep breath and cleared his throat.

'Excuse me.'

The man looked up.

The mirror image again.

'Sir?' Did he add that or did it come from the Other?

'C-could you spare me a few moments?'

'A few, certainly. Please, sit down. Join me!'

'For a moment. We have seen each other before.'

'Have we? Ah, well.'

He sat gazing across the table as the man speared a segment of meat and put it in his mouth. He chewed it, very deliberately, swallowed it and looked across at Matheson.

'What can I do for you?'

Time passed.

Matheson said, 'Do you notice anything about me?'

The Other frowned. 'Notice anything?' Echoing Matheson.

'About us.'

'About us?'

'We . . . resemble each other.'

'Ah, yes. Do we?'

'More than just resemble.'

'More than that?'

'Like a mirror image.'

'Ah, well . . .' Another segment of lamb chop was devoured. The man had nearly finished his main course.

'You do see it?' Matheson said.

The Other considered this. 'People often resemble other people.'

'But this is much more than a mere resemblance. Look, my name is Matheson. Alistair Matheson.' He gave a nervous laugh, trying to make a joke. 'I shall feel very nervous if you tell me your name is Alistair Matheson.'

That would be rather a coincidence,' the Other replied. 'It isn't.'

'Then you are . . .?'

'Martin. Gilbert Martin.'

The name seemed vaguely familiar, but Matheson stopped shaking. There was nothing more to shiver about. This was just a man, merely another citizen, Gilbert Martin who bore a resemblance to himself. Although the accent was different.

'I'm a Scot, Mr Martin.'

'I do detect a very slight burr. You have rid yourself of it remarkably well. No glottal stop, no rasping vowels.'

'And you? You're from down here?'

'Oh, yes. From down here.'

'I'm sorry if I'm intruding.'

'Oh, you're not, Mr . . .?'

'Matheson. As I said.'

'Yes. Matheson, I enjoy company. And all you're saying is most interesting.'

Another hollow silence, dishes clattering in the background.

'I think I saw you some weeks ago in Oxford Street?'

'Possibly. I am often in Oxford Street. Of course I am often in many places.' A small, amused smile. 'I do tend to circulate.'

Matheson's waiter came over. 'Will you be lunching at this table, sir?'

Matheson looked uncertain. The Other – no, not the Other any more. Martin now, Gilbert Martin, spoke. 'Yes, please bring Mr . . .'

'Matheson.'

'Mr Matheson's lunch over here.'

It was done swiftly. The waiter prided himself on his efficiency.

'Very good of you,' Matheson addressed Martin. 'We do look amazingly alike. People will be quite amused.'

'Perhaps.'

'Perhaps they'll think we're twins.'

'Perhaps. Or perhaps we had an errant parent loose in London some forty years ago.'

Matheson frowned. The idea did not entirely appeal to him. 'I don't think . . .'

'Oh, but you must. A perfect solution. And quite delightful. You must think on it.'

Matheson was discovering a puritanical streak in himself. Martin was treating the matter with some levity. Perhaps that was the right, the best way to treat it. Yet he, Matheson, had allowed himself to become almost paranoid because of a small coincidence of nature. He'd been very foolish, he decided. Gilbert Martin was treating it with the correct casualness.

44

'I'm afraid I shall have to leave you in a moment,' Martin said. 'A previous engagement, Mr Matheson. Yes, a previous engagement. I shall leave you to enjoy your lamb chops in peace. You haven't touched them yet. I should do so before they get cold.'

'Yes, I will.'

Gilbert Martin folded his napkin, stared down at his plate and the remains of his lamb chops, and rose to his feet.

Matheson, knife and fork in hand, said, 'I'm sorry to have intruded on your lunch.'

'No intrusion. I like company, as I said. And get so little of the right kind in my job.'

'And that is?' Matheson said, and at once realised he was perhaps being too inquisitive.

'I am involved in certain social work projects. But I'm very glad we've met. Two kindred bodies, if not necessarily spirits.' Martin waved the waiter over. 'My bill, please. And . . . er . . . put Mr Matheson's lunch on it as well.'

He flushed, embarrassed. 'Dear me, no. That is not necessary.'

'My pleasure, sir.'

'Perhaps we'll meet again then and you will be my guest for lunch? I eat here quite often. When I don't have to attend a working lunch.'

'Ah, yes, the civil service is an exacting profession. Especially in the higher echelons. But we shall meet again, Mr Matheson, I assure you.' The Other took the bill from the waiter and gave Matheson a nod of farewell. As he moved off the light caught his face.

Under Gilbert Martin's chin was a small scar, the same cut Matheson had reopened that morning while shaving.

Martin walked smartly out of the restaurant. It was only then that Matheson wondered how Martin knew he, Matheson was a civil servant.

He was sure it hadn't been mentioned during their short conversation at the lunch table.

Chapter Six

Afternoon in the office.

Matheson had in front of him a list of questions on defence matters submitted to the Minister by various concerned Members of Parliament. The Minister required answers within three days. Running his eyes down the list, Matheson could answer half of them without documentary consultation. This he did in an hour, and summoned Miss Lubovious to instruct Stanley Crowther to find the answers to the remainder of the questions and submit them to him in two days. That would keep the Minister satisfied.

He leaned back then, considering his lunch-time encounter. He felt pleased with himself. He had met and faced his double. There was nothing more he need worry about. The likeness was a coincidence; the encounters accidental. He was even prepared to believe that, in the sighting from the window of Margaret Mower's apartment, he had probably been mistaken in imagining the figure in any way resembled Gilbert Martin. He had, he told himself, permitted the whole business to induce a neurotic reaction triggered possibly by his heavy workload, or even by the still recent move from Edinburgh to London. His imagination had been over-stimulated in an unhealthy manner. He probably needed some mild tonic, even a visit to the doctor in the near future. But now the best medicine in the world would be deliberate relaxation.

He accepted his usual afternoon cup of tea from Miss Lubovious, informed her he was not to be disturbed by anyone less than the Minister himself. When she had left the office he sipped his tea and sat back, closing his eyes, feeling warm and comfortable. He would even, he decided, smoke a cigarette. Although he had broken the habit before leaving Scotland, restricting himself to the occasional cigar, he now felt he just might indulge once more in his old vice. He kept a packet of cigarettes in a drawer in his desk for visitors (so he told himself) but so far it had been untouched.

He opened the drawer.

The packet was open and there were only three cigarettes left. Also a minute mound of tobacco in a corner of the desk beside the packet. He frowned. Miss Lubovious . . . no, that was unlikely, she never smoked, hated the smell of tobacco. One of the cleaners was a more likely possibility. They were of course strictly prohibited from opening drawers in desks unless requested to do so. They were also forbidden to smoke although this, he was sure, was hardly an enforceable rule.

He called Miss Lubovious in, told her what had obviously happened.

'I will speak to Mr Varren,' she said firmly. Varren was a kind of senior janitor in charge of all such matters.

'Please do so. It is theft, on no matter how small a scale.'

She turned to go, then stopped at the door. 'Your visitor yesterday . . . he smoked, I believe.'

'What visitor yesterday? I had no visitor yesterday.' Knowing he had spent the day working on assessments.

'The one who came just before I went home. I stayed on but then you told me I could go. But I can always smell cigarette smoke as you know, Mr Matheson. Unless, of course, he smoked his own.'

Alistair Matheson stared at her. 'I had no visitor yesterday afternoon!'

She blinked several times. He'd noticed, whenever she was nervous, whenever she made a mistake, she always blinked several times.

'But, sir . . .'

'Miss Lubovious?' As he uttered her name again, he thought, Such a curious one. Lubovious? Of German origin, he believed. 'I had no visitor yesterday.'

She blinked again, her face like white manuscript paper. 'If . . . if you say so, sir.'

47

'I do say so. You went down to Mr Crowther's office several times yesterday. Perhaps the visitor was his.'

Unconvinced, she said, 'Yes, possibly.'

'There we are then. I suppose this visitor had a name.'

'Er, yes. I . . . perhaps I didn't quite catch it. Something like Marvin. Yes, something like. Marvin, Martin . . .'

The chill was back. Like ice on the spine.

'I know of no Mr Marvin,' he said, saying that he had only that lunch-time encountered a Mr Martin for the first time. Therefore it could not have been Martin in his office yesterday. He straightened up in his chair, trying to dismiss the chill. Coincidence . . . Lubovious's mistake . . . he'd had no visitor late yesterday afternoon, indeed none at all during the day.

She had continued to speak.

'What was that?' he said.

'I said, no, you didn't know a Mr Marvin. Or Martin. Or Martindale. Yes, you do know a Mr Martindale. In charge of the secretarial pool. But it wasn't him. No, of course not.'

'You may go, Miss Lubovious. And, you know, I think you've been overworking. Perhaps you should take a few days' leave.'

'I shouldn't want to do that, sir.'

She left the office, blinking continuously. Of course she'd certainly had been working very hard, perhaps overworking. If he himself had been overworking, it was logical to believe she had also been under stress. He overworked, his secretary overworked. The way of the Ministry.

Alone, he lit a cigarette. And at once felt dizzy, head swimming, room tilting. He stubbed the cigarette out. Shouldn't try and take it up again. Disorientating. Affected the blood pressure. Almost hallucinatory. For a second he'd imagined he himself . . . no, not himself . . . Martin, Gilbert Martin, sitting facing him in the chair in front of his desk. Also smoking a cigarette.

He stared at the ashtray with his stubbed out cigarette still smouldering. Leaning forward he grasped the stub and pressed it hard into the glass.

He sat back in his chair, thinking. Really he'd let this business of the Other get him down. It had affected his nerves

48

more than he cared to admit. So stupid too. A man who resembled him had accidentally crossed his path two or three times and brought him close to some kind of breakdown. Nervous exhaustion at least. Yes, indeed, so stupid. Especially now it was over.

He should tell Randall.

Again, after the inevitable delay, he was speaking to the security man.

'I did tell you I would contact you, old boy,' Randall said, a touch petulantly.

'I know, and I'm sorry. But you see, I saw him again. This time I spoke to him.'

'Spoke to him, did you?'

'Had quite a long chat. Introduced ourselves to each other.'

'You did?' Randall seemed surprised.

'Yes. Saw him having lunch at this restaurant so I went over and introduced myself. Asked me to join him.'

'How nice.'

'He was a very pleasant fellow . . .'

'And probably didn't look in the least like you.'

'Oh, yes, he did. He looked like me. Well, quite like me. Which of course makes everything seem rather ridiculous. At least, all this fuss I've been making.'

'Well, that's nice to know.' Randall was being ironic. Matheson could almost hear his teeth grinding. 'I suppose he gave you his name? I mean, you were introducing yourself to him. And presumably he to you.'

'Yes, he told me his name.'

'And it wasn't, I hope, Alistair Matheson.'

'Of course it wasn't.'

'I *am* relieved. What was it?'

'Martin. Gilbert Martin.'

A short silence.

'Gilbert Martin, you say?'

'Yes.'

'I wish I'd been there.'

Matheson felt irritated. 'You don't believe me?'

'I didn't say that. I think I do believe you. I would like to have been there though. You see, we've been looking for a Gilbert Martin for some time.'

49

'Looking for him?'

'We'd certainly like to talk to him.'

'Why?'

'Some of that is . . . classified. Let's say his name has cropped up in some particular situations.'

'He's some sort of a spy?'

Randall seemed to hesitate. 'I didn't say that. I just said we'd like to talk to him.'

'We being . . .?'

'My lot. The Circus, the Firm . . . both MI5 and 6. Although officially I'm only supposed to know about 5.'

'Inter-departmental feuds?'

Randall sighed. 'They go on.'

'Anyway, my problem is solved. You don't have to go looking for my double any longer.'

'So easy for you. But I do have to keep looking for Mr Gilbert Martin . . .'

Matheson sighed. 'I don't suppose I should expect to understand any of this.'

'Right. Best not to. But if you see him again, I want to know. Give you one consolation though.'

'And that is?'

'We have a rather faded photograph of Gilbert Martin. Funnily enough, he doesn't look in the least like you. 'Bye, old man!'

He heard Gavin Randall replace the receiver, and sat for a long moment before replacing his own.

Ridiculous, he thought. Of course Gilbert Martin looks like me. Even Martin agreed. Randall must be looking for another Gilbert Martin. Yes, that was surely the answer. It couldn't be so uncommon a name.

He relaxed. No real problem then.

Of course, there was Lubovious's story about the visitor he was supposed to have had yesterday. She had to have been overworking. He'd had no such visitor. The woman was imagining things. Have to keep an eye on her. Wouldn't want his secretary cracking up.

He put the thought aside and reached again for the phone. Time to relax.

'Hello, Margaret? Alistair Matheson here . . . Yes, I'm fine. Really. Everything cleared up, you might say. And you?

. . . Good! Look, I know it's rather short notice but are you doing anything this evening? . . . What did I have in mind? I thought, the theatre. And supper afterwards . . . well, I'm sure I can get tickets for something . . . Of course I'll avoid these shows if you've seen them . . . Yes, leave it to me. Pick you up around seven? Fine. See you then.'

They went to see what Margaret thought was a rather inane farce, but Alistair enjoyed it. Donald Sinden played a lubricious Member of Parliament attempting to cavort in a seedy hotel room with his female secretary while his P.P.S., played by Michael Williams, vainly attempts to cover up for him. The inadequacies of the play were compensated for by the excellence of the performances. Margaret could only assume that Alistair was enjoying the spectacle of his masters being lampooned.

After the play she found he had booked a table at the Savoy Grill.

'How very grand,' she said, omitting to point out the Savoy Grill must just be a trifle *passé* these days.

Over dinner he told her about the meeting with Gilbert Martin. 'Such a relief, I assure you. I think you were right when you said I was getting paranoid. And I was letting it interfere with my work. Something I can't allow.'

She smiled to herself. She was finding in him a distinct touch of pomposity. At the same time, something in his story of the meeting with the Other had caught her attention.

'What did you say his name was?' she inquired calmly. Underneath she did not feel quite so calm.

'Who?' he said vaguely, toying with sole *meunière*.

'The man. The lookalike.'

'Martin. Gilbert Martin.'

'How . . . how strange.'

'Is it? Perfectly ordinary name. Probably hundreds of them in the phone book.'

'Gilbert Martin.' She repeated the name. 'Did you ever manage to read . . .'

He interrupted her. 'You know, I told a friend in . . . well . . . in one of the security agencies.'

'I didn't know that.'

51

'I told him what happened. Well, you can't be too careful in a job like mine. Agents of other countries always on the look out for . . . weaknesses. Breaches in our defences, so to speak.'

'Yes, I see that.'

'Anyway, it turns out they are actually looking for someone called Gilbert Martin.'

'You mean he's a foreign spy?'

'Oh, I can't say that. Not for sure. But they want to talk to a Mr Martin. Of course it isn't the same one. Not the same as my Mr Martin.'

'How do you know that?'

'They have a photo of their Martin. Can't be mine because the photo doesn't resemble me. Not in the least. That's what my friend says. Can't be mistaken about a thing like that.'

'No, I suppose not.' She seemed vaguely distracted, appearing to be concentrating on carving her *filet mignon* into small segments.

'Anyway I told him, as far as I was concerned, he could forget the whole business.'

'He agreed?'

'Not exactly. Wants to know if I meet Martin again. That's my Martin, of course. Not his. I don't see the point. But then, these people really are paranoid.'

'I suppose they would have to be.'

'Anyway, it's a small weight off my shoulders, now that I've seen and spoken to him. Just an ordinary character who has the misfortune to look like me.' He laughed at his own joke. 'Oh, and he did make the suggestion, not in the best of taste, that my father might have strayed during a visit to London over forty years ago. Hence the resemblance. Of course, he never knew how impossible that would have been since he never knew my father.'

She did not reply but stared into the middle distance, lost in her own thoughts.

'Another glass of wine?' he said, reaching for the bottle.

She was subdued during the run back to Richmond. He wondered if he'd said something to offend her and, as he drove, searched back through the evening trying to find a place in the conversation wherein he might have offended. He could think of none.

52

'You all right?' he said.

'Oh, yes, I'm fine.'

A long silence. Outside the car it started to rain. He switched on the windscreen wipers. At the same time he was searching for something to say.

'Sorry you didn't like the play.'

'Oh, no. It was . . . well acted.'

'Would you come to the theatre again next week? I could try for the National. Or anyway something different from tonight.' Thinking, something serious would be more in her line.

'That would be very nice.' Still preoccupied. But at least she had not refused. Perhaps she was feeling unwell?

'You sure you're all right?'

'Yes. Oh, I'm sorry. I was just thinking about something.'

'The novel you're writing?'

'Yes, something like that.' It was a simple lie, almost a half truth. Not the novel she was writing but one she had read.

He brought the Aston Martin to a halt at the entrance to her flat.

'Would you like a night-cap or coffee?' she said without much enthusiasm.

He glanced at his watch. It was one-thirty. 'I think it's a little late tonight. Perhaps I could telephone you at the weekend?'

'Yes. Do that, Alistair.'

She suddenly leaned forward and kissed him with some force and passion. He was surprised. It was the first time they had kissed and he would have expected something more sedate. Not that he was displeased. He waved goodbye to her and drove to his own flat with a sense of elation. He decided she was obviously attracted to him. The possibilities pleased him.

He noticed when he went into his living room that the light on the answerphone was glowing. He ran the tape.

It was a flat, almost monotonous voice.

'I shall be in the same restaurant tomorrow for lunch and look forward to seeing you. I think we may have much in common. And I don't mean simply a resemblance. Oh, and do me a favour – don't mention our luncheon date to anyone.

53

Especially your friend Randall. I have my reasons. There will be no trouble. This is Gilbert Martin, in case you don't recognise my voice. See you tomorrow.'

Chapter Seven

The day of the second luncheon.

Some time before going to lunch, Alistair Matheson was summoned to the office of his superior. The Permanent Secretary, still ailing, had forced himself to come to the Ministry. He wanted to ensure that everything was running smoothly during his absence. He also wanted to make his presence felt. If he was forced to retire owing to ill-health, he felt he had to leave his Ministry (for he considered the entire defence establishment his personal enclave) a smoothly functioning organisation. If he were not to fulfill his ambition to become Cabinet Secretary and head of the home Civil Service, at least he would leave the Ministry of Defence as an example of how a Ministry should be managed. He was also unhappy about the assistant transferred from the Scottish Office, and in his view, forced upon him by the Minister.

Alistair led the small group of civil servants into the Permanent Secretary's office. No one sat except the chief himself. The others grouped themselves on either side of Alistair in a perfect crescent.

Sir Gerald Leigh (he had received his K. two years before) had been a very tall man, six feet five to be exact, with a slim elegance. Now he was stooped, losing several inches in stature, and the slim elegance had degenerated into a thin, wasted appearance, the face ashen, cheeks drawn and fallen in, skin parchment-like and yellowing. He was not an old man, fifty-eight could be considered the prime of life in the service, and the nature of his illness had never been revealed to any member of his secretariat. It was however obviously some form of wasting disease and cancer was rumoured.

Sitting behind his desk, Sir Gerald let his eyes run the length of the crescent in front of him. His face was expressionless. This was not unusual. In the eight years he had held his present post he had cultivated a bland, emotionless demeanour. Within the great offices of the Ministry of Defence he had rarely been seen to smile and then only a polite, forced grimace at some pleasantry of his Master's. The severity, it was said, even extended to his home life. Lady Leigh was a pale ghost who only appeared in society on her husband's arm when it was expected of her. (There was a salacious rumour that some years before she had been found in bed with the driver assigned to her husband by the Ministry. The marriage would have come to lurid end had it not been for Gerald Leigh's determination to achieve his K. and preserve a career that would certainly have been blighted in the Divorce Courts). He only relaxed in the company of other Permanent Secretaries and there was purported actually to laugh and even to tell particularly bawdy after-dinner stories.

Now, having surveyed his immediate inferiors, his eyes, icicle cold, rested on the most senior of these, Alistair Matheson.

'Mr Matheson,' Sir Gerald said. 'You have, I appreciate, only been with this Ministry for two months. You were brought here at the request of our present Master. Not, I may say, with my approval.'

Matheson was embarrassed. Such judgements should not be delivered in front of *his* inferiors.

Sir Gerald's address was broken by a fit of coughing, a series of dry, painful sounds. When these had ceased he went on.

'I have been studying your assessments, opinions and judgements which have been submitted to the Minister in my absence. I can only say that if, in both style and content, these are typical of the work done in the Scottish Office, then I would view that Office with dubious emotions.'

Matheson felt nauseous.

'There are standards,' the Permanent Secretary went on, 'which in this Ministry I have created and intend to maintain. Your work falls considerably below these standards.'

Matheson opened and shut his mouth, aware that he must look like a fish floundering out of water.

'No doubt you may in time reach our standards,' Sir Gerald pressed on, 'under my instruction, but it will be a considerable time and entail a consideration on my part which should not be expected of a senior officer of this service.'

The icicle eyes raked the crescent. 'This of course applies to all of you. Had Mr Matheson alone fallen below the required standards, you at least might have been expected to assist him, propel him in the direction I have propelled you. I see no signs of such movement.'

Matheson took a deep breath. Now he could speak, appearing to defend not only himself but his assembled colleagues.

'You'll pardon me, Permanent Secretary, but if such criticism is justified, it would be better perhaps to direct it to me alone as I have been the senior man. And also, rather than generalities, I think it would be more helpful if these criticisms were specific.'

The eyes, underlined by the black circles of ill health, settled again on Matheson.

'Specific, sir? That would be only too easy. Basically, the style of all your papers leaves much to be desired.'

Another deep breath. Matheson's future career, he could see, was fast disappearing.

'The Minister has always appreciated my preparation of advisory papers. I believe he found understanding the new format quite simple, and preferred it so.'

The parchment-like skin facing him wrinkled in a grimace of contempt. 'Simplicity on the Minister's behalf is rarely a virtue. Comprehension of the depths of our purposes may escape our Masters but they permit our equals in other Ministries, and our successors, to interpret our advice in many and various ways. As one of our great predecessors termed it, *economy of the truth* has its values. Multiple interpretations protect our reputations in the future. I also detect a partiality in your opinions which should not be present. Even if that partiality supports the present government, it seems distinctly to represent your personal opinion.'

'But . . .'

'Your personal opinion is of no interest to us! Should be of no interest to the Minister! You will remember that, should a

57

government of a more leftish hue take office, the Service must stand as before. That is, impartial, available and unblemished.'

'We do not have to reveal the opinions of a previous administration.' Matheson felt bound to defend such an unfair assessment of his abilities.

'Nevertheless our opinions must stand in print as being without partiality.'

The Permanent Secretary now hesitated, appearing to gulp deep breaths of air, his hands trembling.

'I have given you my view of the current standard of your work, gentlemen. I have obviously been on sick leave too long. I am back!'

Matheson was irresistibly reminded of old newsreel shots he had once seen of General MacArthur's return to the Philippines at the end of the Second World War.

Sir Gerald went on, 'Let my comments guide you in whatever future work you are called upon to do. But you must realise my opinions will be reflected in my personal assessments of your ability. You may wish to consider at length your possible future in the Service. Thank you. Good morning.'

Matheson watched his colleagues filing out before leaving the office. His face was scarlet, he knew. That such remarks, even if true, which he did not accept, should be delivered in front of everyone was a humiliation. The arrogance and the harsh unfairness he found intolerable. And he suspected he was meant to find it all so. Leigh was trying to get rid of him, that was only too obvious. Also telling him that, with such a report about to be submitted to the head of the Home Civil Service, his career would certainly progress no further.

He was at first in no mood to lunch with a comparative stranger. However, his mood changed before leaving his office, as if a die had been cast. He knew the worst. To hell with the worst! To hell with the Permanent Secretary! He might expect some support from the Minister, but against such vicious detraction it would do little good. However, even if he left the Service, he would not starve. He could live comfortably for the rest of his life.

Nevertheless the judgement of his superior, that he was a failure, rankled. The thought had to be put aside. He determined to try to do so.

58

He went to lunch.

In the trattoria he was shown not to his usual table but to that at which he had first seen Gilbert Martin. His double was already there and rose to greet him, hand outstretched. He noticed with a sudden feeling of awe that Martin was dressed in a conservative dark pin-striped suit, the exact replica of the one he himself was wearing. This only underlined the resemblance. Again, over the lunch table, it was as if he was gazing into a mirror.

'How good of you to come, Mr Matheson,' Martin said. 'Or may I call you Alistair? It seems ridiculous being so formal when talking to the replica of oneself. You don't mind?'

'Not at all,' Matheson replied, despite feeling awkward with the familiarity.

'And you, of course, must call me Gilbert. Now, let's relax. The lunch is on me of course.'

Matheson demurred gently. 'You paid for my lunch last time we met. I insist on this being on me.'

He expected the usual argument with one of them eventually snatching the bill at the end of the meal. It didn't happen that way.

'If you insist,' Martin acquiesced instantly. 'Very good of you. I've already ordered brown Windsor soup and a fillet steak for myself. And you'

After such a morning as he'd had, Matheson did not feel hungry. 'A small mixed salad,' he informed the waiter. 'No soup.'

'You have no appetite. Such a pity. A bottle of Burgundy for me.' A smile across the table at Matheson as he turned back to the waiter. 'Red, I think, with my steak. And perhaps a Chablis for my friend. Oh, yes, you must. St Paul, remember? "A little wine for the stomach's sake." One of the few things on which I agree with Paul. No dessert, I think. And have two large brandies ready with the coffee.' Martin might have accepted the position of guest but he was organising the meal.

When the waiter had departed, Martin faced Matheson again. 'So, Alistair, you have not had a good morning?'

The Ministry would certainly know of his humiliation by the Permanent Secretary, but Alistair was not aware that all

59

the world and his wife would also know of the events of that morning. It seemed he was wrong.

'You're quite right. It has been a trying morning.' That at least could mean anything. Pressure of work or whatever Martin might choose to believe.

'Oh, more than that,' he insisted. 'I can see it in your face.'

Matheson replied with a wan smile. If his lunch companion was fishing for information, he had no intention of providing it.

Martin went on, 'I wouldn't worry about Sir Gerald Leigh. He won't interfere with your career, I'm sure.'

Again Matheson could not speak. He was so surprised at the seeming knowledge Martin had of his morning. Martin must have other friends in the Ministry. One of the other senior officials, perhaps?

The Other seemed to read his mind. 'Of course I don't know anybody else in the Ministry of Defence. I only know of Sir Gerald. And of course . . . he will soon be removed.'

A cold phrase rendered coldly. Matheson inadvertently found himself shuddering.

'Be . . . be removed?' he questioned.

'A matter of time, certainly. And then the establishment people will have to find a successor. You will be the only choice.'

'Oh, no.' Matheson shook his head vigorously. 'In the Home Civil Service, I'm afraid, I don't have superiority.'

'Exceptions will be made, Alistair.' It was said with quiet assurance.

'You also tell fortunes?' he said, trying to be light and amusing.

But Martin seemed to be serious. 'Oh, yes, of course. I'm nothing if not a good fortune teller. Very accurate, I assure you. And it will all happen very quickly.'

'You read hands?'

'Hands, tea leaves, dreams, bumps on the head – phrenology, that is – crystal gazing, the Tarot – I'm especially good with the Tarot – and of course horoscopes. Good at astrology, too.' Martin himself assumed a light-hearted tone. 'A very old hobby of mine,' he went on. 'One has to keep not only up with the times but ahead of them.'

The waiter arrived with his soup. Another brought the wine and at Martin's nod opened the two bottles. He insisted on tasting them both. Again he nodded, this time with approval. The waiter poured.

Matheson found himself laughing at Martin's catalogue of fortune-telling abilities. At least the man seemed to be cheering him up. 'You almost sound as if you believe in all that astrology business.'

'I do, I do. My dear fellow, it's a science. Maybe an inexact one, but definitely a science. Have you ever read J. W. Dunne's *Experiment with Time*? It's all there. He struck on the truth, even if it was just luck.'

'I read Dunne many years ago. I don't see the relevance.'

'The fourth dimension. Time running along a track. Step out of the track and one observes past and future.'

'And how does one step out of the track?'

Martin smiled thinly. 'Oh, I don't say it's easy. Of course Dunne suggested it came in dreams. I could suggest that which you call fortune-telling might be yet another way.'

Matheson could only express amused disbelief. 'Oh, come now, you don't expect . . .'

'I do, indeed. But it takes time to reach a comprehension of such beliefs. In time, I will demonstrate. But let's not get bogged down in such esoteric matters. Tell me, how are you enjoying living in London?'

'It's pleasant.'

'And Chelsea is so full of life.'

'How do you know I live in Chelsea?' He felt a nervous twinge.

'You are in the newest London telephone book, my dear Alistair.'

Relief replaced curiosity. He felt he was being oversensitive this morning after the interview with the Permanent Secretary.

'And where in London do you live?' he asked, more for something to say rather than from any genuine curiosity on his part. Perhaps, he told himself, he was already getting bored with this stranger. After all, that's what he was. A stranger. The only thing they had in common was a remarkable physical likeness, and that was hardly enough to sustain a

61

friendship. Especially when Alistair Matheson was not a man to form friendships easily.

'Catford,' Martin replied. 'I have a large house in Catford. Very large. Too large. And like you, one servant. I manage.'

Matheson pondered briefly on the 'like you'. Was Martin guessing or could he, in some way, know about Dobson? He dismissed the thought, the man was probably guessing, and pressed on with another query, one of the few remaining questions regarding Martin that might be of interest.

'And you have a profession? Apart from fortune-telling?' This was said lightly in order not to cause offence.

'I am fortunate. Not unlike yourself, I have . . . independent means. Unlike you, I have never had any great desire to pursue one of the more distinguished professions. All my life I have been a dabbler. In things that interest me. Also perhaps, I have been a kind of amateur philosopher, indulging in a study of my fellow man. It has variety at least. Otherwise I get bored very easily.'

'You're not married?'

'No. As I said, I get bored easily. Anyway I believe in a variety of experience. And you . . . you're not married?'

'No. Not yet.' The 'yet' was deliberate. Had to emphasise to this stranger that there was nothing peculiar or perverse in his inclinations. Anyway, there was a measure of truth there. Deep down he was beginning to have expectations of Margaret Mower.

The luncheon progressed. Martin's conversation became lighter, easier; he told a few quite witty stories based on his experience of life which did now seem to Matheson to be very different from his own. The lunch was developing into an amusing interlude. Gilbert Martin was revealing real charm. And, because of their likeness, Alistair Matheson felt he could presume that he possessed similar qualities. There was something he had never realised before.

They came to the coffee.

'We must do this more often,' Martin said. 'It's been most enjoyable.'

A small warning signal sounded deep inside Matheson. He ignored it. 'Yes, of course,' he responded. A man must have acquaintances if not close friends. There could be no harm in acquaintanceship.

62

'And not just lunch,' Martin went on. 'I'm not a bad cook, you know. You must come out to Catford. Dine with me. See my house. I have a small collection of interesting artefacts.'

'You collect antiques?'

'In a small way. You?'

'No, not really. Haven't had the time. Like them, though. Give life a kind of permanency.'

Martin seemed amused. 'Yes, yes, permanency. Always there for some of us.'

'And you must dine with me,' Alistair said politely, thinking there would be a nice talking point. The two of them side by side. Charlie and Nan Grove there. Perhaps the Snodgrasses. And Margaret. Seeing their faces on meeting his mirror image.

'Good God!' he could hear Charlie Groves say. 'Wouldn't have believed it.'

Told you so.' Himself enjoying their astonishment.

'Couple of peas in a pod,' Snodgrass would echo the cliché.

'Yes, you must dine with me. Meet a few friends,' he repeated.

'And I shall, of course, invite a few friends to Catford to meet you.' Martin glanced at the wafer thin gold watch on his wrist. 'Now I must go. I don't want to keep you from the nation's business. I shall contact you soon. Very soon.'

Matheson paid the bill and they came out into a sudden outbreak of bright sunlight. Martin blinked.

'Too bright, the damn sun.'

'Better than rain, surely?'

'London always looks better under a gentle downpour,' Martin said, and grasping Matheson's hand, shook it warmly. 'I'll say goodbye just now, Alistair. And I predict your afternoon will be better than your morning. I wouldn't worry about the Permanent Secretary.'

He moved off down Victoria Street, leaving Matheson staring after him until he vanished in the crowd. Matheson felt cold again under the sun. What the hell was all that about the Permanent Secretary. How could he know? The thought was unfruitful, almost depressing. Perhaps Gilbert Martin really could tell fortunes.

Matheson walked back up to Whitehall and the Ministry.

63

The commissionaire saluted him at the door. At least the man recognised him now. It had taken a month before the ex-soldier had realised he was one of the most important people in the Ministry. Third to the Minister and the Permanent Secretary.

The commissionaire was approaching him now. The man was an aging ex-Guards sergeant.

'Terrible thing, sir,' he said.

Matheson was puzzled. 'What's that?'

'Sir Gerald, sir. Oh, we all knew he'd not been too well, but nobody expected this.'

'Expected what, man?'

Outside the building the sky clouded over again.

'Sorry sir. Of course you've been out at lunch. Happened just an hour ago. Terrible.'

'What is so terrible?'

'Sir Gerald, sir. The Permanent Secretary. After some meeting this morning, he was alone, working in his office. Apparently just managed to press the intercom. By the time his secretary went in, he was dead. Stone cold . . . no, still warm, but stone dead. Terrible.'

Chapter Eight

Sir Gerald Leigh was certainly dead; sitting behind his desk, eyes open, looking distinctly uncomfortable, but obviously feeling and seeing nothing.

The Ministry was in panic. Secretaries whispered to each other, senior civil servants ran hither and thither, demanding to know what had happened and, when informed, proceeded to check their workloads. Had the P.S. died with questions unanswered, papers incomplete?

Matheson went quietly to Leigh's office and surveyed the body which had been lifted from the desk and laid on a couch. A doctor, one of the senior officers of the Royal Army Medical Corps, a brigadier with an office in the building, had been called. It could be said that Sir Gerald had gone in style. The Brigadier was a Queen's Honorary Physician.

Matheson waited unobtrusively at the far side of the room while the doctor completed his examination. When he straightened up and turned from the body, Matheson approached him.

'Brigadier?'

He blinked owlishly at Matheson, knowing the Scot was next in rank to the dead man.

'Oh, yes, definitely dead. Definitely.'

'What killed him?'

'Ah, what indeed? Of course he wasn't a well man. We all knew that. Kidney trouble, liver in a bad way too. Gave him an examination myself before he went on sick leave. Mind you, he thought he was fit enough to come back. Probably was. Sick leave did him good.'

65

'So why did he die?'

'Of course, can't say for sure without an autopsy. But I have a fair idea.'

'Heart?'

'Definitely stopped now. But that didn't kill him. No, more like a bolt from the blue, eh?'

Matheson sighed. The Brigadier was noted for his obtuseness. 'Brigadier, what do you think killed Sir Gerald?'

'Comes like a thunderbolt, this kind of thing.'

'What kind of thing?'

'Cerebral incident, almost certainly. A stroke. Pretty massive one. Otherwise it wouldn't have killed him. Which it did. Be sure after the autopsy. Have to be one. Minister'll have to be informed.'

'I shall see to that. And notifying Lady Leigh? I think you should attend to that, Brigadier.'

'Oh, yes, I suppose so. Phone her, perhaps?'

'I think a visit to her home. As soon as the body is removed.'

The Brigadier assented bleakly.

'And take the senior Army Chaplain with you.'

'I think he's on leave.'

'Then phone the Admiralty and get the senior Naval Chaplain. Good afternoon.'

Matheson went to his own office. Miss Lubovious greeted him.

'I phoned the House,' she said. 'The Minister is coming over.'

Lubovious was always good in emergencies.

'Thank you, Miss Lubovious. I'll be in my office when he needs me,' he said, and went into the room shutting the door firmly behind him. He sat at his desk and stared straight ahead.

'Like a bolt from the blue!' the Brigadier had said.

'I wouldn't worry about the Permanent Secretary,' Gilbert Martin had told him. Also had said of Leigh, 'He will soon be removed.'

What the hell had Martin meant? How the devil had he known?

Or was he, Alistair Matheson, becoming paranoid again. What was it Martin had said about telling fortunes, about

66

being psychic? Not that Matheson believed in that kind of nonsense, not really. Of course there were people who could do things, were supposed to have unusual talents. What about Uri Geller? Well, what about him? A world-shattering ability to bend spoons. And Matheson had once seen a documentary film about that woman in Russia who could move things around a table without actually touching them. Telekinesis, that was it. What the hell had Geller bending spoons and a woman in Russia moving matchboxes around a table to do with Gilbert Martin?

Coincidence . . . Martin's predictions had to be. After all, Gerald Leigh hadn't been well. (Had he mentioned that to Martin? He couldn't remember . . . not for sure.) More than not being well, Leigh had obviously been seriously ill, it was obvious now. Stupid to dwell upon what Gilbert Martin had said. Indeed, was he sure Martin had said that? He thought about the lunch. He could remember for sure they'd invited each other for dinner. No date, but invitations verbally issued and talked about. Certainly he'd said he'd had a bad morning. Martin had tried to cheer him up. That was all. Perfectly natural.

The intercom buzzed.

He flicked the button.

'Yes, Miss Lubovious.'

'The Minister's back from the House. He'd like to see you in his office at once.'

'I am on my way.'

The Minister's office was the largest in the building. Naturally the way things were. The Minister himself was standing behind his desk, a man of medium height, with sandy-coloured hair and gold-rimmed spectacles. He was five or six years older than Matheson but in fact looked ten or fifteen years his senior. He looked stoop-shouldered. He would be. He'd served in the cabinet of the previous Prime Minister as Secretary of State for Scotland. They all had stoops, the members of that cabinet.

The Minister looked up as Matheson entered, peering myopically over the gold rims.

'Ah, Alistair, come in. Sit down.'

Matheson sat in front of the ministerial desk.

67

'Tragic,' said the Minister. 'Tragic. Not that he was a well man. Far from it. Would insist in coming in this morning, though. Too conscientious. Might have been alive if he hadn't been. Oh, God, I'll have to visit his wife.'

'I instructed the doctor and a chaplain to visit Lady Leigh.'

'Good, good. Soften the blow. But I'll still have to see her. Courtesy. What a bloody nuisance. Only met her once. Struck me as a very emotional female. Oh, lord! Maybe get the P.M. to go along with me. Certainly the Cabinet Secretary.'

The Minister daubed his brow with a handkerchief from his breast pocket. 'Trouble is, neither you or I have been here very long,' he went on. 'Not that Leigh was much help. His illness, you know. You'll have to take over for the time being.'

'Yes, of course, Minister.'

'You've been doing the job anyway since his illness. And very competently.'

'Thank you, Minister.'

'Oh, I can judge a man, Matheson. Always been able to. Why I brought you from Scotland. And you haven't let me down. Yes, you'll be acting Permanent Secretary. I intend to have a word with the Cabinet Secretary, in his capacity as Head of the Home Civil Service. I understand there is even more protocol in the Service than anywhere else. All that rubbish about Buggin's turn. Worse than a bloody trade union! I am going to request that you be promoted Permanent Under Secretary to the Ministry of Defence. There! Your full title, as best man for the job.'

Matheson thought, the late Sir Gerald would hardly have agreed. Thank God he'd not reached the Minister before dropping dead.

'Of course I can't promise anything, Alistair.' The Minister veered from first to second name terms and back again. 'You Civil Service boys have your own methods. But I can even take it to the P.M.'

'Very good of you, Minister.'

'In my own interests. You and I think alike, man. Ideal in government. Good. Now, let me see . . . You've been handling everything anyway? Yes, you have. Well, keep on. Oh, unless Lady Leigh objects, better get Crowther to help her with the funeral arrangements. Be glad to have it taken off her hands, I shouldn't wonder. Get him planted soon as possible.'

'Of course.'

'And make sure my time-table is free for the funeral. Yes, well, that's everything for now, Alistair.'

Matheson went to the door feeling elated. He might just get the job of P.S. if the Minister pressed it hard enough.

'Oh, one other thing. If I can get you the job as P.S., it'll mean your K. within a couple of years. A thought, eh? Sir Alistair.'

'If that happens, I should appreciate it,' Matheson replied diffidently.

He went out, elation mounting. *Sir Alistair Matheson.* Always on the cards if everything had gone as he'd planned, but he'd never been sure of it. Retired too soon, or without achieving rank, he might have had to be content with a C.B.E. But not now. Not if everything went well.

He felt sure it would continue to go well.

Margaret Mower said, 'How strange!'

Finishing his work at the Ministry that afternoon, Matheson had returned to Chelsea where Dobson had run a bath for him. While the manservant was doing this, Matheson told him of Leigh's death.

'Most unfortunate, sir,' Dobson said impassively. Of course everything Dobson did was effected with this bland impassive air. It came of modelling himself on Wodehouse's Jeeves. He would ask himself in any situation: 'What would Jeeves have done?' and then do it. Matheson too was a Wodehouse addict and recognising every move Dobson made as being based on Jeeves, found it most disconcerting. Alistair Matheson was no Bertie Wooster.

'I may become Permanent Under Secretary, Dobson.'

'In that event, may I extend my congratulations, sir? Will you be eating at home tonight?'

'Yes. No. No, I think I'll visit a friend.'

At this point he'd phoned Margaret and suggested they dine together again.

69

'Not tonight, Alistair,' she'd replied. 'Tonight I'm washing my hair, and while it's drying I intend to do some proof-reading of my new book.'

'I did want to see you.' He sounded crestfallen. 'Rather a lot has happened.'

'I tell you what,' she responded sympathetically. 'You have dinner and come on here afterwards. I'll have a drink waiting for you and you can tell me all that's happened.'

Thus, having dined alone, he ended up sitting in a deep armchair in Margaret's flat, brandy glass in hand, relating the day's events. She sat on a divan in a red dressing gown, a towel around her damp hair.

'How terrible,' she'd said of Leigh's demise.

And 'How strange!' she said on hearing about Matheson's lunch with Martin and the latter's hints at what was to come.

'As if he was foretelling the future. Oh, not directly, but definitely hinting, suggesting, whatever . . .' Matheson said, eyes wide, as it was difficult to believe all he was saying himself. 'And . . . and of course, he was right. Or approximately right. Astonishing.'

'Indeed,' Margaret agreed. 'Astonishing. More than that. Very, very strange. And you say, close up, he still looks like you?'

'Yes, even more so. Mirror image, did I tell you that? Anyway, he is. Of course one gets used to it. Takes it for granted.'

'I'd like to meet him,' Margaret said thoughtfully.

'Oh, I am sure you will.'

'You're seeing him again.'

'He invited me to dine at his home. I don't know whether he wants me to bring a partner . . .'

'Oh, I couldn't go. Never go to a stranger's home unless specifically invited. Make it a rule.'

'But if you came as my partner?'

'The guest of a stranger? No. Never liked that. You can end up being the guest of someone quite horrendous. Speak your mind and it becomes too easily a quite ghastly occasion.'

'Of course I should have to reciprocate. Invite him to my place. You wouldn't object to that?'

'No, I shouldn't.' A long pause. Then she said, 'Alistair?'

70

'Yes?'

'This man, Gilbert Martin . . .'

'What about him?'

'You remember I told you about that book . . . Hogg's *Memoirs and Confessions of A Justified Sinner*?'

'Yes, you did. Hogg was a fellow Scot, wasn't he?'

'You never read it?'

'I've been rather busy . . .'

'Remember I told you it was about a man who met the Devil, and the Devil looked exactly like him?'

'A kind of horror story? Not really my kind of thing.'

'The Devil's name in the book was Gil-Martin.'

She was staring at Matheson, waiting for a reaction. He sipped his brandy thoughtfully. Then he started to laugh.

'Oh, really, Margaret! What are you trying to say?'

She stared bleakly down at the carpet. 'I don't know.'

'Gil-Martin indeed. That's funny.'

'Odd. And he looking so much like you.'

Matheson swallowed the rest of the brandy and stood up. 'So you're telling me I have encountered the Devil himself, and he's asked me to dinner at his home in Catford?'

'I didn't say that. It's just so . . . so . . .'

'I think you should give me another brandy, and take one yourself.'

She refilled his glass and poured herself another.

'But, Alistair, you have to admit it's strange.'

He laughed again. 'A coincidence. I think Mr Martin will be rather amused when I tell him I have a friend who believes he may be the Devil.'

'I don't! I've said it. It's just . . . funny.'

'Funny, odd, strange, peculiar . . . all the words. Must mean something. We civil servants are accused of being verbose, of publishing papers no one understands, of verbal obscurity. You novelists profess to write good clear prose. Yet what do you mean: funny, odd, all these words?'

She stared up at him. 'Of course, you're right. I don't know what I mean.'

'You believe in the Devil?'

'No, of course not.'

Again Matheson laughed, a dry sardonic laugh. 'I'm the one who should believe in that gentleman. I think my father

71

did. Made a deal of money but retained his Presbyterian beliefs. My mother was different. She believed in the natural superiority of her class . . . she married beneath her . . . but her beliefs wouldn't include "Satan, old Hornie, Nick or Clootie" – that's Robert Burns. No, her family's definition of the Devil would have been a member of the Labour Party. I think my beliefs are probably closer to my mother's than my father's. Of course when Harold Wilson was in power, as a civil servant, I worked for his government. Wilson wasn't the Devil. Wasn't even a minor demon. Simply a pragmatist. Mind you, Mother wouldn't have been too sure about Tony Benn. I rather like him.'

He realised his discourse was drifting away from the subject. He changed tack. 'Anyway, the voters of Catford would hardly like the thought that the Devil lives in their midst.'

She nodded wearily. 'Oh, I know I'm being stupid. But it's so much of a coincidence.'

'There must be quite a few Gilbert Martins in the phone book.' He looked around. The telephone was on her desk next to her word-processor. Under the phone were the volumes of the London telephone directory.

'Yes, but they don't all look like you, Alistair,' Margaret insisted.

He took one volume of the directory from under the phone and started thumbing through it.

'There you are,' he said after a moment. 'Rows and rows of G. Martins. And there Gilbert Martin, Gilbert Martin, and another Gilbert Martin. And here. Gilbert Martin, 5 Lower Cotton Street, Catford. That'll be him.'

'Of course it will,' Margaret said. 'I didn't say he didn't exist.'

'But one thing still puzzles me.' Matheson rubbed his chin. 'It was as if he knew Leigh was going to die. As if he knew . . .'

'I may not believe in the Devil,' Margaret said, 'but I do believe there are people with certain gifts., I suppose I believe in some aspects of the paranormal.'

Matheson nodded as if making up his mind. 'I must talk to him again.'

'What are you going to do?' she went on. 'Phone him? Ask him if he can truly foretell the future?'

'No.' He smiled. 'Hardly on the phone. Have to see him. And soon.'

'Alistair, don't . . .'

'Don't what?'

'Let this become another obsession. You did, you know, when you first saw him. The resemblance did seem to take you over.'

He looked down at her, seemed to straighten up and smiled. 'Of course not. But I am curious.' He looked at his watch. 'Time I was going. Eleven o'clock already. I have to be at the Ministry early tomorrow.'

She saw him to the door. He felt suddenly awkward, saying goodnight at once being a problem. She solved it for him by standing on tip-toe and kissing him on the mouth. As she did so her mouth opened and she ran her tongue along his lips. At first he was taken aback. They had not yet reached this kind of intimacy; he could not have been sure she would have wished it. But she obviously did.

'Phone me,' she said. 'Soon.'

In the street he sat in tthe car for some minutes. He told himself he shouldn't have brought it. How many brandies had he had? Three. Too much. And yet they had had no effect. His head was quite clear.

He started the car and drove off.

Thinking again about Gilbert Martin and his powers of perception. They must be no more than that.

He drove along the King's Road without stopping. He passed the turn-off to his house. Without further thought he drove to Catford.

It took him some time to find Lower Cotton Street. It was after midnight when he brought the Aston Martin to a halt outside number five.

Chapter Nine

The first visit to the house on Cotton Street.

It was one of a long row of terraced houses that had seen better days. Sometime back in the reign of Victoria or Edward these large mansions had been the suburban equivalent of Eaton Square. But the idea of wealth gravitating out of Central London had never caught on. It had remained the fashion to live in the West End when not on the country estate. Thus Catford's elegance had been left to decay. Many of the four-storey houses in Cotton Street had been split into bedsitters or rather seedy hotels. Some were derelict, some had been taken over as offices by local small businesses.

Number five, however, looked to Alistair Matheson's nervous eyes as if it was one of the derelict buildings. The windows were dark and seemed to be uncurtained. The door, the original of heavy wood, possibly oak, bore old-fashioned brown stains but in places the varnish had given way to whitish patches as of dampness.

Matheson parked the car across the street and, stepping out, walked slowly to the opposite pavement. Wondering as he walked what possible excuse he could give to Martin for calling at his home after midnight.

'I was just passing and thought I'd drop in' didn't sound very convincing.

'Curious about you. I just had to come and see for myself where you lived' was at least the truth but he could hardly say that. Nor could he make some excuse about his car breaking down . . . too much of a coincidence that it should have happened in Cotton Street exactly opposite number five.

Thus he hesitated at the foot of the six steps that led up to the door. There was no nameplate merely a brass figure, five, tarnished and discoloured, at the side of the door.

Slowly Matheson climbed the steps. Below the brass numeral was an old fashioned bell-pull, also in brass. And in the centre of the door at waist height was a brass-trimmed letter slot.

Turning, he peered back along the street, delaying any decision about ringing the bell. The street was deserted. One or two lights in adjacent buildings were all high up on the third or fourth floors and threw little illumination on to the street. Of course there were street lamps but they seemed remarkably ineffectual, merely casting small pools of light on the cracked pavements below them. At least two of them had ceased to function.

He turned back to the forbidding barrier of the door. Telling himself he should drive away, go home, wait until he was invited. Certainly he should not be here after midnight, uninvited.

Looking around again, this time with a furtive glance, he swung back, stooped, and pushed the letter box open, peered through. Into darkness.

Not, it seemed, ordinary darkness but much more, a deep, solid blackness, a physically tangible segment of nothingness. But then what had he expected? Perhaps some welcoming glimmer of lights, the warmth of a distant electric bulb? There was none.

He straightened up and reluctantly turned again from the door. Now he had to decide: ring the bell, face Martin, wake him from a comfortable bed with some stupid excuse which the man would be too clever to believe? Or go back to his car and drive back to Chelsea, metaphorical tail between his legs? Then he felt at once tired, bone tired, the sour taste of brandy at the back of his throat. Too much brandy. Too little sleep. He leaned against the door.

There was a loud, creaking sound and slowly it swung open. Matheson stumbled backwards, only stopping himself from falling by grasping the lintel. Steady on his feet again, he swung around and stared into the blackness. His nostrils were at once assailed by a musty smell, the odour of dust and dampness. And the door had been open which was strange in itself. In London at this time of night who would leave the front door of their house unlocked?

He reached out, feeling the side of the door, searching for an electric switch. At first he found a bare wall. Somewhere, he told himself, there must be a switch. He felt in his jacket pocket and, producing his cigarette light, flicked it on.

It flared as the flame caught the threads of a spider's web by the wall then died to a small flame, as if it was barely alight in the cold draught Matheson could feel on his face. Then he found the light switch and turned it on.

The light was yellow, high up towards the ceiling and not too bright. Nonetheless Matheson blinked, bedazzled even by this dim illumination. It came from a solitary bulb, unshaded, hanging from a small cord in the centre of the ornate ceiling. Amidst the ornamentation were more webs and long hanging threads of webs. The spiders had made number five home.

Matheson looked around. Bare floorboards in a bare hall. Bare but for accumulations of dust in corners, even mounds in the centre of the room. There was no furniture but on one wall to his left what had once been a large, heavy tapestry. This too was shrouded in dust but patches on it where the dust had accumulated and fallen to the floor with the force of its own weight revealed a one time richness, a deep red satin fabric interwoven with gold and silver threads. Curious, Matheson walked over to the tapestry and with the back of his hand struck at the dust. A cloud rose and fell leaving a segment of the design on the tapestry clear. A face, part human, part animal, horned and rampant, was delineated in front of him. At the feet, or was it hooves, of the creature was partly revealed a female figure, cowering, arm raised to ward off the creature, the lower part of its body still enshrouded by dust. Now Matheson could see there were also ragged holes in the tapestry where it had worn away or been torn.

He turned to contemplate the staircase at the end of the hall, bare stairs leading upwards. To one side of these a passage led to the rear of the house. And at each side of the hall, double doors led presumably to the living areas of the ground floor.

He walked to the foot of the staircase and peered upwards into dimness where the light from the solitary bulb could barely reach. He could just make out the balustrade stretching up to the first floor and beyond into darkness again. There was, at the very top, an area lighter than its surrounds, possibly a skylight.

Somewhere to Matheson's right there was a scuttling sound. He spun around, movement catching the corner of his eye. Then another movement, behind the tapestry. He strode over and kicked it. The rat scurried out and across the room, vanishing into some aperture on the opposite wall.

Matheson felt nauseous. What was he doing in a derelict house in Catford at one o'clock in the morning? Of course it had to be the wrong house, Gilbert Martin couldn't live here. Nobody could live here except possibly squatters, derelicts, down-and outs – and there was no sign of them. So this was number five Lower Cotton Street, so he Matheson had misheard the number. Martin could have said twenty-five or thirty-five, that was certainly the answer. A misheard number.

Then he remembered. The telephone book at Margaret's house at Richmond: Martin, Gilbert, 5 Lower Cotton Street, Catford. And a post code number which he had forgotten. And a telephone number, also forgotten. But he could not have been mistaken about the address.

He went to the right and threw upon the double doors. The light from the hall met the blue of whatever light came from open, unshuttered windows, spilling across another empty room. A large marble fireplace stood against one wall gaping openly at bare boards. Again the smell of dust mixed with another even more unpleasant odour filled Matheson's nostrils. As if someone had defecated somewhere in the room. He shut the doors quickly.

The front door was still ajar. He had an impulse to run back and out into the comparatively clean air of the street. He should not be here, he thought, and how would he explain his presence if a beat policeman should investigate the open door?

'I was calling on a friend and the door happened to be open?' Hardly a satisfactory explanation. Not very convincing even from a senior civil servant.

He moved back to the foot of the stairs and started to climb. They creaked beneath his feet. Somewhere outside he heard the sound of a police siren diminishing into the distance. He continued to ascend, the thought coming to him that he should be nervous. Indeed, he was surprised he wasn't. Curious, yes, or perhaps inquisitive was a better word. But he could tell himself he was too down-to-earth to be afraid of a house. Basically he was simply puzzled as to why Martin had given him the address of an empty house. Unless . . .

He reached the landing on the first floor. Dimly he made out a light switch. Again a bare bulb hanging from the ceiling flared into life. There were three doors on the landing. The nearest opened on to what he presumed to be a large drawing room. There was no furniture in the room and no bulb in the light socket. The only light came from a large bay window and revealed bare boards and another expansive marble fireplace.

Unless . . . he had allowed his mind to roam . . . unless Gilbert Martin had recently bought the house and not yet moved in. If this were so, and it would seem to be the only explanation, then it would be some considerable time before the house could be made habitable.

The second door led to what seemed to be a small study. Again minus light bulb. The third door led to yet another large room and against two of the walls he could make out shelving, from floor to ceiling. A one-time library, now without a book in sight.

On the second floor were three bedrooms, bathrooms en suite. There was a fourth bathroom at the end of the landing and here another solitary bulb was still functioning. The bath was a very large Victorian affair, brass fittings covered in dust and green with verdigris. The lavatory, on a raised dais, resembled nothing less than an elevated throne. There was an enormous oblong cistern and a long chain, the handle broken off and lying on the floor.

The third-floor lights did not function. He could just make out a number of doors leading to what he presumed might be servants' bedrooms. There was another bathroom too, smaller and less imposing than the one below.

He climbed to the fourth floor. Not knowing why he was exploring, not knowing what he expected to find. The skylight provided the only light here, the frosted glass cracked and leaking, a damp puddle bearing witness to the recent rain. There were two small rooms, both filled with what he could only presume was junk. A number of crates, an ancient perambulator and large armchair, one of its casters gone and the whole canted to one side, were the only things he could make out in the dim light in the first of these rooms. The second was small, containing two large chests covered in dust and nothing else.

The third room was at the end of the landing and, as Matheson approached the door, an aroma like burning wax assailed him. His eye dropped to the floor and he noticed at the crack beneath the door a line of light, shimmering and flickering.

Someone was in the room and burning a candle!

Matheson took a deep breath and gripped the handle of the door. His hand was trembling. Not with fear, he told himself. With a kind of anticipation.

He turned the handle and pushed the door open.

There was another loud creaking sound and he stepped into the room.

A pair of red-rimmed eyes stared up at him from the centre of the room.

The old man was crouching over a solitary candle which was protruding from a battered tin can. Thin grimy hands were close around the flame as if seeking whatever heat it gave off. The man was dressed in a heavy coat, rumpled and stained, once expensive but now frayed at collar and cuffs. A greasy soft hat perched on a mop of long, even greasier hair. The cheeks were unshaven and grubby.

The eyes blinked. The man continued to stare, saying nothing.

Matheson had to break the silence. 'You! Who are you?'

The old man's mouth curved downwards. 'Not doing nothin'.'

'What are you doing here?' The question followed the answer.

'Nothin',' the man repeated, starting to whine. 'Said so. Not doin' nothin'. 'Cept warming' me hands.'

'Who are you?' Matheson repeated his original question.

79

'Me? Who're you, eh? Who're you?'

'I'm . . . I'm a friend of the owner's.'

The man gave a low wheezing sound. Matheson realised he was laughing. 'Somebody actually owns this dump?'

'Yes. Now who are you and what are you doing here?'

A grimy hand ran through greasy hair. 'I'm keepin' warm, wha' do you think?'

'You're squatting?'

'So? You want me on the street, don't you? You'd rather I was in a cardboard box under Charing Cross railway bridge, would you? With them others. Squeezed up like sardines. Where I could die of pneumonia, eh?'

'There are hostels!'

'"Are there no prisons? And the workhouses, are they still in operation? The Treadmill and the Poor Law are in full vigour, then?"'

'What are you talking about?'

'Not talking. Quoting. Scrooge. Chas. Dickens. *Christmas Carol*. See, not an uneducated man, me. Not ignorant. Read a bit, me.'

'And the quotation is hardly relevant.'

'Not to you it's not. All dressed up an' nowhere to go, eh? What *you* doin' here anyway? In the middle of the night.'

'I was . . . looking for the owner.'

'At one o'clock in the morning? Oh, I heard the chimes not long ago. Sure I did. One o'clock. Witching hour. No, that's midnight. Witching hour plus one. Things supposed to come out in the night.'

The old man had turned away from Matheson now, staring into the candle, gazing into the very heart of the flame.

'Don't stare into the candle! You'll damage your eyes!'

Another wheezing chuckle. 'Too late for that, Mister. Damaged long ago. Man tried to blind me. Tried to pull them out. Oh, yes, he did.'

'Don't talk rubbish, man!'

'Oh, he tried. Like in King Lear when they went for Gloucester. "Out, vile jelly!" Eyes out, there an' then. Bleedin' sockets left. 'Course that's only a play. Fellow tried it on me for real. Gougin' . . . that was the word. He was trying. But I stopped him . . .'

80

'I think you should stop this nonsense,' Matheson said, deciding the old man was patently mad.

'He din't get away with it, no! See, there was this nail just lying there . . . six-inch nail it was. Shoved it right into his belly button. Rusty, it were too. Shoved it right in the whole six inches. Stopped tryin' to get my eyes then. Screamed – that way, y'know. Stuck pig. I was twistin' the nail too. Down through the belly. Right down to . . .'

'That's enough. Quite enough. Time you were out of here.'

'Wantin' the place for yourself, eh?'

'Don't be stupid!'

'Can't call me stupid just because of your good suit, fancy collar and tie. They all start off like that . . .'; His tone suddenly changed. 'Anyway you wouldn't want to stay here. No, you wouldn't. Deceptive house, this. Things happen. Oh, they do. Things happen . . .'

'What are you talking about?'

'Off kilter, this house. Why I'm the only one that squats here. Oh, yes, seen things, this house. Things bein' done. Things still to be done. Filled with anticipation, this house. Of past and future. Same thing, past and future. Like Dunne's experiment . . .'

Matheson wasn't sure if he'd heard correctly. 'What did you say?'

'Said the house was off kilter. On the edge. Sometimes goes over the edge. Don't want to be here when that happens, you don't.'

'And you do?'

'Oh, me, I know. So I can hang on. See these fingers? All torn and bloody. With hanging on.'

Matheson shook his head in an attempt to clear it. This was ridiculous. The old man was in some kind of personal unbalanced fantasy and Matheson was close to being taken into it with him. The strangeness of the house was responsible. Ridiculous! Standing in a deserted house listening to a rambling derelict at one in the morning . . . it was as mad as the old man himself.

'I'm going,' he said.

'You're going,' the old man responded.

'Yes, I am.'

81

'Good. Your own good. Best thing to do.'

'And I suggest you collect whatever belongings you have and go yourself.'

The old man shook his head. 'No, no, no, no. No need. Roof over my head.' Nodding towards the candle, its flame flickering. 'Own central heating. No need to go. An' I'm used to the place.'

'I told you, I am a friend of the owner's. Doubtless he intends to move in shortly. Then you'll be thrown out. Or arrested for breaking and entering . . .'

The old man shook his head. 'No. Can't get me on that one. Door was open. As it was to you. No breaking, just entering. And that's not a charge itself, see. Know the law, too. I'm here. Possession is nine points of something or other . . .'

'I shall inform the first policeman I see that you are squatting here. He'll get you out. Probably you'll end up in a prison cell.'

'Least I'll have a roof over my head.'

Matheson turned on his heel and went out of the room, feeling sick and dizzy, a vertigo caused by the flickering candle, so he told himself. Also wondering whether he should have ejected the tramp himself, forcibly taken the old man from the house. Still it wasn't his business. Gilbert Martin would want the old man out. Let him do it when he moved into the place. Nothing to do with Alistair Matheson.

He went down the four flights of stairs quickly. Almost running. Curiosity sated, wanting to be out of the house. This house. Away from the place and whatever it contained. One tramp and a deal of dust. Wanting to be well away.

At the foot of the stairs he stopped and looked up. Without any reason. Without knowing why. Dimly he could see the skylight and a shape below it, leaning over the topmost balustrade.

'Least I'll still have a roof over my head,' the old man was calling down, a delayed echo of his last sentence.

'Not for long!' Matheson called back. 'Not in this house, if you're wise.'

He turned and headed towards the front door which was still open.

'Goodnight, Mister,' the man called down again. 'Goodnight, Mr Matheson!'

He stumbled across the hall to the door and out into the night street, sick again with wonder. How could the old man know his name? He hadn't given it. Had he misheard? Imagined the name?

As he imagined he had suddenly recognised the old man's voice.

Chapter Ten

Gavin Randall said, 'You should have told me you'd seen him again. I said I should be informed.'

They were sitting in the lounge of Randall's club. They'd lunched and were drinking coffee in the spacious lounge overlooking St James's Park. The room was empty except for an elderly member dozing at a large window at the far end of the room, *The Times* draped across his face.

'Of course I intended to inform you,' Matheson said, his face reddening. 'But, after all, you said your Gilbert Martin doesn't look in the least like me so I imagined it couldn't be of interest to you.'

Randall stared pensively at the fingernails on his right hand. 'You're telling me what I'm interested in?'

'Oh, come now, Gavin . . .'

'It's an acknowledged fact that two people describing the same man will come up with entirely different descriptions. Probably to do with the point of view.'

'You believe my Gilbert Martin is the man you're looking for?'

'I didn't say that. I won't know the man I'm looking for until I find him. And even then I might not know.'

Matheson took a deep breath. 'And he might be the wrong man. Wouldn't it help if you told me why you are so interested in this man. What has he done?'

Randall was silent for a moment. He ceased to contemplate his fingernails and took a sip of coffee.

'The matter comes under the heading of need to know,' he finally broke his silence. 'And of course again one might not know what he has done until one is face to face with him. As you may have been.'

'As the one person who has been face to face with him, surely I might be told what you *think* he has done?'

Randall changed the subject abruptly. 'Tell me again about this house in Catford.'

Matheson described for the second time the events of the previous night. 'Of course, what I can't understand is why he should tell me he lives there? After all, if he invites me, as he suggested he would do, to the house for a meal, he'd have some explaining to do.'

'Of course he may have recently purchased the property and could be in the process of redecorating.'

'He certainly hasn't started redecorating anything yet.'

Randall pursed his lips, a look of mild amusement on his face. 'Maybe he revels in the simplicity of poverty. That's rare. A kind of perversion thought up by the wealthy. If, of course, the house really is his.'

'The question of what is real and what is not real keeps intruding,' Matheson said wearily.

'My perennial problem, Alistair. What appears to be real, what contrives to be real, what is real? And is reality itself not questionable?' Randall sighed. 'Everything in life is so ambiguous. In my profession even more so. However, one goes through the motions. When I left you for a few minutes during our lunch after you told me of this, I put a phone call through to my office. They will have found out by this time who owns the Catford property, how long it has been owned, who, if anybody, is supposed to live there, and so on.'

'I shall be interested to hear.'

'Of course you shall. We will go back to my office. They should have all the information by now.'

Matheson frowned. 'I have to be back at the Ministry . . .'

'You need not concern yourself about rushing back, Alistair. Oh, I know, with Leigh's death you have grave problems of state. Of course such portentous matters are so important, in the end they take care of themselves. It's the ultimate exercise in pragmatism and the ideal recipe for government: Do nothing. Time resolves all problems. I have made your excuses to your secretary. The Ministry will expect you when you arrive.'

85

The civil servant affected astonishment. 'You take a lot on yourself. The problems at the Ministry of Defence are massive . . .'

'Of course they are. Always. But, however trivial, my problems have priority.'

'You say so . . .'

'Authority of the Cabinet Secretariat. They overrule God. After all, we have the Archbishop of Canterbury on our side. Direct line. Upwards.'

Matheson's reply was ice cold. 'I too can be pragmatic. There is a possibility I could be appointed permanently to Leigh's post. My taking time off with you just now seems ill-advised, to say the least.'

Randall laughed. 'My company can only enhance your career prospects. My problem goes to the top of any list.' He suddenly sprang to his feet, exhibiting an energy he had never previously shown to Matheson.

'Come along. My office. Bestir yourself. Awaken your sense of adventure. You are on the edge of a different world. As if you are being invited to visit Langley, Virginia. Or be shown around the Lubyanka. Only our tea is better and you have considerably more chance of getting out unharmed.'

Outside the club, Randall flagged down a taxi and instructed the driver to take them to Century House. Randall's office was on the sixth floor, a tiny, modern space with room for a desk, three chairs, a filing cabinet and little else. It was as different from Matheson's expansive wood-panelled homage to Victorian diplomacy as the moon to the earth.

Randall caught Matheson's appraising look.

'Sit down, old man. Mousetrap, this place, compared to what you're used to. Yes, mousetrap's the word. Catch a lot of mice though. But in modest circumstances. Now, let's see what my people have found out.'

Matheson took a seat. It was wooden, slatted and liable to fold itself flat. Very uncomfortable. 'Look, Gavin, what is this all about. Is Martin some kind of enemy agent?'

'I didn't say that.'

'That's the trouble. You haven't said anything at all. I *have* signed the Official Secrets Act. I know a great many of our country's secrets. And, incidentally, Gilbert Martin has never tried to prise anything out of me.'

'Glad to hear it.' Randall pressed a button on his desk. A young woman entered, smiled wanly and placed a folder on the desk. She withdrew.

Randall opened the file. Without looking up he said, 'You'll take a cup of tea? Don't say no. They bring it automatically. It's supposed to make strangers feel relaxed. I used to think they drugged it, but they don't. No need with the English. Oh, and the Scots and Welsh of course. Tea itself is a drug to the . . . British. You'll notice I didn't include the Irish. At least the Fenians. Tea has no effect on their natural aggression. Nothing has.'

Matheson did not reply. There seemed no point. Randall would come back to the subject in his own good time.

'All we know on the subject is here,' Randall went on, running his eyes down the top page. Then he looked up at Matheson. 'Marvellous job, this. Especially since Le Carre made it so realistically romantic. Often wish I could wander around looking Byronically miserable like Alec Guinness as George Smiley. Now, about your friend . . .'

A pause, purely for dramatic effect.

'The house at Catford is owned by Gilbert Martin. He purchased it some five years ago. As far as we know it is his place of residence.' Randall looked up at Matheson. 'Thanks to your information we have just confirmed this. However, it is possible he has other residences, owns other properties.'

'I'm quite sure he does,' Matheson said. 'No one could live in that place.'

'Your tramp was living there.'

'Hardly living. Squatting maybe. Existing even. Not living.'

'In residence anyway.'

'Surely you have some way of finding out any other property Martin might own?'

Randall shrugged. 'Gilbert Martin is not an uncommon name. There must be quite a few Gilbert Martins who own property. Also our Mr Martin may own any amount of property under different names.'

'Then why the Catford house under his own name?'

'You know him as Gilbert Martin. He would hardly give you an address known to be owned by someone else. Also, it

87

may be that he uses it as a London address only. May consider it an investment. Buy a derelict house in London, keep it a few years, decorate it when he's ready to sell and make a large profit. Why not?'

Matheson gazed at the window. The office Venetian blinds obscured any possible view of the London skyline. 'I'm confused,' he said.

'Of course you are. Ours is a confusing business. We are perpetually confused. And, indeed, of necessity thrive on confusion.' He turned to another page in the file. 'I suppose I shall have to tell you something of Gilbert Martin.'

'I *have* been asking you.'

'We have to choose our time. Let's see. No, best not mention that. Where to start? Ah, yes, five or six years ago. One of our people was investigating possible leakages of information from GCHQ, Cheltenham. Young Monty Wallingham. Good lad. Excellent at black-bag jobs . . .'

'What on earth?'

'Oh, intelligence slang. Means he's good at everything from bribery to burglary. Anyway, we'd become very sensitive about GCHQ since Geoffrey Prime was caught in '82 selling secrets to the Russkies. This time there was nothing definite. Just rumours. Monty was sent down to look around. Supplied with bleep-boxes and everything.'

'Bleep-boxes?'

'Used for telephone tapping among other things. Officially the tapping is quite illegal. We do it all the time. Anyway, you realise we were trading on other people's toes.'

'I don't.'

'In theory this was an MI5 job.'

'You aren't MI5?'

'Good God, no. MI6. Dealing with overseas business. But we'd had the name of a man called Gilbert Martin from Germany and France, and now it had cropped up at Cheltenham. So Monty went there to listen. From there he went off to Morwenstow in the south-west . . . GCHQ have a base there. Apparently one of the operatives at Morwenstow had encountered a lookalike.'

'A lookalike? Now wait a minute . . .'

'Patience, Alistair. This operative, a man called . . .' Randall consulted the page again '. . . yes, called Alwyn

88

Makepeace, reported he'd struck up a friendship with a man who looked exactly like him.'

'You're joking?' Matheson said, and then added, 'You're not joking.'

Randall's secretary came in, deposited a cup of tea in front of each of them, gave Matheson a very small smile and went out.

'Told you tea would appear, wanted or not. Where was I? Ah, yes. Not joking. Monty became very edgy. This man looked like Makepeace, could perhaps take his place and lay his hands on some pretty useful information. That was the thought.'

'You're suggesting Martin is going to try the same trick with me?'

'Didn't say that. Suppose it's possible. Don't see an old dog like you letting it happen.'

'You're damn' right I wouldn't!'

'Not talking about you just now. Talking about Monty. Not that it happened in Morwenstow anyway. But this Alwyn Makepeace was a strange character. Oh, he had full security clearance and he'd dutifully reported meeting Martin. Never did tell us how, mind you. Also we found Makepeace dabbled.'

'Dabbled? Dabbled in what?'

'Exactly. In what? Esoteric interests. Perhaps esoteric activities.'

'For God's sake, meaning what?'

'Touch of the old bogulars. My word for seances, spiritualism, all that kind of thing. Bogulars. Seems probable that's how he met Martin. You don't go in for that kind of thing, by any chance?'

'Good God, no!'

"Didn't think you did. Not you, not the bogular type. Anyway they'd met and now Monty Wallingham went down to Morwenstow to check what was going on. He met Makepeace who seemed to have changed his mind. Oh, this man Martin had struck up a friendship with him all right. But it had turned out, according to Makepeace, to be quite harmless. Martin never asked about Makepeace's work. Kept everything purely social. They merely bumped into each other for a drink now and then, played the odd game of snooker at the local pub and occasionally went to seances at the home of a woman called Nelly Garton. And nothing happened at these seances. Well, apart from contact with the spirit world . . . Makepeace's phrase, not mine. Monty at first began to wonder whether this Martin was maybe MI5 and we were treading on each other's toes. I checked with MI5 . . . delicate business, they're so touchy . . . and found they had no man in Morwenstow. Although they apparently were also quite interested in the name Gilbert Martin. A big row developed. Whose jurisdiction? Settled by the Cabinet Security Committee. Since we'd come across the name overseas, they allowed us to continue the investigative operation.'

'And MI5 were out?'

'Officially. But you never know with those buggers. Might just carry on behind our backs. Anyway Monty Wallingham was told to keep at it on account of the Cheltenham rumours. But we seemed to be barking up the wrong tree. We heard from him that Makepeace knew Martin had a cottage just outside the village. Fern Cottage, it was called. I always remembered that name. It was the last thing we heard from Monty.'

'What do you mean?'

'Two days after that last communication Monty Wallingham was found in a ditch. Minus his head.'

'His head!'

'We never found it. Identified him by fingerprints.'

'Murdered, of course?'

'Not so. According to autopsy and inquest, he'd been hit by a lorry on the road. Lorry stopped and the driver was quite ill afterwards. Said Monty had jumped out in front of him. After checking him out, we had no reason to doubt the story. Monty's chest was stoved in and by a freak the head was severed.'

Matheson sat riveted. 'Surely when you never found the head . . .?'

'The body was thrown on to the edge of some swampy ground. Local fen or something like that. District constabulary reckoned the head had been sucked into the marsh. Might reappear, might not, they said. And closed the case. Of course, we didn't.'

Matheson grimaced. 'It's like fiction. Seances, headless bodies, spies . . . something out of Dennis Wheatley.'

'Yes, isn't it? Terrible prose writer but a good story teller. Wheatley worked with intelligence during the war, did you know that? He would have appreciated this business,' Randall was still serious. 'Anyway, I went down myself to talk to Makepeace.'

'Was he dead too?'

'Not dead exactly. He'd had a kind of breakdown. found in his bed that morning. Had to be taken to the local hospital in a coma. Five years later he still is.'

'What . . . what caused it?'

'God knows. The surgeons didn't. I also went to see the spiritualist Nelly Garton. No help there. A very vague, fey lady. Remembered Makepeace and confirmed he'd become friendly with one of her other customers. But she didn't remember the man's name. Wasn't unusual for her. Maintained she never knew half the people that came to her seances.'

'And what about Martin?'

'We never found him. But what was really strange was that we never found Fern Cottage where he was supposed to be living.'

'Why was that?'

'For one very good reason. Makepeace had been there, Monty had seen the place, yet when we went looking for it we couldn't find it. You see, none of the locals had heard of it. It was on no maps or land registers or anything. There was no cottage even remotely like the description Monty had given us. Fern Cottage simply did not exist.'

Chapter Eleven

Later. Considering the visit to Randall's office.

Fantasy, Matheson told himself. It's all fantasy. But then, that was the kind of world people like Randall lived in. A world of lunatic plots, complex plans, double crosses, betrayals, suspicions, back stabbings – real and metaphorical, moles, murders and mayhem; a world that should only exist in a paperback novel and perhaps only did. Alistair Matheson smiled to himself, a strained tight little smile. Perhaps it wasn't so different for the world of politics and the civil service. Excluding the murders, but certainly with a degree of polite mayhem.

Add to it, in this case, seances, headless corpses, disappearing cottages, and people who looked like other people. Something out of Edgar Wallace or E. Philips Oppenheim. Yes, certainly those two rather than the Len Deightons, the Ian Flemings and other more modern writers. Gavin Randall's world was indeed as picaresque as Oppenheim's. It could have nothing to do with the Gilbert Martin Matheson knew. That Gilbert Martin who looked like him. Not like the man called Alwyn Makepeace. Unless Makepeace also looked like Alistair Matheson? Which he didn't. Or Randall would have mentioned it.

And the happenings at the house in Catford now seemed like some kind of aberration in the natural flow of life, a waking dream verging on nightmare. Thinking of it, Matheson could not but wonder how much of it was some quirk of the imagination fuelled by the amount of alcohol consumed. He was sure by now that he had only imagined the old tramp who had called out his name. More likely a few words of abuse, distorted by the echo in the empty house.

At the end of the meeting Randall had repeated that Matheson must inform him of any further contact with Gilbert Martin, and emphasised he must tell no one of what he had learned in Century House. Matheson had reassured him of this, making one mental reservation. He wanted to tell Margaret what had happened. He felt he was entitled to one trusted confidant his office, he phoned Margaret.

'Dinner tonight?'

'I really shouldn't . . . I've still got pages of proofs to correct.'

'A small celebration. Please. Tell you about it over dinner. Nothing formal.'

'You're simply playing on my curiosity. What can I say?'

'Pick you up at eight. Quiet dinner some place peaceful.'

He replaced the receiver and sat back smiling smugly. Thinking, what was it Dr Johnson had said about Scotsmen on the make? He would paraphrase it. No sight so pleased with himself as a Scotsman who had made it. At least he was honest. And could say that the whole stupid Gilbert Martin business was over. He told himself it no longer concerned him. Merely the effect of a physical resemblance, however startling. He was no longer startled.

Another thought had been growing in his mind. A senior civil servant's prospects were surely enhanced by marriage. Not, of course, that that was the principal consideration. He was distinctly attracted by Margaret Mower. And she was so eminently suitable.

He called Miss Lubovious in and asked her to reserve a table at Tonio's for two. Tonio's was a small, comfortable and expensive Italian restaurant close to where he lived just off the King's Road.

The table was in a discreet alcove. Only one other table in Tonio's overlooked theirs or could be seen by them and it was unoccupied when they arrived.

Matheson ordered aperitifs. After they had ordered, they sat back. For the first time in days, he felt relaxed. He told Margaret about his temporary promotion and his hopes of its becoming permanent.

'I'm so pleased for you,' she said. 'The last weeks you've allowed that Gilbert Martin business to become a strain, and I haven't helped.'

'Why should you say that?'

She pursued her lips. 'Oh, all that business about the *Justified Sinner* and Gil-Martin couldn't have helped. Stupid of me to have mentioned it.'

He demurred. 'No, no, added a certain spice.'

He then divulged all he had told Randall. And all Randall had told him.

She listened, mouth slightly open. 'That's a fantastic story,' she said when he'd finished.

'Fantastic is the word. I don't know or pretend to know what happened to his Monty Wallingham . . . except that he lost his head in a car accident . . . and Alwyn Makepeace, well, he had a breakdown. But what it has to do with my Gilbert Martin I'm damned if I know.'

'The house in Catford, though, that sounds pretty strange.' Margaret's brow furrowed.

'Yes, but you know how much I'd been drinking. For me, quite enough. So there was an ancient squatter in a derelict house . . .'

'Gilbert's house. Your friend Randall confirmed it. And Randall suggested Martin could have bought it as an investment. He's perhaps intending to redecorate it before inviting you to dinner. And now I hope I'm included in that invitation. I'd like to meet your Mr Martin after all you've told me.'

He liked the way she included herself in Martin's possible invitation. It showed she was thinking the right way, his way.

The dinner arrived. The food was good and they seemed to have the restaurant to themselves, at least until they reached the coffee. Matheson ordered two large brandies and the drinks arrived just as a party of four began to occupy the nearby table.

Margaret raised her glass. 'To you, Alistair, and your new appointment. I'm sure you'll be confirmed as Permanent Secretary.'

He raised his glass and, as he did so, looked across at the adjoining tables and the four new arrivals.

94

The glass never reached his lips. His arm seemed to freeze, brandy dripping on to the table cloth. The figure furthest from him at the next table waved cheerfully across at him.

Slowly he lowered the brandy glass, eyes riveted at the raised hand and the face beneath. Margaret followed the direction of his gaze.

'Someone you know?'

He nodded slowly, saying nothing.

'I think he's coming over,' Margaret observed.

The man seemed indeed to be excusing himself from his three companions. These were two women and another man. The women were young and attractive, one blonde, one brunette. The other man was also young, fair-haired, almost girlish, an androgynous creature; and laughing at something his male companion was saying as he rose and squeezed round the back of the blonde's chair to head in Matheson's direction.

'Who is he?' Margaret said.

Matheson replied from between clenched teeth, his face pale and tense, 'Don't you know? Don't you see?'

For a second, when he'd first looked across, he'd thought there was no table, only a mirror in which he could see his own reflection. Then he realised there were four people at the other table. And one appeared to be himself, which wasn't possible.

Margaret stared at him puzzled, 'I don't think I've met . . .'

'Of course you haven't met. Not him. But you can see, can't you?'

'See? See what?'

'Him! Me! Alike as . . .'

Gilbert Martin had reached their table. 'My dear Alistair, what a pleasant surprise!'

Matheson nodded dumbly.

'Of course,' the new arrival went on, 'you live quite near here, don't you? And tonight you'll be celebrating. I shall intrude but for a moment. May I add my congratulations.'

'For . . . for what?'

'Your promotion, of course. The new P.S.'

'Acting P.S.'

'A quibble my dear fellow.' Matheson being congratulated by Matheson, the second only under another name. 'A mere quibble.'

'How did you know?'

'Oh, I knew. Friends like yourself in high places. Not so high as you, perhaps, but many knowing friends.' Martin swivelled around as if only from the hips and bestowed a wide smile on Margaret.

'You must excuse me, but I did so want to congratulate my friend Alistair.' A wave of the hand in the air, a broad gesture. 'Oh, no need to tell me who you are? Margaret, of course. You don't mind my calling you Margaret? He's talked so much about you.'

This last piece of information took the smile from Margaret Mower's face. Whether or not she hoped for a progression in her relationship with Alistair, she certainly did not wish to know that he had been discussing her with strangers.

But Martin was undaunted by the disappearing smile. 'So nice finally to meet you. And may I say you are every bit as beautiful as Alistair said. He did not exaggerate. And so talented too. I've read all your books.'

Margaret's smile was restored. Not that she believed him. She knew to take flattery with a pinch of salt. But then, she liked the saline taste.

Before she could reply, however, Martin had taken a step back. 'Must return to my friends. Don't want to impose. Be delighted if you cared to join us, but I won't wish to break up an intimate dinner party for two. Perhaps another time, eh? See you soon, Alistair. Have a proper chat then.'

He backed away and returned to his place at the other table. His companions were talking volubly and he at once joined in, making some remark which caused them all to laugh. For a moment Margaret thought they might be laughing at Alistair and herself, but surely if they were doing so at least one of them would have looked in their direction? Nobody did.

It was only then that she realised her companion had barely spoken and was now sitting, forehead creased, staring across the table at her.

'What is it?' she said.

96

'You saw him?'

'I could hardly not see him. Who is he? He never actually mentioned his name.'

'You know who he is?'

'No, I don't!'

'The resemblance, Margaret, the resemblance! That's him. Of course it is. You can see . . .'

She answered in a tone of mild exasperation. 'See what?'

'Me! Him! Gilbert Martin. My double. Like talking to myself . . .'

'That's Gilbert Martin?'

'Who else?'

Her turn to be silent, Matheson's to become exasperated. 'You saw?' he said. 'You saw him!'

'Yes, I saw him.'

'Well?'

'And you tell me that is Gilbert Martin?'

'Of course it is. Who else?'

'And I believe you, Alistair. If you tell me, I believe you . . .'

'Well of course!'

'But, Alistair, he isn't . . . really in the least bit like you!'

Chapter Twelve

Later that evening, in Alistair Matheson's flat.

They left the trattoria shortly after Martin had visited their table. As they went he stood up and gave a small bow which neither Matheson nor Margaret acknowledged.

They walked along the King's Road in silence for a few moments until finally Matheson suggested they call into his flat for a final drink. To his surprise Margaret accepted. He was surprised because he'd felt they were on the brink of an argument; this to do with her refusing to acknowledge the resemblance between Martin and himself. It wasn't mentioned until he had shown her around the flat and they were in his drawing room, drinks in hand.

'I like the flat,' she said. 'Very nice. I like your taste. It lacks one thing, if you don't mind my saying so.'

'Say,' he said coolly.

'It needs a woman's touch.'

He knew he should have been pleased by this remark, encouraged certainly in areas he had in mind. Yet, in his present mood, he found himself resenting it. There was nothing, he told himself, wrong with the flat, the decor, or the furnishings. He at least could see nothing to criticise. What did she mean, a woman's touch? Frills around the edges of things? God, woman would put frills around the edges of the world. Pink too, yes that would certainly be the dominant colour. Oh, hell, not pink, please! Yet, he thought, she had no frills, pink or otherwise, in her own apartment. Why inflict them on him!

'What do you mean?' he said hoarsely.

'Just what I said.'

'My servant Dobson does rather well I've always thought.'

'Of course he probably does. Everything is spotless, no sign of dust, everything in its place. That's the trouble.'

'I don't follow.'

'It's . . . it's too perfect. Too hygienic. Too unreal, inhuman. Because of that, it lacks comfort. A woman would add what is missing. Perfection is never comfortable. I'm sure, Alistair, you want a cosy, comfortable home, a place you can relax in.'

He bridled visibly. 'I can relax perfectly well here. I like things to be hygienic. I'm sorry you don't like the flat . . .'

'But I do! It's bright and pleasant. It just needs . . .' She gave a small shrug '. . . the woman's touch.'

He changed the tenor of the conversation. 'I think you're shortsighted.'

Margaret laughed. 'I'm not in the least shortsighted.'

'You couldn't even see the likeness . . . the remarkable likeness . . . between Martin and myself.'

She became quiet. 'No, I didn't.'

'I find it's as if I'm looking in the mirror.'

'I don't see it.'

He turned away. The evening was going wrong. Not at all as he'd planned it. Because Martin had turned up at the restaurant. No, because she couldn't see that which was so obvious to him. But surely not only to him? That was a fantastic idea. Quite grotesque. That only he could see Martin as a mirror image.

'Alistair?'

He turned back, trying to appear nonchalant, concealing the strange concept in his mind. 'Yes?'

'It's ridiculous. Arguing about a comparative stranger. Does it matter who he looks like, your Mr Gil-Martin?'

'Gilbert Martin.'

'I'd like another drink.'

He refilled their glasses.

'Thank you,' she said, traces of a smile at the corners of her mouth.

Nothing more was said. Not then. She came to him and they kissed. She with considerable passion, he emulating her but nervous. It had been so long and he felt clumsy and awkward.

Afterwards he realised she had led him to his own bedroom. She had taken the initiative and he was at first embarrassed and then, after some thought, resolved he would be content she should do so. She started to undress him and after a while he started to undress her.

They made love twice that night. The first time was a failure, he was too nervous, too anxious, and it was over too soon. Later she started to excite him again, her tongue everywhere, her hands moving across his body, caressing, grasping . . .

She broke her silence, then, muttering, whispering to him, at him, surprising, shocking him with her gasping exhortations, her language raw and coarse. For the second time he entered her almost viciously, stimulated by her words and movements. They moved together now and it seemed to go on and on until they lay, covered in sweat, gasping and satiated.

'That was good,' she said. It was all she needed to say. He agreed.

Later, in the small hours, they were both awake. He told her of his fantastic idea about Martin. Could it be that only to him did the man appear as a mirror image?

'That's ridiculous,' she said.

'I'm telling you it's fantastic,' he replied. 'As much as your *Justified Sinner* story. As much as Martin being the Devil.'

The thought in words made him shiver which surprised him.

'Your friend Randall seems to think he's a spy from what you told me.'

'I suppose he does. You know, you shouldn't have been told that.'

She giggled, an unusual sound from her. 'Told what?' Wide-eyed. Playing the child.

'You learn fast.'

'All women learn faster than men. The men just hate to admit it.'

'Nonsense on both accounts.'

100

'I thought you'd say that.' Another thought crossed her mind. 'Hadn't you better tell Randall about the meeting tonight?'

'I suppose I should. He keeps telling me to do so, and so far I haven't done a thing. I'll phone him in the morning.'

'Strange story he told you. About the man being decapitated. And the other man who had a breakdown.'

'Alwyn Makepeace. An unforgettable name. Wait a minute. Something I didn't tell you. Something I'd almost forgotten. Makepeace claimed that the Gilbert Martin he met looked exactly like . . . like himself. Another . . . mirror image. Is . . . is it possible?'

She sat up in bed, breasts bare, staring ahead. 'Funny,' she said. 'Another old legend.'

'What?'

'Not that Hogg's Gil-Martin is a legend but the Devil in a novel. But something else. A Shapechanger!'

'What the hell is that?'

'Old legend. Crops up in folklore all over the place. American Indians believe in it. So do hougans.'

'What are hougans?'

'Voodoo priests.'

'Oh, yes, that will be it.' Caustic as only a Scotsman can be. She looked down at him. 'You're laughing.'

'Yes, I am. And so should you. Voodoo? Shapechangers? Red Indians? It'll be horror comics next. We're both going crazy.'

She giggled again. 'Are you sure?'

'Oh, it's all right for you. You're a lady novelist. You earn your living by fantasy. By story-telling. Me? I'm a senior civil servant. Very practical. Very down-to-earth. Supposed to be. Also don't believe in folk tales or horror stories. Except in fiction . . .'

'What about the house in Catford?'

'He owns it. Getting it decorated probably.'

'The old man who knew your name?'

'Martin must have told him. Look, if Martin is some kind of agent, as Randall seems to think, the whole idea may be to compromise me in some way. I'm quite an important person, Permanent Under Secretary now. A way in to the country's defence secrets . . . Yes, that could be it. As Makepeace would have been a way in to GCHQ.'

She was nodding her head now. 'Yes. And the lookalike business – looking like Makepeace, looking like you – could be some kind of hypnotism or brainwashing. To get to you as he got to Makepeace.'

Matheson looked dubious. This was something he had never considered. Nor would he do so now. 'I first saw him in the street and spotted the resemblance. How could he have hypnotised me? No, that's not possible.'

'It is if you met him before.'

'I didn't!'

'And he erased the memory of the meeting from your mind?'

'Really, Margaret, we're going into fantasy again.' He paused, brow furrowed. 'Pity Monty Wallingham was killed. He might have learned something.'

'But isn't Makepeace still alive?'

'Randall said he had a breakdown but he didn't say he was dead. Now, wait a minute. Makepeace is like me. Thought the man looked like him. I should like to talk to Makepeace . . .'

'Then why don't you?'

'I don't know. Hadn't thought about it.'

'Think about it now,' Margaret insisted.

'If he's still alive, it might be an idea. I'll be talking to Randall tomorrow. Tell him I've seen Martin again. If I can find out what happened to Makepeace . . .'

They both lay back, a decision made. After a while, they tried to make love again but didn't succeed. It seemed Matheson was not, as yet, a three-times-a-night man.

The next morning he arranged a taxi to drive her home before he went in to the Ministry. Late that afternoon he phoned her.

'I've spoken to Randall,' he informed her. 'Told him about our encounter with Martin.'

'And?'

'He was interested. Said he would . . . take steps.'

'What does that mean?'

102

'When you speak to intelligence people, you never expect to understand what they mean. If they intended merely to cross the road to get to the other side, they would tell you they were taking steps. Which I suppose in one sense would be true.'

She absorbed this and changed the subject. 'What about Makepeace? Did you ask him?'

'I had to be circumspect.'

'You didn't ask him.'

'Oh, but I did. Very casually. "Whatever happened to that fellow in the Wallingham business? Makepeace or whatever?" Did it as a pure aside.'

'And probably alerted him at once.'

'I did not. All Randall would say was that Makepeace went into an asylum of some kind. For how long, he didn't know. Might be still there.'

'Where?'

'Didn't say. Might not be there. Might be dead. Or released.'

'Not much help, all that.'

'Didn't expect him to be. Intelligence people never answer questions, even the most innocent ones. Then they know they can't get into trouble.'

Margaret was exasperated. 'Then what was the point?'

'Off chance he might let something slip. He didn't, so I did my own investigating.'

'How?'

'You forget, I'm a very senior official in the Home Civil Service. A person of some considerable influence.'

'I'll try not to be overawed.'

It was Matheson's turn to be exasperated. 'I'm merely explaining so as you will understand. There's no need to be sarcastic.'

'So tell me what happened.'

'Alwyn Makepeace was a civil servant too. Apart from intelligence records there had to be his ordinary civil service records. I asked and obtained them.'

He paused, took a deep breath and said, 'How would you like to go down to the West Country for the weekend?'

'Very nice. But what has a dirty weekend to do with . . . .?'

103

'Margaret, as a senior civil servant, and unmarried, I can have an affair. I can pass the weekend in rural surroundings with a lady companion. But it cannot be referred to as a dirty weekend! As to what it has to do with the matter in hand, Alwyn Makepeace was sent to a nursing home in Exeter after his breakdown. As far as his records go he is still there.'

'So it's not even a dirty weekend. Not even simply a weekend in rural surroundings. It's merely part of your investigation into your present neurosis.'

'If you don't want to come . . .'

'I didn't say I don't want to come. The Imperial and the Royal Clarence are among the better hotels in Exeter. I suggest you book a double room . . . and if you have to adopt a *nom de plume*, please not Smith, Jones or Brown.'

The weekend.

'It's good to get away from London,' Margaret said.

It occurred to Matheson that, for all her reputation and ability as a novelist, she could come out with all the customary clichés.

The drive to Exeter was pleasant, the sun forcing its way through grey clouds. They left London early on Friday morning (he had taken two days from three weeks' leave long due to him) and were well on the road west before breakfast. They reached Exeter just after two o'clock in the afternoon and, turning off the High Street at Broadgate, drove up to the Royal Clarence Hotel.

Matheson registered under his own name which caused Margaret's eyebrows to go up in surprise. Once in their room alone, she challenged him.

'Your own name, eh? Very courageous. I should be impressed.' She was standing at a window gazing at the excellent view of Exeter Cathedral.

'No need,' he said. 'A practical necessity. If anything urgent crops up at the Ministry, they have to have an address and telephone number, in case of emergencies.'

'So no doubt you put *Mr and Mrs Matheson*?' A touch of sarcasm.

'As a matter of fact, I didn't. Just put my own name and address.'

104

She frowned, considered this and bridled. 'So I don't even exist!'

'You exist. You are here. Your name simply does not appear therefore you are not compromised.'

He saw she obviously couldn't make up her mind whether she approved of this or not.

He went on, 'Now to find out where we are going. From the civil service files I gather the place Makepeace was put into was called the Royal South Devon Hospital. Somewhere off the Magdalen Road.'

The hotel receptionist directed them to the Magdalen Road and the Hospital.

'Of course, it's not an actual hospital,' she said.

'What exactly do you mean by that?' Matheson said.

'Well, it is . . . or certainly it was for, well, you know . . .'

'I don't know. Which is why I'm asking.'

'It's a loony . . . I mean, it's for the mentally disturbed.'

Matheson nodded, his face expressionless, and led Margaret out to the Aston-Martin. Ten minutes later, as they drove up the large square red-brick building, the clouds finally managed to shut out the sun and rain started to fall. They hurried into the building.

The entrance hall was large and cold. Green walls surrounded stone floors. A formidable woman, white coat over a black dress, stood behind a reception desk.

'Can I help you?'

'I wish to enquire about an inmate . . . a patient, I mean.'

'You are family?'

'No. I am a senior member of the patient's former profession.'

'And the name?'

'Makepeace. Alwyn Makepeace.'

'You understand we are not permitted to give out information regarding patients?' The woman's mouth was a thin straight line.

'I don't wish for information. I wish to speak to Mr Makepeace.'

'You would, of course, have to get permission.'

'From whom?'

'The senior consultant. Or the Registrar.'

'I will see the senior consultant then.'

'He won't be here until Tuesday.'

'The Registrar then.'

'I doubt if he'll see you without an appointment.'

Matheson gazed with ever increasing annoyance at the woman and then glanced at Margaret at his side. Her face was bland, expressionless, or did he detect the trace of a smile? He decided to use some pressure.

'My name is Matheson. I am Permanent Under Secretary at the Ministry!' Careful not to indicate the exact ministry. Leave her with the impression he might actually be from the Ministry of Health.

It appeared to work. The woman paled and without further ado lifted a telephone. In minutes another attendant, this time male, showed them into a large office. The man behind the desk rose, hand outstretched.

'Cody,' he said. 'Conrad Cody. Registrar. You're from the Ministry of . . .?'

'. . . Defence,' Matheson cut in.

'Oh, I thought you were from the Ministry of Health?'

'No. My name is Alistair Matheson. You can check with the Ministry of Defence. Er, this is Miss Mower, my assistant.'

'Please . . . please sit down. I must say I cannot see what we have to do with the Defence Ministry . . . Would you care for some tea?'

Matheson accepted the tea on their behalf. It might help to relax Dr Cody. Over tea, he explained, 'Your patient Mr Alwyn Makepeace worked for the Ministry.'

'Ah, yes,' said Cody. 'I understood he worked in communications.'

'Directly linked to Defence.'

'Of course, of course. You understand the nature of Mr Makepeace's condition.'

'We understood he had a breakdown some years ago,' Margaret said, feeling completely left out of everything so far.

'A "Breakdown" is not a word we use. It is meaningless,' the doctor said primly.

106

Matheson glared at Margaret and cleared his throat. 'Of course we realise that. What exactly is the matter with Makepeace?'

'Was the matter? A number of things. Difficult to describe them in layman's terms. Mental diseases are divided into psychoses, considered insanity, and neuroses, considered nerves, by the layman. The main neuroses are anxiety, hysteria and obsessional. Certainly at the beginning Makepeace suffered from obsessional neurosis, a very severe type of neurotic illness. These can be characterised in a number of ways. Compulsive feelings that certain acts must be done, and, in Makepeace's case, certain thoughts must be thought . . .'

'Such as insisting that someone else was his physical double?' Margaret again, ignoring a second glare from Matheson.

'You obviously knew him,' Dr Cody continued. 'When Makepeace came here, at first, he was very obsessional. But he responded to treatment.'

Cody's brows furrowed. 'And we thought he was close to being released. You understand, he could release himself at any time. He had agreed to come in here but we couldn't keep him, not unless he was certifiable. Which he wasn't. Not then.'

'You're implying he is now?' Matheson asked.

'I didn't say that. I . . . don't know.'

'But something happened, didn't it?'

'Mr Matheson, I have told you as much as I can. There is, as you know, a degree of confidentiality between physician and patient. All I have told you already was known by his immediate employers at the time he came here. The rest is between myself and Mr Makepeace.'

Matheson took a deep breath. He straightened up in the chair. Doctor, patient confidentiality indeed. Confidentiality was something he knew all about. And knew the attitude to take when those in the service needed discouraging from maintaining it.

'Dr Cody, this is no trivial matter. Makepeace held a position of great importance in the defence of this nation. If he was or is ill, we are entitled to comprehend the nature of his illness. Even if we have to get a judge to so instruct you.'

107

It was bluff, Margaret knew, but could not but admire Matheson's execution of such a tactic. Cody's face had flushed and his eyes flickered around his office as if seeking a way out. There was none.

'I'm sure there is no need for such a measure,' he said. 'Of course anything I tell you is in complete confidence . . .'

'Of course.'

'Well then . . . latterly, when treating Makepeace and feeling we were having some success in ridding him of his obsessional problems, we began to notice other hitherto unrecognised aspects of his personality. Psychopathic symptoms were being uncovered . . . you understand the phrase psychopathic personality means roughly someone who has different standards of behaviour from those accepted by society?'

Matheson's turn to frown. 'What form did these symptoms take?'

'The basic one, of course, of a complete disregard for other's feelings. That's minor, irritating but not necessarily perverse. But with Makepeace there was an increasing interest in cruelty, in a desire to inflict pain. Although here he had no opportunity to do so, there were indications . . .'

'And now?' Matheson said.

'Now?'

'How is he now?'

'I'm afraid I have no idea.'

'What do you mean?'

'As I said, we couldn't certify him.'

Margaret said, 'Despite the psychotic tendencies?'

'Certainly. There was no evidence. We merely suspected, and were concerned. But he insisted he was able to function now in the outside world and we couldn't deny him. It seems he was right. We've had no reports of his being anything other than normal. But of course I thought you knew that. Alwyn Makepeace discharged himself over a year ago.'

Chapter Thirteen

'Of course we know where he lives,' Dr Cody said.

Matheson looked up but it was Margaret who spoke. 'Can you give us his present address?'

'Naturally we made sure we had that information, just in case.'

'In case of what?' Matheson asked.

Cody looked away uneasily. 'We felt some kind of eye should be kept on Makepeace. I suppose I should say we were . . . we are concerned about his suspected psychosis. So when he gave us his new address, we arranged he go on the local G.P.'s panel and informed the doctor of his case history. A natural precaution in case he should become . . . ill again.'

'Ill,' Matheson said flatly. A statement not a question.

'If there were any recurrence of symptoms, then the G.P. could refer him to us again. I'm glad to say there has been no such occurrence in the year since he left us.'

Matheson frowned. 'But if there had been and Makepeace had not gone to his local doctor, you would not have known?'

Cody straightened up behind his desk as if to indicate he could be as pompous as his male visitor. 'We believed we had established a kind of trust between our patient and ourselves.'

Margaret expressed her surprise without any of Matheson's pomposity. 'You're serious. You believed you could trust a psychotic?'

'A *possible* psychotic, Miss Mower. And remember, we were treating Makepeace primarily for obsessional neurosis. Now I'm afraid I've told you pretty much everything possible. The healing of mental illness is not yet an exact science. There are subtleties you would not understand.' He went on in this vein for another minute before rising from behind his desk. 'Now I'm sure you'll excuse me? I have a great deal of work.'

'You were going to give us Makepeace's address?'

'Was I? I'm not sure that ethically I should . . .'

Matheson assumed his civil service face again. 'Doctor, Makepeace was a former civil servant with some responsibility in highly confidential areas. His department should have been informed when he was discharged from this place and his new address should have been forwarded to that department.'

'I . . . I can't be sure we were so informed. I shall consult my files and if that is the case, I shall so inform them at once.'

'In order to save time we'll take the address now.'

Cody looked uncertainly from one of his visitors to the other. Margaret could only admire the assumed authority in Matheson's voice. Awkward in other things, she thought, he had a magnificent assurance when playing the senior civil servant.

'Yes, of course,' the doctor said and went out of the office.

He returned a few moment later carrying a buff-coloured file. 'Here we are. Cherry Lane Cottage, near Widecombe on the Moor. That's Dartmoor. I remember Makepeace said he wanted peace and quiet. Where else would one find peace and quiet but on the moor?'

They drove to the village of Moretonhampstead, and at the tiny post office, Matheson asked directions to Cherry Lane Cottage.

'Oh, that'll be Mr Makepeace,' the post mistress said. 'Don't see him very often. Once a fortnight. Cashes his pension cheque, buys a few things and goes off.'

'He's a pensioner?'

'Not a senior citizen's pension. More likely an early retirement one. Such a nice man, Mr Makepeace. But very quiet.'

'How do we find Cherry Lane Cottage?'

'Ah, yes, how indeed. Just keep driving along the B3212. That's the road right across the moor. You'll see the sign for Cherry Lane Cottage after you pass the Widecombe sign. Well, that is, you might see it. The rain makes it so easy to miss, especially when it's misty like it is today. And it's not really a road up to the cottage, just a track. Of course if you do miss it, you'll go right on to Two Bridges and Princetown, where the prison is. Now don't you go far from the road if you go looking for the cottage. With that mist you could get lost easily. And don't try it at night.' She grinned cheerfully. 'You might not be found for weeks.'

'Or we might meet the Hound of the Baskervilles,' Margaret said, returning her grin, turning from the rack of postcards she had pretended to be studying.

'Dartmoor ponies, you might,' said the post mistress seriously. 'But I don't know nothing about any dogs on the moor. Has somebody lost one?'

There was no answer to the question. They left and were on the moor again, moving slowly through the thickening rain.

'I've never been on Dartmoor before,' Margaret said. 'Neither has that post mistress, I think. No dogs on the moor indeed!'

'I've been here. Years ago. Motoring holiday John O'Groats to Land's End,' Matheson said. 'On a decent day, I rather liked the moor. Bleak like the Highlands. Plenty of high ground but no real mountains.'

The mist broke for a few moments as if on cue and Margaret could see the high ground away to the horizon on their right.

'Up there,' Matheson nodded, 'and beyond lies what Conan Doyle called the Great Grimpen Mire. They say it can suck down a moor pony. I hope you're keeping your eyes open for that sign?'

They nearly missed the sign. It had indeed tilted over. A wild moor pony was rubbing itself against the sagging wooden post. The drizzle had stopped but mist clung to the ground and to them, a damp and chilling shroud. The pony studied them for a moment and then came over to peer at them from behind a low stone dyke as they parked the car.

Another signpost close by indicated that the traveller was ill advised to feed the ponies. Margaret scowled at this.

'What's wrong with feeding them if they're hungry? I have some chocolate.'

'Keep it. Feed that one and when he's eaten your chocolate, he'll want more. And when he can't get any more, he's quite liable to kick in the side of the Aston Martin. Come along, this must be the track.'

111

It was a rough path between clumps of grass and rock. It led upwards into the mist. Somewhere there was the boom of a bittern. Margaret closed with Matheson, taking his arm.

'Sinister, isn't it?'

'Just mist. Keep to the path and we should be all right.'

They kept to the path, and were faced with a problem when it divided into two, one track heading on upwards, the other twisting around an outcrop of rock and heading northward into the deeper mist.

'Which path do we keep to?' she said.

'Straight on, I think.'

'It's getting thicker. And darker. What did that woman say about night on the moor?'

'It's only late afternoon. And it's just the mist. Would you rather wait in the car?'

'Alone? In this mist? You're joking!'

They climbed onwards. She became quite breathless. 'Why . . . are we . . . going to see this . . . man anyway? I think . . . I've forgotten.'

'Because he knew a man called Gilbert Martin and claimed he and Martin looked exactly alike.'

Quite suddenly the outline of a cottage rose up in front of them.

'There we are, Margaret. Cherry whatsit Cottage.'

'It doesn't look real. The mist makes it look like . . . like . . .'

'Like what?'

'Like a film set. One of the old 1930s horror films – *The Bride of Frankenstein*. All dry ice, grey cycloramas and damp-looking cardboard rocks.'

As they approached, the mist cleared and the cottage defined itself. It was a typical aging edifice of rough stone with a thick wooden door, fading green paint peeling from the wood. On each side of the door was a square window with four thick, glass panes. A slanting roof of cracked wet slates was broken only by a lone chimney. No smoke issued from it.

'You're right,' Matheson nodded. 'Universal Studios, 1934. With Karloff in those enormous boots being pursued by villagers carrying flaming torches. And Ernest Thesiger lurking in the background. Used to like these old horrors.'

112

They were in front of the wooden door now. Matheson lifted his fist and knocked firmly on the peeling wood. The door swung open.

'I suppose they don't bother to lock doors in the country,' he said, hesitating. 'Nothing worth stealing, I imagine.'

'So what do we do now?'

Matheson rapped his knuckles on the wooden door frame and waited, staring back along the track they had just followed. Not that he could see anything. Except fog. Almost tangible, swirling, wreathing, distorting what vision there was.

'No one seems to be at home.' Margaret said, stepping sideways and staring at a patch of ground below the right hand window.

'Should we go in?' Matheson, still hesitant, looked at her as if for support.

'Better than waiting out here in the dampness,' she replied. 'You know, there's the beginnings of a vegetable garden here.'

'I imagine one has to do something, living in the wilderness. Although why on earth he should choose to live out here, God knows.'

'To do with his mental state? A kind of reaction against society. A form of agrophobia perhaps.' She turned and rejoined him. They went into the cottage.

It consisted of one large room with bare stone walls. To the right the fireplace, stone and steel and ashes, and a thick slate mantelpiece on which stood candles in brass holders and an oil lamp. Above the fireplace an ancient fowling piece. In front there were two armchairs, circa the early fifties, cracked plastic once pretending to be leather. A trestle table, looking remarkably new, held another lantern, a half empty bottle of milk and a large mug. Against the rear wall was a basin and a small calorgas cooker, and another side table held two pots, a frying pan and several china dishes. On a shelf above there were tins of ham, corned beef, peas, carrots, and two tins of pineapple. Beside the tins was a lettuce, none too new, green leaves turning brown and curling up at the edges. Next to it, a bowl containing some dubious-looking old, new potatoes.

In the centre of the rear wall facing the front door was another door, key in lock, obviously leading to the rear of the cottage.

To the left was the sleeping area, a camp bed, unmade, blankets and sheets in an untidy mass; at one side a large, very old wardrobe slanting over the bed. At the other side a bedside table on which stood another oil lamp and against the wall a bookcase, tattered paperbacks providing a splash of colour.

'All one needs if one has to go back to nature,' Matheson said, superciliousness covering a nervousness he was loath to reveal. 'I suppose the . . . the usual offices are outside at the rear.'

'I suppose,' Margaret said. 'But where is the occupant?'

Matheson strode over to the back door. 'Not out at the usual offices, anyway. The door's locked on the inside.'

'Maybe he's taken a stroll,' she suggested.

'In this weather?'

'Alistair, some people actually like the great outdoors, mist, mud and rain included.'

'Yes,' he replied dryly. 'We even have people indulge in that kind of perversion in Scotland. Shall we step outside and see if we can spot Mr Makepeace? Even a neurotic enthusiast couldn't go far in this kind of weather. Unless he's planning to emulate a pony and disappear into the Grimpen Mire.'

They went outside. The mist seemed to be thinning. Rocks at the side of the path they had climbed were taking on distinct outlines now.

'All we need is the howling of Sherlock's hound,' Matheson said. 'To complete the effect.'

But Margaret did not reply. She was staring beyond the area where the vegetable garden seemed to extend into the mist.

'There!' she said. 'At the end of the garden. Someone standing there!'

Matheson peered into the mist and took a few steps forward. His right foot sank into a damp patch of ground. He looked down at what had been a shining patent leather shoe, now mud-encrusted, and cursed under his breath. He limped onwards, aware his footwear was ill adapted to the moor. The shape at the end of the garden became clearer.

He said, 'Damn! It's only a scarecrow.'

Avoiding the damp patch, Margaret came up beside him. 'Very practical. Keep the birds off his vegetables. I suppose you're right. He can't be too far away.'

She gazed around and then her eyes returned to the scarecrow. 'It's a very big scarecrow.'

114

'Yes, it is.'

Matheson moved forward slowly to within three yards of the scarecrow and then stopped abruptly. Margaret heard his sharp intake of breath.

'What is it?'

'Stay . . . stay there,' he said. 'Stay!'

She could see the scarecrow was very tall, the pole that made up its backbone over seven feet in height. A tattered raincoat fluttered some feet off the ground, seemingly wrapped around the body of the dummy. Margaret could just make out something scarlet on the coat.

She moved forward again.

'No!' he called, voice on the edge of panic. 'For God's sake, don't come nearer!'

She stopped, frightened by his tone.

Matheson stood ashen-faced, staring up at that which they had presumed was a scarecrow.

The body of the man had been raised off the ground, his hands lashed together around the top of the pole. Someone had driven a long nail through the wrists and into the wood. At the ankles the body had again been tied to the pole over a foot from the ground. The tattered raincoat had been tied around the shoulders. Under the raincoat was a once expensive sports jacket wide open at the front, and stained. Under the jacket, the shirt was also wide open. Below the shirt, the trousers hung limply around the hips. The fly, a twisted zip fastener, was open.

Coat, jacket, shirt and trousers were soaked in a thick damp, oleaginous scarlet.

Matheson could only judge that the blade of some sharp instrument had been thrust into the body just below the throat . . . it had to have been very sharp indeed as it had then been drawn down deeply from the entry point through the chest, navel and stomach to the crotch. As if the man was about to be filleted.

Matheson turned away, phelgm rising in his throat. He started to retch, knowing they had finally found Alwyn Makepeace.

115

Chapter Fourteen

Alwyn Makepeace didn't look in any way like Alistair Matheson. Not now; not before either. Despite the manner of his dying, his face was unmarked. Nor was there any expression of pain or horror there. The face was that of a middle-aged man, slightly baffled, above all, in death, serene.

'Not in the least like me,' he told Margaret later.

That was after he'd brought the police to the cottage and insisted on the scene-of-crime officer calling the Chief Constable. Of course, questions were asked.

'Why?'

'Why are you here?'

'Why did you want to visit Alwyn Makepeace?'

'Had you met him before?'

'Why were you making enquiries at the hospital in Exeter?'

To all these questions were added the word 'sir'. But then Alistair Matheson was not an ordinary suspect. Indeed, it became apparent the he could not be held to be a suspect at all. Apart from his position as a senior civil servant (and that did not mean he was not a suspect, after all somewhere at some time in recent history surely senior civil servants have committed obvious crimes; certainly espionage for foreign powers; and therefore possibly in history they may well have committed murder) he had an alibi. The time of Makepeace's death was estimated quite precisely at around the hour Matheson and Margaret Mower had spent with Dr Cody.

The Chief Constable, Sir Alan Carfax, arrived and joined the investigating officer, Chief Inspector George Trevayne. After a time, Matheson and Margaret were driven back to police headquarters in Exeter where further questions would be asked. They were not shown into an ordinary interview room but were taken at once to the large comfortable office of the Chief Constable. They were offered food and drinks and settled for coffee and rolls. An hour later they were joined by Carfax and George Trevayne. Another offer of coffee was followed by more questions but each deliberately phrased to turn the interview into more a discussion than a cross-examination.

Carfax started, 'You knew Makepeace, Mr Matheson?'

'Knew of him. Never met him.'

Trevayne took over at once. 'Yet you came all the way from London to see him?'

Alistair Matheson had been thinking for the past two hours how he should frame his story and had instructed Margaret to leave all the answering to him.

'That's not quite accurate. Miss Mower and I had decided to spend a restful weekend here in the West Country. Before I left London I heard that Makepeace was in hospital in Exeter. I knew something of his case and decided to visit him. Dr Cody told me he'd been discharged and was living at the cottage on Dartmoor. Since we'd already decided to drive over the moor . . . Miss Mower had never been on Dartmoor . . . I thought we should look in on Makepeace. You know what we found.'

The Chief Inspector looked from Matheson to Carfax and back.

'You heard, in London, that Makepeace was in Exeter? From whom?'

Matheson took a deep breath. He'd determined from the beginning that he was not going to mention Gilbert Martin. The only link between Martin and Makepeace was through Randall. To mention Randall would be to bring in the security services. If they wanted to come in, they would do so when they heard of Makepeace's murder. That would be up to them. Not Matheson's responsibility. Also to bring Martin in would be to tell a story these police officers would certainly consider quite incredible. Also it would cast a shadow over his own integrity.

He replied disarmingly, 'After we'd decided to come down here, I came across Makepeace's file.' He thought, they

117

would never discover he had requested the file. 'I'd heard about Makepeace's case and it interested me. Pure curiosity, I suppose. But he was a former civil servant, had been a sick man, so I decided to call on him.'

'Can you tell us what his case was?' said the Chief Constable. 'Save us a bit of time.'

What the hell actually was Makepeace's case? He realised there was no easy answer; Randall had been deliberately vague. He had to make it up as he went along.

'Alwyn Makepeace had a responsible job with GCHQ. He also dabbled in Spiritualism. Not the safest hobby for a man who might become a security risk. I believe . . . and this is only hearsay . . . he was investigated. Insisted he was no risk to security, of course. But . . . well . . . he felt he was being persecuted by the security people. Over a period of time. He became extremely upset.'

He took another deep breath and plunged into further partial improvisation. 'I believe he complained to his superiors. You will understand his complains became common knowledge in the Home Civil Service. I, as a senior civil servant, heard about them and was curious. I think most of us were. Of course, I was in the Scottish Office at the time.'

'Most interesting,' Carfax said. 'Be curious myself. Please go on.'

'In the end, the security people were more or less proved right. Makepeace became quite obsessional, had a breakdown. He insisted it was worry over the investigation. Security maintained he was unstable to start with. A case of which came first, chicken or the egg? To get out of it, he took early retirement and voluntarily committed himself to hospital. That appeared to be the end of the matter.'

'Was there a security leak?' asked Trevayne.

'To my knowledge, they never found any evidence of one. It was one of the reasons I wanted to call on him. A lot of us in the Service felt he'd had a raw deal.'

Margaret was looking at Matheson with an expression of awe at the back of her eyes. Later, when they were alone, she was to say, 'You should be writing fiction rather than me. That story sounded almost convincing.' Matheson was able to defend it as the partial truth. But then she did notice that,

118

since the Martin business, he was developing a glibness she reckoned hadn't been with him previously. He was developing an imagination.

It was Trevayne who now put a key question to him. 'Do you think all this business years ago could have anything to do with his murder?'

'You're the detective,' Matheson replied. 'I couldn't answer that. Of course you'd doubtless have to consult the security people.'

'Yes, we will.'

'I must say,' he went on, 'I can't get over the fact that this should happen just before I called on him. I mean, since nobody knew I was coming, it wasn't as if . . . well . . . it might have been done to stop him talking to me.'

There was silence. Matheson felt he had perhaps overplayed his hand. It was the Chief Constable who came to the rescue.

'Coincidence. Happens all the time in so many cases. Seen it often over the years. Confuses until we discount it.'

'I suppose it would have been understandable if Makepeace had committed suicide,' Matheson said, making conversation quickly. 'In view of his possible instability.'

'Only trouble with that is you'd find it difficult to nail your wrists to that wooden pole before you disembowelled yourself,' Trevayne said with a distinct touch of acidity.

'Yes, of course.'

Another pause. Carfax ordered more coffee and chatted to Matheson about the problems of the Ministry of Defence. Also the problems for civil servants in their dealings with politicians.

'After all,' said Carfax, 'we're the professionals. Damn politicians are only passing through, so to speak.'

Coffee delivered, he then seemed to try and reassure Matheson. 'You'll be relieved to know Trevayne here has his own theory about what might have happened.'

Matheson was genuinely interested. How could he not be, under the circumstances? Any theories of his own might include Gilbert Martin and he steered away from that thought.

Trevayne said, 'There have been reports of gypsies and tinkers on the moor.'

119

Margaret couldn't be silent any longer. 'Oh, not that old one! When in doubt blame the poor sodding gypsies.'

Trevayne scowled, his face reddening. Matheson looked dubious which seemed to encourage Margaret – not his intention at all.

'Have you had much experience with gypsies and travelling people, Miss Mower?'

'No, but . . .' Margaret flushed now.

'I'm aware that among many so-called thinking people there's a deal of sympathy for them. Fair enough. Many are hard-working people who follow a way of life much misunderstood by the rest of us. But I have to point out to you that recently there have been outbreaks of theft and violence among one particular group of travelling people.'

'I still think you're looking to an easy solution, Mr Trevayne.'

She found Matheson was now glaring at her. As if to say 'Leave it alone.' She looked away.

'We've had reports of some pretty peculiar practices among this particular group.'

'What kind of practices?' Matheson said, instantly curious.

The Chief Constable coughed loudly and exchanged a look with Trevayne.

'On information received,' Carfax said, clearing his throat, 'a child was kidnapped for dubious purposes. This particular group of travelling people . . . I call them that rather than gypsies because I don't believe they are true Romanies . . . are reported to indulge in some fairly esoteric activities.'

'What does that mean?' Margaret, defiant.

'Witchcraft, for want of a better word. Rituals carried out at night. The kidnapped child was picked up by our people in time. Couldn't prove it had been kidnapped . . . they claimed he'd wandered into their camp. But then there were more and more reports of lights moving on the moor, ritual dancing naked at night . . . that kind of thing.'

'Nude dancing at night? In this weather?' This time Margaret sounded incredulous.

'The weather varies.' Trevayne replied dryly. 'Anyway, we've some evidence that these rituals have taken place. And the way Makepeace was killed . . . you have to admit it has a ritualistic quality?'

Before Margaret could say anything further, Matheson replied quickly, 'Yes that could certainly be said.'

'Anyway,' said the Chief Constable, 'that indicates the way our investigations might lead. And of course at the same time we are going to look into Makepeace's relations with his neighbours. Admittedly he was a recluse but there may have been some bad blood along the way. Especially when there are questions regarding the poor man's mental stability. However, I see no need to detain you and Miss Mower any longer. It's a pity this business has put a damper on your weekend.'

'A bigger damper on Makepeace's don't you think?' Margaret said tartly.

'You'll leave your London addresses in case we have to contact you,' Trevayne said, but was interrupted by his superior.

'No need. Mr Matheson can always be contacted at the Ministry. And he will be in touch with Miss Mower should it prove necessary.'

They drove back to the hotel in silence. Matheson was vaguely irritated by Margaret's questioning of Trevayne's theory about travelling people. That it might have delayed their release even by minutes was an annoyance. They'd had nothing to do with the killing of Makepeace and he was sure the police appreciated the fact. He wanted away from officialdom; wanted time to think his own thoughts, to consider positions and possibilities.

In their hotel room, Margaret was the first to speak. 'You're annoyed with me?'

'Yes.'

'But it's so easy for these people to pick on gypsies or tramps when there's a crime they can't solve.'

'I've always believed the police are surprisingly efficient and knowledgeable,' he said, in one of his more pompous tones.

'Oh, yes. What about the Birmingham Six and the other four?'

'And the Scottsboro' boys and Dreyfus and Oscar Slater and so on. There are always miscarriages of justice. But we can talk about then now because they have been admitted.'

'Much consolation to the wrongly accused!'

'Anyway the police were not condemning all gypsies. Trevayne was merely indicating that there was some dubious group nearby who would obviously be worth investigating.'

'There's someone also worth investigating – your Mr Martin. Whom you didn't even bother to mention.'

He swung around to her, his face hot with anger. 'Oh, yes, I should mention a man who looks like me but doesn't look like me, who also looks like Makepeace but doesn't. Who is under observation by the intelligence services, and who may, according to you, be . . . what was the word? . . . a shapechanger?'

'Well, there is some truth . . .'

'They'd have me committed as unstable if not stark raving mad. Let them find out from Randall anything that might be valuable. I have no intention of making a fool of myself.'

They said very little more before going to bed. They lay side by side, in the king-sized hotel bed without touching. There was no repetition of their previous night together. Margaret could not erase from her mind the image of the body they had at first believed to be a scarecrow. It took her a long time to fall asleep. It was even longer for Matheson. He lay staring at the darkened ceiling, able barely to follow a large crack that ran from one corner to another, twisting and turning into a shape like a profile; his own profile in reverse. So like his vision of Gilbert Martin.

And his mind was filled with questions, jostling each other, echoing at the back of his brain. Who was Martin? Why was Martin? What had happened to Alistair Matheson since he'd met this man in Oxford Street in broad daylight on a dull spring day? Why had Makepeace died? How did the man's horrible death relate to himself and to Martin?

Finally he slept fitfully. There were nightmares but in the morning he could no longer remember them.

They drove back to London.

Chapter Fifteen

He dropped her at Richmond.

'You'll be in touch?' she said, a question rather than a statement.

'Yes,' he replied, momentarily unsure that he meant what he was saying.

In his own flat in Chelsea he poured himself a large whisky and sat down, gazing at a blank television screen. After a time he switched the set on and found himself staring at the large mouth of Esther Rantzen. He changed channels. Some sort of American mystery film. He watched without seeing.

More time passed.

He was wondering why he wasn't hungry. He'd eaten nothing since breakfast in the Exeter hotel. It was now past nine o'clock. He should think about food. Yet he had no interest in eating. Perhaps, he told himself, somewhere at the back of his mind was the image of Alwyn Makepeace, dead and used as a scarecrow.

Makepeace, who thought he'd met a man called Gilbert Martin who looked like him, had died like that. Should he, Matheson, be concerned? He too had met Martin who looked like *him*. Would he end up like Makepeace, a gutted scarecrow? The thought induced a feeling of nausea.

The doorbell rang.

He rose slowly, reluctantly. Wanting to much to be left alone; wanting to curl up in the armchair, womblike, and sleep. Alone and warm and safe.

The doorbell rang again. Insistent.

He stood before it, the thought coming to him that the caller might be Gilbert Martin. What to say, how to react?

I've just seen a dead, mutilated man and I blame you for his death. He took a deep breath and opened the door.

Gavin Randall said, 'You're back.'

'Who told . . .'

'We keep an eye on our people, Alistair. Especially when we have problems. May I come in?'

In the lounge he looked pointedly at Matheson's empty whisky glass and sat down.

'Would you like a drink?' Matheson said.

'Whisky'll be fine, old man.'

With drink in hand, Randall settled back in the armchair and looked at his host.

'You went to visit Makepeace.'

The directness of the statement should have surprised Matheson but it didn't. If anything, he resented Randall's certainty.

'I went for a quiet weekend. When I realised I was near Makepeace I enquired about him at the hospital.'

'A quiet weekend? And you found Makepeace was living on Dartmoor?'

'Yes.'

'So you went there to visit him?'

'If you know about it, why ask me?'

'Just making sure of my facts. Why, Alistair? Why all this trouble to meet a man you didn't know?'

Matheson could be honest now. 'I . . . I was curious.'

'About Makepeace? I told you about him.'

'I wanted to see for myself. If Makepeace thought Martin looked like him, then surely Makepeace must . . . must look like me?'

Randall laughed. It was a hoarse laugh. The whisky had made him hoarse. 'But haven't you been told Martin looks like neither you nor Makepeace?'

Matheson stared down at the carpet and shook his head. 'I've seen Martin, face to face. He does look like me. To me anyway. I don't understand why . . . why others can't see it. And you, you people, what are you doing about anything? I told you about Martin. What have you been doing?'

'You think we're doing nothing? Have you also thought that Makepeace may have been killed because *you* were going to see him?'

124

'No, I didn't think that. I don't think it! Nobody knew I was going to see Makepeace. Certainly not Martin!'

'He might have followed you . . . might have got ahead of you.'

'Why? Why kill him like . . . like the way he was killed then? Easier just to shoot him or stab him. Why that way?'

'Perhaps *pour encourager les autres*.'

'Anyway he's certainly keeping well ahead of you and your people. What have you done?'

Before replying Randall took a gulp of whisky. He had a small smile on his lips. 'Oh, we've taken steps. Always a good thing to do – take steps. And make enquiries. Keep weather eyes open. Be ready for all eventualities. You see, we too are good at civil service jargon. Oh, yes, and I have a man keeping an eye on the house in Catford.'

'What's he found out?'

'Early days. House is derelict. Confirms what you told us. Hardly livable in. No immediate sign of your old squatter. Perhaps you scared him off.'

'That's it!'

'So far. Our man's still there. Something else may develop.'

They fell silent. An uneasy silence. To do something, Matheson topped up Randall's whisky glass and poured himself a second drink. Randall accepted the topping up with an amiable nod. Time to try another tack, Matheson told himself.

'Gavin, I've signed the Official Secrets Act.'

'You said that before. Hasn't everybody? If they haven't, they should.'

'I am a senior civil servant. Surely you can tell me what's going on?'

Randall, still amiable, shook his head. 'Can't do, old man. Not your sphere of interest or concern.'

'I'm the one the man's spoken to. Surely that brings it into my sphere of interest? And especially my concern.'

'There might be another reason why I can't tell you anything.'

'And that is?'

Another long pause before Randall replied. And then, when he did, he looked away bleakly.

125

'Because we don't know.' An embarrassed admission. Delivered with so little embarrassment. Alcohol had its effect on Gavin Randall.

'For God's sake . . .' Matheson said but Randall interrupted him.

'See, Makepeace's death makes it serious.'

'Certainly. For Makepeace.'

Randall frowned. 'If this Martin character had anything to do with Makepeace's death, for whatever reason, then he made a massive mistake. He has left himself open to a murder charge.'

'This wasn't just murder! The man was gutted from neck to crotch. Again, why kill someone like that?'

'We have to find out. Whoever did it might simply be insane. But now, you do realise how important it is that you inform us if and when Martin contacts you?'

'Of course I do! How? The trouble is, the man just turns up. What can I do? Say: "Excuse me but will you wait here while I phone my friend in M.I.5?"'

Randall drained his whisky glass. 'M.I.6. Of course it's not always easy. But you must try harder. If he turns up, as you say, you must inform us as soon afterwards as you can. And if he makes an appointment with you, for lunch or anything else, you must clear it with us. You understand this?'

'Of course, I do. But, Gavin, supposing he does invite me to dinner at Catford . . .'

'Won't happen there. Not for months. State of the house, as I said. Anywhere else he invites you to dine, clear with us.'

'Yes, all right. But if he does ask me, I . . . I want to go.'

'We'll see.'

'I want to go because I want to know – why me? What it's all about. Is he trying to infiltrate the Ministry or whatever?'

'We'll consider all that.' Randall rose unsteadily. 'Time I wasn't here.' He grinned. His face was very red.

He went on, '"When I was coming down the stairs, I met a man who wasn't there. He wasn't there again today. I wish that he would go away." Tha's the whole thing in a nutshell.'

Matheson realised the intelligence man had already been drinking before he'd arrived. First time he'd ever seen Randall drunk. The man's voice was starting to slur now that he was on his feet. With the slurring came a swaying of the body.

126

'I hope you've got a driver with you, Gavin. You shouldn't be driving.'

'Can drive perfectly well!'

'You've had quite a lot to drink.'

'Two small whiskies. All you gave me.'

'And how much did you have before you came here?'

'Ah-ha. See, it's the curse of this intelligence business, Alistair. They . . . they were all heavy drinkers. Burgess, MacLean, Philby. Only one who always looked sober was Blunt. An' he just looked . . . looked . . . wha's the word? Blunt, that's it! Blunt always looked Blunt. Of course they were on both sides. I'm only on our side. Whatever side that is. Best get home. You remember about him, Gilbert bloody Martin, you tell us.'

'Have you got a driver with you?'

'G'd God, no. We're not senior boys like you. Not Permanent Under-Secretaries. Oh, no. Definitely lower ranks.'

'I'd better drive you . . .'

'No! No, no no no. I'm perfectly all right. Haven't far to go. Remember what I said. Whatever that was. But it was important. G'night, old boy.'

He went, increasingly unsteady as he did so. From the window, Matheson watched him climb into a large Ford Sierra. A long moment passed before the engine roared, the car came to life and moved off.

Randall driving.

Later, how did Matheson know what happened? Did he see it in a dream? Imagine it under the light of day? Hear it from Randall?

The M.I.6 man found himself blinking as he peered at the road ahead. Must be careful, telling himself as he drove not to hit anybody. Could get away with drink and driving if he was stopped by the police. Matter of areas in which he was important. Oh, not like Matheson, not that important, but in a different way. Yes, he could get away with it. Unless he hit someone. Then he might be in trouble.

Anyway, why should he not drink? Pressures on him. Pressures on all of them. Agents of the country, even agents of foreign powers, all of them drank too much. K.G.B. men,

127

sodden with vodka the lot of them; C.I.A. up to their ears in branchwater and rye; the French on brandy; all of them had to relieve the pressures. That was the excuse anyway. Maybe . . . and he giggled when he thought of this . . . maybe it was just that, an excuse. The real reason, that they all liked the damn stuff. And why not?

He was driving north from Chelsea. He had an apartment at the top of Highgate Hill. Not as expensive as Chelsea, but who cared? Gavin Randall had his life. Flurries of activity and excitement interspersed with long days and long nights and a few obliging women he knew. He wasn't married. Why should he be? All those married agents whose wives went off with other men or complicated everything when the husband defected and had to make arrangements for the wife to follow. Not that he, Randall, would ever defect. He was positively Land-of-Hope-and-Glory, British bulldog, best country in the world type. No defecting to the East, or what he had once called it – defecating to the East. Same difference.

He nearly drove through a red light. Saw it and jammed the brakes on just in time. Funny look from a policeman on the kerb. Pay attention. Shouldn't drink and drive unless you were thirsty.

He drove on.

Stopping easily at the next set of lights. Hyde Park Corner. Still a deal of traffic around and it must be nearly midnight. Big cities never sleep. Such obvious thoughts come out of alcohol.

The car door opened and closed.

Randall took his eyes from the road and turned to stare at the passenger seat. The figure was in darkness.

'You've been drinking,' it said.

He shook his head. The voice was strangely familiar, known and yet not quite recognised. He couldn't see the shape of the man who had climbed into the passenger seat but he was instantly alert. Or knew he should be but for the whisky having its effect. Reactions slowed down, perceptions blurred. Indignation rose.

'Who the hell are you?'

'I thought you were looking for me.'

128

The traffic lights changed to green. He must have hesitated because the car behind him flashed its lights impatiently. He moved on.

'I don't know you,' he said to the man in the passenger seat.

'Surely you do?'

They drove around Marble Arch and into Oxford Street. A flare of neon lit up the car. Randall took his eyes from the road and looked at the man in the passenger seat.

And saw himself.

'No!' he said.

'No what?' the man said.

'Who . . . who are you?'

'You know who I am.'

'You . . . you're me!' Such a stupid thing to say.

The car veered into the centre of the road.

Too late he saw the heavy lorry looming up in front of him, bearing down on the Sierra.

Chapter Sixteen

Another week at the Ministry.

Alistair Matheson is plunged into work. The debate on the defence estimates is coming up in the House and the Minister demands to be briefed on a wide range of issues.

Tuesday found Matheson in Number Ten Downing Street, waiting outside the Cabinet Room. The Minister came out to receive a sheaf of documents from his Permanent Under Secretary.

'Sorry about this, Alistair. Landed you in the hot seat at the worst time of the year. Thank God, after this the House goes into recess. Right, you have everything I need?'

Matheson went through the sheaf of documents, item by item. His Minister was pleased. At that moment the Prime Minister came downstairs heading for the Cabinet Room and stopped to chat with his Minister of Defence and the Permanent Under Secretary.

'Matheson, isn't it?' said the Prime Minister. He was a thin grey man. When he smiled his lips twitched, the only indication that he was actually smiling. The eyes remained distant. He affected a manner that served to indicate: We are all equal under the sun. But he was a Tory and his manner almost certainly an affectation. Underneath, he considered himself born to rule.

'Yes,' the P.M. continued. 'You came down from Scotland with Ian here?'

The Minister of Defence nodded. 'Couldn't do without him. He's proved it since Gerald Leigh died.'

'Good, good. Well, come along, Ian. I need your support in Cabinet today. Rumours the natives are getting restless.'

With a brief nod to Matheson the Prime Minister took his Minister of Defence by the arm and they disappeared into the Cabinet Room. For the first time since the weekend, Alistair Matheson felt good. His existence had been acknowledged at the very fountainhead of power. His life and career seemed set fair.

Except, of course, for the Gilbert Martin affair.

The week continued.

Matheson went through the motions of his job with some kind of enthusiasm. He tried to keep the events of the weekend out of mind. After all, the death of Alwyn Makepeace had nothing to do with him.

He tried to avoid contact with Margaret Mower. He was still, he had to admit to himself, attracted to her. But her participation in the weekend made him uneasy. As if she was somehow linked to Gilbert Martin. Not that he believed she was. Not that he knew what to believe. In a quiet moment, after a hard days' work, he sat down in his living room in the Chelsea flat and considered all he knew, asked himself all the questions. It was a Thursday night.

Who was Martin? What did he want? Was he some kind of foreign agent trying to infiltrate the Ministry? Randall's involvement seemed to indicate that might be the case. Not that he'd heard again from the security man since the Sunday visit. What else? Who killed Makepeace and why was he killed? Did Martin kill him? No evidence there except for the link Randall had pointed out. Was that valid? And why had Makepeace been killed in such a horrible way? And again, who was Martin?

The telephone rang.

'Alistair?'

'Who is this?'

'It's me, Margaret.

'Hello. How . . . how are you? Didn't recognise your voice.' It was true. She sounded different. Or perhaps he was forgetting how she did sound. In four days? How could he? Unless he wanted to do so.

'How are you, Alistair? I thought I would have heard from you.'

'Up to my ears in work.'

131

'Ah, yes.' She sounded almost wistful. 'Nothing else happened?'

'No.' No need to tell her about Randall's call on Sunday.

'Well . . .' she said, and hesitated.

'Well . . .' he echoed her. At once all seemed awkward between them.

'I've been thinking,' she said. 'There's someone else we could try and speak to.'

'Who?'

'You mentioned that intelligence man . . . what's his name?'

'Randall.'

'Yes. He told you that Makepeace had been involved with a medium before he went into the mental hospital. Nelly something or other.'

Matheson frowned. Something he had forgotten. What was the woman's name?

After a moment it came back to him quite clearly. 'Nelly Garton,' he said.

'The Psychical Research Society usually has some record of these people. If you like, I could contact them and see if I can find out if she still practises. Would that be the right word?'

Matheson was interested despite himself. Perhaps he had been preparing to break with Margaret. Had she sensed that? Was this her way of keeping the relationship going? Or was she genuinely interested in the whole business.

'If you want to contact them, by all means do so.' How grudging that sounded. Yet she should realise that being with him when he'd discovered Makepeace's body, being with him when they'd encountered Martin in the restaurant, could just link her to the man. Of course it wasn't her fault but he wished to be rid of Martin and everything about him. That seemed now to include Margaret.

Yet he had enjoyed her company. And more, he had to admit.

'I appreciate you're very busy,' she went on. 'So I'll see what I can find out about this Garton person. Perhaps at the weekend you'd like to come to me for a quiet dinner?'

He hesitated. He was hesitant a great deal these days.

'I'm not sure about the weekend, Margaret. I may have to work with my Minister. Very busy, you understand.' He'd never yet had to work over the weekend with the Minister, rarely would unless there was some big conference on. It was the Ministers who worked at their red boxes at weekends not the permanent civil servants. So why turn her down? Did he just want to be on his own, away from her, away from a companion with whom he found dead bodies. There was a thought.

'Next week then?'

'Better. Much better. Ring me then.'

'I'll ring you if I find out anything about Nelly Garton.' This was said coldly and directly.

'Yes, of course. She may be worth talking to. That's if she's still alive.'

'You mean if she hasn't been carved up like Makepeace?' Even more cold, almost vicious in tone.

'I didn't mean that. I imagine she wouldn't be a young woman and in five years anything might have happened. But look, Margaret, I have to go. Do tell me what you find out and we'll talk about dinner next week. Goodbye just now.'

He hung up feeling mildly ashamed of himself and determined he must get this whole business from his mind. Concentrate on something else, anything else.

He switched on the television set and tried to loose himself in following Hercule Poirot in an obfuscating murder investigation. The end credits were just rolling up when the doorbell rang.

There were two men in raincoats, trilbys, and expressions of determined intensity.

'Mr Alistair Matheson?' the smaller of the two asked. The smaller man was over six feet tall. The other man was at least six foot four.

'Yes.'

They were civil servants, he could tell; he could always tell. Part of a breed (almost giants in this case) that might just as well have their occupation printed on their brows.

'I wonder if you could spare us a few minutes? We're . . .'

'Policemen.'

'You were expecting policemen?'

Matheson smiled sourly. 'We are fellow members of the civil service. I can almost always recognise our . . . breed, shall I say? Especially the police variety. I suppose you'd better come in. This will be about the Dartmoor business, I've no doubt.'

He ushered them into the sitting room.

'And what can I do for you? I did imagine I'd told the Exeter police all I knew.'

The smaller giant cleared his throat. 'We may be at cross purposes, Mr Matheson. I'm afraid I know nothing of any Dartmoor business though you may wish to tell us of it. By the way, I'm Chief Inspector Claypole and this is my colleague, Inspector Burns. We're Special Branch.'

Matheson was mildly surprised. Special Branch, of course, was the active arm the security services used. Had they now come into the Makepeace murder?

'Of course, anything I can do,' he said. 'You know who I am?'

'Of course, sir. P.S. at the Ministry of Defence. Sorry to bother you, of course.'

'But if it's not to do with Dartmoor, what is it to do with?'

'Tell us about Dartmoor, Mr Matheson.'

He told them about the discovery of Makepeace's body. Exactly what he had told the police in Exeter. No more, no less. Nothing about Martin. Definitely nothing about Martin. When he finished, Claypole nodded.

'Thank you, sir. Very upsetting. But I don't see how it has anything to do with why we are here. Still, we'll bear it in mind. It's really an Exeter police job.'

'If it's nothing to do with that, then why have you come here?'

Claypole cleared his throat. He seemed embarrassed. 'You're acquainted with Gavin Randall?'

Matheson concealed his surprise. What had Randall been up to? 'Yes, of course. Old friend. Met him some years ago when he had cause to come to Scotland when I was at the Scottish Office. We keep in touch.'

'And you've seen him since you came to Defence and London?'

'Yes, I have.' Careful now, Matheson told himself, alarm bells ringing in his head. What were they after?

'When was the last time you saw Mr Randall?'

134

'Sunday evening. He called in for a drink. And . . . and a chat.'

'Would that be to do with Mr Randall's profession? You will know what that is?'

'Yes, I know. We often talked a bit of civil service shop, you might say. Nothing specific, of course. Nothing to do with details of his profession. Nothing top secret. Very punctilious about that, both of us.'

'You have no knowledge of anything he might be working on concerning the Ministry of Defence?'

'No. Nothing like that.'

The lie direct. Or was it? Was Gilbert Martin trying to infiltrate the Ministry through him? But to what end? There was no way Martin would get anything from him. But anyway, if he was concealing the truth from these Special Branch characters it would be because of Gavin Randall. Gavin had always instructed Matheson to say nothing without clearing it with him. There was rivalry in the intelligence services and more that occasionally crossed wires. And why should these policemen, Special Branch or not, be brought into the Gilbert Martin business without Randall's own agreement? Above all Matheson had no desire or inclination to talk of Gilbert Martin. Not to people he didn't know.

'Look, perhaps it's time you told me what this is all about,' he said.

The two Special Branch men looked at each other but Claypole was still the one who spoke for the two of them.

'We're not quite sure, sir. You see, Mr Randall has been missing since Sunday night.'

Another shock. Somehow it didn't fit in with anything that had happened or he'd expected to happen. A new twist. Unless . . . and the image of the dead Makepeace came to mind.

'What time did he leave you?' Claypole asked.

Matheson felt perspiration break out on his forehead. 'Oh, back of nine, I think. Couldn't be sure of the exact hour.'

For the first time the taller man, Burns, spoke. 'Could it have been any later? Or earlier?'

'I doubt it. Couldn't be sure, of course. It was just a casual call.'

135

Claypole stepped in again. 'That would indicate you were the last person to see Mr Randall.'

'Hardly that, unless Gavin . . . well, if he'd had an accident. And then surely someone responsible for the accident . . . would have been . . . the . . . last person . . .' He realised what he might be saying. A person responsible? For what?

He added, 'Unless he was taken ill.'

'We have nothing to indicate he was taken ill. We have checked hospitals and so on.'

'Could he have collapsed in his home? Perhaps be lying . . .'

'We have entered his home. No sign.'

Matheson surveyed the two giants. 'Then I'm afraid I can't help you. But it is most distressing. I . . . I like Gavin Randall.'

'There were no physical signs that he might be ailing?'

Somewhere in the back of his mind, Matheson's initial uneasiness was growing. 'No, again nothing. He seemed much as normal.'

Burns, cutting in again. 'Did he talk politics at all to you?'

'God, no! Would have bored each other stiff. Anyway, aren't we all suppose to be impartial?'

'Nothing was said on Sunday to indicate he might have intended to go away?'

'Go away where?'

Then the implications of the question registered. 'You don't mean you're thinking Randall might have taken off? Gone to Russia? Gone over? Another defection. Surely that kind of thing went out with the Cold War?'

'It's still rather chilly out there. And of course we have to consider all possibilities,' Claypole said.

'But that's preposterous! He was a British intelligence officer . . .'

'So was Philby. And Burgess. MacLean was a Foreign Office civil servant.'

'No, he was in the Diplomatic Corps. There is a difference.'

Claypole ignored this. 'Man in Mr Randall's occupation disappears, we're called in. For that matter, if *you* disappeared, we'd also be called in.'

136

'But I haven't disappeared,' said Matheson, and then realised he must sound quite pleased with himself for not disappearing.

Claypole was not amused. 'You can tell us nothing then, sir?'

'Only that I'm sure Randall would never defect. Not much point in going off to Russia anyway. Not now. I think you'd be barking up the wrong tree there.'

Burns replied, 'We bark up lots of wrong trees. Until we get to the right one. Which we usually do.'

'Perhaps his disappearance might be connected with whatever he was working on? Surely you should find out.'

'We have thought of that,' Claypole said caustically. 'Unfortunately, apart from routine departmental work, Mr Randall was between assignments. Although one or two of his colleagues believe he might have been following up something on his own.'

'What does that mean?'

'That he might have stumbled across something which puzzled him but not so strongly yet as to report it to his senior officer. Of course, he wouldn't mention anything like that to you?'

'No. Nothing like that.'

A lost opportunity to bring everything into the open. Yet he had to convince himself he was right to say nothing. When Randall did turn up he wouldn't be happy to know Matheson had told the Special Branch everything. And what could he tell them? About Gilbert Martin? He'd already decided how stupid that would sound. Anyway, Randall had said he'd put somebody on to the house in Catford. Let Special Branch find out that way.

Burns moved towards the door, Claypole following him.

'Well, thank you for seeing us, Mr Matheson. If you can think of anything Mr Randall may have said that might indicate where he could be, we'd be glad to hear it. I'll leave my card on your table here. You can phone me at any time.'

'And if Mr Randall turns up?'

'I'm sure we'll learn of that even before you, Mr Matheson.'

'Yes, of course. In that case, I'd be pleased if you'd let me know. As I've said, he was a friend.'

Claypole stopped at the door. '*Was* a friend? Why the past tense?'

Matheson felt the perspiration on his brow again. Why had he used the past tense?

'Was? Is? Merely a slip of the tongue, I assure you.'

He showed them out without further conversation. Outside the door Claypole nodded and went down the stairs followed by his taller colleague.

Back in the sitting room, Matheson poured himself a stiff whisky. Where the hell was Randall? Another question among so many. Was it possible Gavin Randall was going to end up like Makepeace, found dead in some grotesque way? No, surely not. Randall was a professional, he could look after himself. Even against Gilbert Martin he should know what to do, what course of action to take.

At least Martin had not appeared for some days now. Perhaps he had gone for good. There was a thought devoutly to be nourished.

It was not to be so.

The next day Matheson was in the House of Commons. The Minister had asked for his presence while under investigation by the Select Committee on Defence.

It was an easy meeting. The Committee was aware that both the Minister and his Permanent Under Secretary had only recently taken up their posts and had given them a gentle passage. The questions asked were not difficult, simply indications of the directions their interests would take as the Minister settled into his job.

After the meeting the Minister invited Matheson to have tea on the terrace of the House. It was one of those few days that indicate the coming of summer. The sun was overhead, the Thames glinting, its rays slivers of gold on the water. The air was warm but not too warm. London on a late spring day was all it should be.

Matheson was finishing his tea when the Minister rose to greet a colleague.

'John! Nice to see you.'

'Ian. Had to say hello. Haven't seen you since you took over Defence. All congratulations and so on. P.M.'s made a good choice.' One of the few Scottish Tory members with hopes of elevation to the ranks of junior minister, being effusive as a matter of policy.

'You know my Permanent Under Secretary, Alistair Matheson?'

John didn't but said, 'Of course, of course. I'm showing a friend here around the House.' He indicated a figure looming up behind him. 'We're in luck. I'm able to show off I'm acquainted with a member of the Government and the Cabinet no less. This is the Minister of Defence and his Permanent Secretary. Allow me to introduce Mr Gilbert Martin.'

Chapter Seventeen

It became cold on the terrace.

The man called Gilbert Martin shook hands with the Minister.

'Delighted to meet you, sir. Followed your career with interest. Defence problems have always held a particular fascination.'

'Oh, well, thank you,' said the Minister with assumed diffidence.

'Indeed, yes. Fascinating. Defence of the Realm and all that. Very necessary.'

He'd barely acknowledged Matheson's presence. But when the M.P. was button-holing the Minister on a question of business, Martin turned and fastened his gaze on the civil servant. With a cold smile.

'Nice to meet you.' As if they hadn't met before.

Matheson said, 'Haven't we . . .?'

Martin took his hand, shook it and drew him away from the two politicians. He said *sotto voce*, 'Of course. But I didn't want to embarrass you.'

'What are you doing here?' Matheson hissed.

Martin replied, wide-eyed, 'Merely a sightseer. Seeing how they all function. Where the power is – what there is of it. I'm fascinated by power. But, of course, isn't everybody?'

What's he talking about? What's he really doing here?

Matheson took a deep breath. His hands were shaking. 'I found Makepeace,' he said.

Martin's face revealed nothing. 'Makepeace? Who is Makepeace?'

'Alwyn Makepeace. On Dartmoor.'

'Alwyn Makepeace?' Martin said. 'Ah, yes, I believe I did once know somebody of that name. Years ago. A sad man. Highly sensitive.'

'And now highly dead.'

'You say so? How sad. But then, he spread sadness all around him.'

The M.P. called over, 'You ready, Mr Martin? Want to get you seated in the Strangers' Gallery before it all starts, Question time, y'know.'

'Right with you,' Martin replied, and turned back to Matheson. 'We must have a meal again soon, Alistair. And I haven't forgotten I invited you to dinner. Soon, very soon. Be in touch.'

He moved away and then appeared to have an afterthought. 'By the way, I wouldn't worry about Randall. He has been accommodated.'

They moved away. Matheson stared after the departing duo, shivering even more now. The Minister sat down again and stared at him. 'Amazing!' he said.

'Minister?'

'The likeness.'

Matheson felt a sense of relief. 'You . . . you noticed?'

'Could hardly fail to. Astonishing. Never come across that before. Such a close resemblance.'

'I'm relieved,' Matheson said. 'I thought I was the only one who could see it.'

'Could hardly fail to,' the Minister replied. 'Why, he could be my twin brother.'

That evening Matheson worked late and then walked, his mind spinning in convoluted circles. What was it Margaret had said? In Hogg's book. Gil-Martin resembled whoever he was with, whoever he wanted to be.

Insanity? Or fiction?

Gil-Martin . . . the Devil in another guise.

Gil Martin, a character in a fiction.

Then, who was Gilbert Martin? The name was coincidence surely? And the Minister was mistaken, of course he was. Martin had a certain resemblance to Matheson. Not to the

141

Minister. Not at all. Didn't look in the least like the Minister. Any other thought was insane.

Or Alistair Matheson was . . . having a breakdown? Not insane, God, no! He would deny that emphatically. But he'd been under a strain. It was possibly having an effect. Had to be something like that. After all, what was the alternative?

The legend made flesh.

No! Never, never, never, to believe that – there was the way to insanity.

He came to his club. He'd walked from Whitehall to St James's. It was a warm spring night, a haze of heat over the city still, darkness falling late. Few people were in St. James's at this time. The lights from the large windows of the Regency building cast yellow light on the pavements.

Not that he was a member, not yet. But the club had a reciprocal arrangement with his old club in Edinburgh. Here he was now a temporary, honorary member. As if on sufferance. Soon he could become a member; his fellows in the Service had put his name forward. He'd never liked the temporary or the honorary thing. Only visited the place twice since he'd come to London. And a third time tonight.

As if the place had become a haven: safe, solid, secure. Couldn't be touched in there by fear or fantasy. He went in.

The porter acknowledged his arrival. 'Evening, sir. Nice to see you again.'

The first time he'd visited the place, he'd explained to the man who he was, why he was there, mentioned the reciprocal arrangement. The man acknowledged him pleasantly enough, arranged for a waiter to show him around. The second time he'd thought the porter wouldn't remember. But the man had, as if he was chosen for his ability to absorb faces like blotting paper.

He glanced into the reading room, the vast space, almost a caricature of itself: panelled walls, leather armchairs, elderly members barely awake or fast asleep under open newspapers, empty whisky glasses on the tables beside their recumbent figures. Aging ravelled sleeves of care being knitted up.

He went to the bar. It was more modern and with some activity. A small buzz of talk, members facing each other across small tables; a few figures at the bar, the barman

142

leaning back stifling a yawn, then grateful to see Matheson's entry. Something to do, someone to serve.

'A Macallan, I think. A double,' Matheson said.

The malt whisky was placed in front of him. He looked around the room. Unfamiliar faces except for a fellow civil servant across the room, a man he barely knew.

'Good evening!' from a figure at his elbow.

Matheson turned, fearful that he might be faced again with the ubiquitous Gilbert Martin. With relief he found himself looking down into the moonface of a small round man in a dog collar.

'You may not remember,' the clerical gentleman said. 'We met the first time you were here.'

He remembered. Charlie Grove, also a member, had introduced him to the little man.

'Of course I remember,' Matheson said. 'May I buy you a drink?'

'Very nice of you. A small whisky would be most pleasant.'

'A malt, Your Grace?' said the barman. The little man nodded.

And Matheson remembered further. The man was a Bishop. C. of E. The suffragan Bishop of Storford.

'You're enjoying living in London?' the bishop said.

'Yes. Quite well.'

'I suppose you Scots will always yearn for your native heath.'

'Sometimes. But not too often. My native heath is the City of Edinburgh.'

The bishop's whisky appeared and they chatted for some minutes. About what Matheson later could not recall. But somewhere during the chat, the thought came to him.

'Could I talk to you, sir?'

The bishop eyed him. 'I was under the impression you were doing just that?'

'I have . . . a problem. Could we sit down?' Matheson indicated a table in an isolated corner of the bar.

The bishop, raising a quizzical eyebrow, acquiesced and they took their drinks to the table.

'I've a feeling,' said the cleric, 'you are going to ask me to talk shop.' He gave a small sigh. 'My kind of shop,' he added.

'Yes. Your kind of shop.'

'I would point out that I am a Church of England cleric. Not a Roman. Personally quite low church really. I don't hear confessions, my dear Matheson.'

'This is not a confession.'

'Thank goodness. I've no doubt confessions have their value . . . like talking to a psychiatrist . . . but I find them embarrassing. However, do go on.'

Matheson took a breath. Suddenly it seemed insane, the question he was going to ask. He was about to make a fool of himself. And this because of something Margaret had said. Nevertheless, he had to ask the question.

'Do you believe in the Devil?'

Matheson felt himself flush. And facing him the bishop flushed, equally embarrassed.

'Do I believe in the Devil? You mean, do I believe in evil?'

'Not exactly.'

'Of course I believe in evil. And not just abstract evil. Very concrete. Look at Hitler. The Holocaust. A rabbinical friend of mine maintains the one thing the Holocaust did for the twentieth century was to reaffirm the existence of evil.'

'No! I mean, do you believe in the Devil? As an entity.'

'Oh, come, now, you mean as a personality? My dear fellow, I'm known in the church for having some advanced ideas. My name has been mentioned in the same breath as my friend the Bishop of Durham. I hardly think a belief in Lucifer or Satan, fits in with the modern teachings of the church. Such a belief would be rather a retrograde concept.'

'You believe in God?'

'Well, yes. As a great spirit of the Universe. As something so vast as really to be beyond definition.'

'"God created man in his own image,"' Matheson quoted.

'Never quite sure about that one,' the bishop replied. 'Sometimes inclined to think man created God in his image.'

'What about Christ?'

'What about Christ?'

'Son of God? God as man?'

Storford pursued his lips. 'Well now, it's not so simple. The question is often asked: Who was Christ? Son of God? Reforming rabbinical teacher? Wise man?'

144

'But as a Christian, surely you must believe he was the Son of God?'

To the pursed lips were added the furrowed brow. 'I have to be careful. You see, you're entering into an area of great debate today. And of course we clerics have to take great care. The danger in expressing unorthodox and advanced theses is that one may do damage to those with simple faith.'

'But if Christ existed . . .'

'Oh, I'm sure he did!'

'Existed as the Son of God made flesh, then surely the Devil can do the same?'

A small chuckle from the Bishop. 'Aren't you attributing God's talents to the Devil?'

'I have to repeat my original question. Do you believe in the Devil? As an entity?'

The bishop suddenly became serious. 'My dear Matheson, are you perhaps undergoing some great spiritual crisis?'

Matheson paused before answering.

'Maybe,' he finally added. 'Or maybe I've simply met the Devil? In person. In the flesh.'

The bishop shook his head with great emphasis. 'No! No, I will not accept that. A man perhaps. A particularly evil individual. Yet, possibly. But the personfication of Satan . . . no, I cannot accept that.'

'Because you daren't?' Matheson leaned forward to within inches of the man's face. 'Because if you do accept what I'm saying, it would tear great holes in your cosy modernistic concept of religion?'

'I think, Matheson, behind all this is a kind of extreme Scots Presbyterianism.'

Matheson was suddenly calm now. 'Yes! Yes, that's it. Back to the true belief. You people have debated that belief out of existence. You're taking the true mystery from Christianity.'

'You are a believer, my dear friend,' the bishop said gently. 'Nothing wrong with that. Not that I would have believed it of you. Such a strong faith.'

'And so very recent. At least for me.'

'And I thought it was a spiritual crisis.'

'Oh, but it is, Your Grace. You see, I don't know whether I believe in God or not. Probably don't. Never have. But I do find myself believing in the Devil, because I've met him. The thing I don't know is why he has chosen me and for what purpose. But whatever it is, I'm very afraid.'

Later, he realised the bishop was convinced he was about to have a nervous breakdown. Storford tentatively suggested he visit a psychiatrist. Also reluctantly bought him another whisky, believing him to be already drunk, and suggested he go home and have a good night's sleep.

Matheson left him, feeling both depressed and oppressed. His discussion with one of God's representatives on earth had elicited the suggestion he seeks psychiatric help and a good night's sleep. Was this not somewhat inadequate in view of the problem he had laid before the cleric?

Also, as he walked home, he could only believe his talk with the bishop had been a mistake. He, Matheson, was a senior civil servant and yet he had left with a member of the established church the impression that he was, if not mad, at least extremely eccentric.

He considered this as he walked home along the Embankment. He needed the fresh river breeze in his face, and though this time it was not raining the night sky was heavy and dark with clouds.

The attack came near Dolphin Square under the shadow of the tall apartment blocks. The first he knew was the sound of running feet behind him. He half turned to see two figures bearing down on him. The figures defined themselves as two large youths.

They leaped upon him.

As he fell to the pavement, he thought, This is farcical. He'd spent the evening discussing evil and now he was experiencing one aspect, modern urban violence.

Pain shot across his chest. He'd been kicked viciously.

'Get 'is fuckin' wallet!' a coarse Cockney voice.

And another replied: 'I'm tryin', I'm tryin'! Get yer boot out of the way.'

Another kick, this time on the calf of his right leg. The pain was agonising.

He felt hands on his jacket, pulling it aside, fingers groping for the inside pocket and the wallet. And he was thinking, Take it and go. Another kick, one to the head, could so easily kill him . . . he kept his eyes tightly shut.

Another voice. Loud. Clear. Angry.

'No!'

The youth, lying over him, feeling for his wallet, was suddenly raised up.

Matheson opened his eyes. Above him was a street light and though his vision was temporarily misted he could see the shape of the youth somehow rising into the air, arms rotating in some kind of desperate struggle. Then the youth, now raised high, was cast aside, seemed to be propelled through the air, out of his vision. Matheson heard a scream and the crash of a falling body. On the pavement he twisted around, trying to see what was happening. He saw the second youth towering over him, boot raised, this time to kick him in the face.

The blow never connected.

The second youth seemed to be dragged backwards, arms flailing. And in one hand a knife appeared, a large flick knife, glinting in the street lamp. The youth was attempting to stab whatever or whoever was behind him. But then the knife disappeared. The second youth's scream was louder, deeper, more horrific.

Matheson rolled over into the foetal position, not sure what was happening.

The scream became a terrible wail and then he heard more footsteps trying to run, staggering, shuffling, and disappearing into the distance.

Gingerly, he sat up. A stab of pain in his calf seemed to emulate another pain in his chest. He looked around. The youths had gone. The knife glinted again on the pavement some yards away, lying beside something else, small, dark, liquid. He looked around and seemed to see a shape in the darkness, the bulk of a man.

Then the voice, almost a whisper, in his head.

'They had no right. You defended me tonight with the small priest. I remember such things. I am not unappreciative.' The words were serious but as an addendum: 'Now go home and have that good night's sleep. The pain will go.'

Unsteadily Matheson rose to his feet, surprised to find the pain was gone. He faced the bulk of the man.

'I have to thank you.'

147

'No need.'

'But who am I to thank?'

'Come now, Alistair, you know that.'

The figure was gone. As if dissolved into deeper darkness. There were footsteps receding. Then Matheson was alone again.

He turned towards Chelsea. As he did he saw the knife again on the pavement and something else.

There were still fingers around its shaft. Fingers attached to a hand that ended in a puddle of blood.

The mugger's hand had been torn off at the wrist.

Chapter Eighteen

He slept fitfully. Dreaming of the severed hand.

He had no desire to go to work. His bruises ached. He wanted to phone and tell them he was sick, but didn't. He was in charge now. An example had to be set. And there was much to do.

In his office, just before midday, Miss Lubovious came through on the intercom. He was buried in a sheaf of proposals for the merging of regiments.

'A personal call for you sir, Miss Mower. Are you in or out?'

He resisted the temptation to say he was out, reluctantly lifting the receiver.

'Margaret?'

'Alistair. Sorry to phone you at work but I've done it – located Nelly Garton. Through the psychical research people. She lives in London now.'

'Oh, yes. Very good.' Was it? Did he want to go on digging deeper? So far it had led to an eviscerated corpse and a severed hand, not a result devoutly to be desired. What else could happen?

'She still consults, the Garton woman. I've made us an appointment for this evening.'

'This evening!'

'Well, I thought it would be a good idea. Of course if you're not free, I can cancel . . .'

'You should have consulted me first.'

Silence. Then a cold reply. 'I was under the impression we were doing this for you.'

'Yes, of course, but . . .'

'Has something else happened? You've seen Martin again?'

'Well, it's just . . .'

'What's happened?'

He was afraid to say it. As if, by doing so, the event would recur. He could feel the ache in his chest and his leg. Like toothache in both places; not agony but a dull pain. And he could see the hand, fingers still around the knife, ending in the pool of blood.

'Alistair, what has happened?'

'Can't tell you. Not over the telephone.'

'Then tell me tonight. I'll be at your place at seven-thirty. We see Nelly Garton at eight. She's not very far from you. At World's End. Oh, and by the way, she charges £75 a session.'

'Good God!'

'In cash. If you haven't got it handy, I can go to the bank.'

'I shall bring it with me.' Grudgingly. Playing the careful Scot.

It seemed appropriate the medium should live at World's End. On the edge, one might say. He wanted then to say, forget it, leave it alone, I've had enough. But it wasn't up to him. Martin would appear whenever Martin wanted to appear. Matheson knew he had no choice. The thing, whatever it was, would never go away – not unless he found a way to force it to do just that. He had to see Nelly Garton whether it helped him or not.

He gave a deep sigh. 'I'll see you at seven-thirty then.'

'And you'll tell me what happened last night?'

'Goodbye just now, Margaret.'

Seven twenty-five. Margaret, early and excited.

'So tell me,' she demanded.

He was donning a sports jacket. More suitable for a visit to World's End than his dark suit and striped trousers.

'You're early,' he said.

'I wanted to be sure I was on time. Should I have waited outside for five minutes?' Very edgy. Not too happy with him.

'Of course not. Would you like a drink before we go?'

'Perhaps later. I may need one later. Are you going to tell me what happened?'

150

He hesitated. As usual. So much of his life wasted in hesitations. He told her. With certain omissions.

'. . . it was Martin's intervention that saved me when they attacked.'

'You're sure? I mean, he hadn't set them on you in the first place?'

'No, I'm sure he didn't. Well, almost sure.'

'Did they hurt you?'

'Not really. Two or three bruises. They might have really hurt me but . . . he turned up in time.'

'How did he . . .?'

'He surprised them. One took off after he . . . he hurt the other.'

'Badly?'

'Yes.'

'He didn't kill him?'

'No, he didn't kill him. Time we were going.'

In the King's Road, looking for a taxi, she persisted. 'What did he do?'

'Never mind. Just don't ask again. Ah, here's a taxi. You have the address?'

It was a side street, a dead end terminating in a brick wall behind which was a junk yard. In the dying light a gasometer loomed. The houses were the usual small artisan's semi-detached residences built some time before the First World War. In many parts of London they had been gutted, the interiors remodelled and the houses resold at considerable profit as bijou residences for the up-and-coming couple. But not this house.

In front of its aging façade was a small oblong of soil, in this case uncultivated. Grass had given up the struggle to grow, leaving the oblong as mud. The façade itself was of chipped brick, still soot begrimed.

As the taxi arrived, it was still daylight but grey clouds, disgorging a thin drizzle of rain, were fast bringing on premature night.

Matheson paid the taxi driver as Margaret surveyed the building bleakly.

'Not exactly encouraging,' she said.

'Unfortunately, a great many of our fellow citizens choose to live like this,' Matheson replied.

151

'Most of them are forced to by economic circumstance.' Margaret protested, echoing her parents' once held Fabian Society principles. 'And many others are much worse off thanks to your government.'

She was needling him and he knew it. Why? He had done nothing to cause her to do so. He had done nothing for some days. Not since their night . . . Also he had said nothing. What could she expect?

'Not my government,' he said sourly. 'I am only a permanent servant to whoever you people choose to vote into power. Shall we go in?'

She nodded curtly. He told himself she was asking, how could she have given herself to such an arrogant, pompous, self-centred prig? What had she seen in the man? There was nothing visibly attractive to her at this time. At that moment he didn't much care for her.

He rang the doorbell.

His ring was answered by a young girl in a creased skirt and grubby jumper. She was about thirteen, wore thick-spectacles and had a distinct cast in one eye.

'Yeah? What do you want?' The accent was American cockney encouraged by too many transatlantic movies on television.

'My name is Matheson. This is Miss Mower. We have an appointment with Miss Garton.'

'You mean Missus Garton? Oh, yeah, she's expectin' you.'

They were grudgingly shown into a small sitting room at the front of the house. Aging armchairs were bedecked with antimacassars, something Matheson had not seen since his grandparents' house in Edinburgh. The mantelpiece and a side table were covered in small framed photographs, some of them turning yellow. A large tinted photograph hung above the mantelpiece depicting a man in the khaki uniform of an infantry sergeant in the Second World War. Heavy curtains covered the windows and looked as if they were never opened. The only and inevitable concession to modern living was a large television set in one corner of the room, below it a video recorder and beside that a record player.

'You're to wait 'ere,' said the girl and left them.

In silence. For a time.

152

Margaret broke the silence, looking around the room. 'It's like going back fifty years in time. Wartime utility furniture, except for the television.

'Maybe time has just stopped.'

The silence was resumed and extended. Matheson let the pause go by and then spoke. 'What the devil are we doing here?'

'I believed I was helping you. Regarding Martin.'

'Martin! Martin, Martin, I'm sick to death of the man. Who is he? Why has he brought us to this place? Why do I think he looks like me when . . . when nobody else sees it? What *is* the man?'

'I thought that's why we were here? To try and find out.'

Matheson shrugged hopelessly. 'Find out what? Why? Why should some crazy woman know any more than we do? You know everything was fine until I saw him. Until I met him . . .'

'Alistair, don't! Whatever's happening, you'll come through it.' Her sympathy and affection for him returned. 'I think you should have a talk with your friend, Randall. After all, he has his suspicions about our Mr Martin.'

'Randall has disappeared.'

'What?'

'I had a visit from Special Branch. They're looking for him. Hasn't been seen since he visited me last Sunday.'

The door opened and Mrs Nelly Garton came in.

She was in her seventies, barely five feet in height, with a wizened face under dyed blonde hair merging at the roots to white. Her eyes, peering up at them questioningly, were a faded blue. There was something birdlike about her. Thin arms about to start flapping. Thin lips twitched under a hooked nose as she spoke. Again a cockney accent came through, blurred by an attempt at gentility.

'You'll be Mr Matheson and Miss Mower, eh? You want to consult me?'

Margaret replied, 'Yes. I made the appointment.'

Nelly Garton looked from one to the other. 'You want me ter hold a seance?'

'We wish to ask you some questions,' Matheson said.

The woman looked up at the photograph above the mantelpiece. 'I don't give readin's. I don't tell fortunes. I'm a

153

psychic. A medium. If I can help yer, it would only be through a seance.'

She turned from the photograph to face them. 'Me late husband,' she went on. 'Killed at Salerno in the war. I knew it before it happened. One of the reasons I don't tell fortunes. See too many things you don't want to see. He's still close by, mind. Yes, we're still together, just on different planes. It's a comfort, like. Do you want me ter hold a seance?'

'I just want to know . . .' Matheson started to say, but Margaret interrupted him.

'Yes, please.'

Nelly Garton looked Margaret up and down. Head to toe. Then a glance at Matheson and back to Margaret.

'Only three of us. Best with a couple more. Just wait here.' She went out of the room.

'Why did you say you wanted her to hold a seance? I simply want to question her about Martin and Makepeace. And Monty Wallingham.'

Margaret's lips were tight. 'Because I don't think that's the way to get her to talk,' she hissed.

'Oh, you read characters now?'

'I'm telling you, Alistair, you ask her direct questions now and I think she'll clam up. But in a seance, when she's in a trance . . .'

'You believe all that rubbish?'

'I believe she believes it.'

'Oh, for God's sake!'

'Just as I believe you think Martin looks like a mirror image of you. Despite the fact that no one else can see it.'

That silenced him. He turned away petulantly.

A few moments later Nelly Garton came back into the room.

'I've asked Mr Buller and his wife to join us. Next-door neighbours. Always ready to oblige. Cost you an extra fiver each but I didn't fink you'd mind. A'right?'

'Yes, of course,' Margaret replied.

Matheson glared.

Mr and Mrs Buller were small, but not quite as small as Nelly Garton; round and plump, but cheerful. Eyes like silver sixpences, the old type, set deep in round cheeks. They

154

looked more like brother and sister than husband and wife. In this case, like had married like. Almost Dickensian, they were, the Cheerybles, only this time husband and wife.

'Hope we haven't caused you any inconvenience,' Margaret said politely.

'Only too happy,' said Mr Buller, beaming.

'Do love havin' them,' said Mrs Buller. 'Love a good seance, so I does. So does Mr Buller.'

'Only too happy,' Buller repeated.

'If you would help me with the table, Mr Buller,' said Nelly Garton. 'We'll put it in the centre of the room as per usual.'

'Happy to,' said Buller. He seemed in a permanent state of euphoria.

Matheson, still not happy, stepped forward, his politeness a reflex action.

Mrs Garton waved a hand in the air. 'No need, sir. Mr Buller knows exactly where the table goes.'

Once it was in position and the chairs placed around it, Mrs Garton allocated seats.

'Mr Matheson on my right hand, Miss Mower on my left. Mr and Mrs Buller at their usual places.'

Matheson sat almost scowling across the table at Margaret.

'Now a bit o' music appropriate to the situation, like,' Nelly Garton went on. 'Used to use Mantovani in the old days but now I gone a bit classical. O'course played very quiet. Young Nige Kennedy doing his *Four Seasons*. Discovered that recently. Dead right for what we want.'

She switched on the record player. The music was low and not unpleasant. Mrs Garton sat down at the head of the table.

'Mr Buller, if you would be so good?'

'Happy to.' Buller rose and, going to the door, switched off the light. The room became pitch black. The small man felt his way to his seat.

'All correct, Mrs Garton.'

'Thank you, Mr Buller. Now if you'll all be good enough to clasp each other's hands and place them on the table, we can begin.'

Matheson felt her small round knobbly hand creep into his.

'I have to ask you, when I am in a trance state, to be quiet and not disturb the medium as it can be dangerous. That's me,

155

as you'll be knowin'. Also be very patient. Everything takes time. If you feel you has to speak to each other, a loud whisper is all right. But only after I gone into the trance state.'

They waited, the darkness all embracing. Apart from Vivaldi from Nigel Kennedy's violin, there was no sound except for Mrs Garton's heavy breathing and the slight trace of a wheeze from Mr Buller.

Still they waited.

Inside his head Matheson felt restless and impatient asking himself questions again. What am I doing sitting in this stupid little room, in World's End of all places, waiting for a stupid little woman to go into a trance? How could anyone believe such nonsense? How could . . .?

'You was always frightened of this kind of thing, wasn't you?' It was Nelly Garton, not in a trance as yet but seemingly somewhere inside his head.

She went on, 'You was nine when the stupid woman gave you the ouija board to play with.'

He hadn't thought about that for over thirty years. Now it was back in memory . . . he could see the damn board as if it were yesterday, remember the obscenities it had spelt out and how he had said them out loud until his mother, hearing them, hearing her nine-year-old son shouting those words, had screamed and slapped him across his face, the one and only time she had ever done that. It wasn't even as if he understood what he'd been saying. He'd screamed to her that the board had done it; that he'd never heard the words before in his life, didn't know what they'd meant or where the board had brought them from. She hadn't believed her son. Why should she? He must have known the words. Board games don't spell obscenities of their own accord.

'She wouldn't believe you, would she, Alistair?' Mrs Garton's voice again. How did she know his first name? How did she know about something that happened to him when he was nine years old?

He heard himself say, 'She wouldn't believe me.'

'Nobody ever does, first time,' Mrs Garton said.

'First time?'

'First time it comes to you. The . . . the other side . . . the evil . . .'

156

'The evil that men do'. Always easy to quote Shakespeare to himself, Matheson thought.

'Not men. Something else,' Mrs Garton said, inside his head again. 'From outside.'

Silence again. A long silence. Mrs Garton's breathing became deeper. Matheson, still asking himself how she could know about the ouija board.

Mrs Garton started gulping air loudly.

Mr Buller whispering. 'She's under now.'

A briefer silence.

Then a voice Matheson had never hard before, a deep almost masculine voice coming from Nelly Garton.

'So here we are, all together again.'

Mrs Buller whispering this time, 'That's Freddie, her husband. He comes through as her control quite often.'

'Is that Gladys there?' The voice of Freddie Garton again.

Mrs Buller said, 'Oh, yes, I'm here, Freddie.' And then, in a whispered aside to Matheson, 'Never knew 'im when 'e was alive. But I feel 'e's an old friend now.'

'Effie sends her best to you, 'said Freddie Garton. 'Says you forgot to visit with your dad. He was quite upset over on this side.'

'Couldn't manage to the cemetery this month,' Mrs Buller replied to the darkness. 'Buller was down with the 'flu. But I'll be visiting him next month, promise.'

Buller leaned towards Margaret, whispering by way of explanation, 'Her dad. Been dead twenty years but knows when she don't visit 'is grave.'

Margaret nodded. Not that she could be seen. Her thoughts echoed Matheson's. What the devil were they doing here, listening to inane trivia supposedly from beyond the grave? She could visualise Matheson in the dark, glaring in her direction.

The voice from Mrs Garton continued: 'But we've got strangers with us. Have to find out what they are wantin'.'

Mrs Buller whispered. 'You can ask questions now.'

Matheson cleared his throat. Stupid, he thought, being part of this. But he could certainly reach Mrs Garton.

'Did you know a man called Makepeace? Alwyn Makepeace,' he said.

157

The silence was almost deafening.

Moments passed.

Finally the voice of Freddie again. 'He's come over. This side. Dead. Not nice, the way of it. Not . . . not . . .'

The voice faltered.

'Someone . . . someone else . . . strong . . . no, something else . . . too strong . . . can't go on.'

The voice disappeared with a strangulated choking sound.

'It's freezing,' Margaret said loudly.

'Shh!' said Mrs Buller. 'Not so loud.'

Suddenly from the medium there issued a low moaning sound, as if someone were weeping profusely.

'God, God, God!' Another voice now, out of the weeping.

'Who . . . who is that?' Mr Buller whispered, almost fearfully.

'God! To do that to a man . . . to do it to me,' the voice wailed. 'He opened me up . . . gutted me like a fish. I watched him. Oh, Christ, the pain . . . the pain. It took so long to die.'

'It's Makepeace!' Matheson said.

The room was filled with sound. Not words but a combination of moans and wails building up to a long unbroken scream.

They were shivering now as an icy wind blasted through the room.

'Who . . . who is it?' Margaret said, speaking loudly above the sound which seemed to pulsate all around them.

As suddenly as it had come all sound ceased except for the heavy breathing of the participants and a hoarse rattle from the throat of the medium.

'She doesn't sound right,' Mrs Buller whispered, on the edge of tears. 'We never had that before. See if she's all right, Buller.'

'No!' Buller replied. 'Could be dangerous.'

The third voice came from the medium then. A voice Matheson recognised.

'Didn't think you believed in this kind of thing, Alistair.'

His own voice but not his voice. Different yet the same. He'd heard it before.

Gilbert Martin's voice.

158

'You recognise my voice? Or is it your voice? Or something else's? Don't let on to the medium. She wouldn't like it. Might damage her like Makepeace was damaged.'

'Who is that?' Margaret said.

'Don't you know, Miss Mower? Could be Alistair's voice. Or mine. Or the Other's. You're ahead of Alistair, Miss Margaret Mower. You know who I am. He only wonders and, like the song, worries.'

The voice sang now, not unpleasingly. 'April again. One worries and wonders . . .' The singing stopped but the voice went on. 'Quotation. "How potent cheap music can be." Ain't it the truth? Who am I? So many names. Almost as many as God. There's the Lord of the Flies, the Lord of Misrule . . . how inaccurate. Depends on what you consider misrule. Still, always there when the lights go out.'

'I know,' Margaret said.

'I'll see you soon then,' said the voice. 'Oh, yes, Alistair first and then you.'

A long throaty laugh. And then, continuing: 'How disgusting to have come through her. She has the talent, but the smell of sweat and stale lavender water sickens me. Time to go. See you eventually and soon, Margaret.'

The voice faded.

And then Nelly Garton screamed.

159

Chapter Nineteen

The seance was over.

Mr Buller switched on the lights. The room was in disarray. Pictures aslant on the walls. Ornaments on the floor. Broken china. One of the heavy curtains was torn – quite a feat considering the thickness of the material.

Nelly Garton was on the carpet, her chair on its side next to her. After the scream she had apparently collapsed in the darkness. She lay on her back, eyes open but glazed and unseeing, her mouth also open, her breathing loud, gasping, stentorian.

'Oh, God!' Margaret, fearful, knelt at her side.

'Is she dead?' Mrs Buller, eyes round, sat as if frozen to her chair.

'Making that noise, I hardly think so,' Matheson responded acidly. Despite his sarcasm, inwardly he was shaking. If he had thought Nelly Garton a fake, he had revised his opinion. And it frightened him. Indeed, everything about Martin frightened him. And Mrs Garton was part of Martin's story. He was in no doubt that in some way Martin was behind all that had happened during the seance.

Margaret was taking the recumbent medium's pulse.

'I think we should call the doctor,' she said.

'Oh, no, I wouldn't do that,' said Mr Buller.

Mrs Buller echoed him. 'Wouldn't. No, no!'

Mr Buller explained, 'Mrs Garton doesn't believe in doctors. Won't have them on any account.'

'Won't have them.' Again his wife echoed him.

160

'Heal thyself. Her motto,' Buller went on. 'Mind you, seen her out before. Conscious. Semi-conscious. But not quite like that. That's heavy, that is.'

'I still think we should call the doctor,' Margaret persisted.

Matheson said, 'If they say she doesn't like doctors, then listen to them. The woman's obviously not dead or dying. And you bring in doctors, you bring in . . . other people. That means questions and maybe even the police and then newspaper people.'

'But if the woman needs a doctor . . .'

'I . . . I don't wish to be involved in this kind of nonsense, and possible attendant publicity. It would hardly go down well with my masters in Whitehall.'

Margaret glared at him. 'How can you say that if this woman's seriously ill? She might have had a stroke or God knows what!'

From the floor came a groan.

'There you are! She's coming round.'

It was indeed so. Nelly Garton, eyelids flickering, gave a second groan and sat up.

Matheson said. 'She'll say "Where am I?" now.'

Leaning on Margaret's arm the medium came unsteadily to her feet and stared at Matheson. 'I knows exactly where I am. I wonder if you knows where you are an' what's happening to you?'

'That's why we came to you,' Margaret said. 'To find out.'

Unsteadily at first, Nelly Garton looked around and then righted her chair and sat down with a sigh.

'I knew why you was 'ere,' she said.

'You really all right?' Mr Buller peered anxiously at her.

'Of course I'm all right, Buller.'

'Of course she's all right, Buller,' his wife dutifully echoed the medium.

'You can go now,' Nelly said. 'That's all for tonight. Take her . . .' a nod in Mrs Buller's direction '. . . and go.'

'We can go, Buller. That's all for . . .'

'Yes, dear.' Buller took her by the arm. 'Time to go back next-door. Come on.'

The Bullers went to the door. Buller turned and opened his mouth but Nelly Garton anticipated him. 'You'll get your money later, so you can piss off now.'

161

The Bullers went. Nelly turned to Matheson.

'I knows what went on when I was under the old 'fluence. I don't always know but I did this time. I could hear it all.'

'You know about Martin?' Matheson said.

'I knows about him you call Martin. I knows about him whatever he's called. And I don't want to know. I had enough of knowing him once before. So you two can put down the cash you owe me and the Bullers and get out of here. Get out of here right now!'

'But you haven't told us anything,' Margaret protested.

'You heard all there was. Tell you this, though: keep away from him. From the man calls himself Martin. He's . . . he's not right . . . shouldn't be 'ere. Shouldn't be allowed. Not right or natural. Not that one.'

It was Matheson who spoke next. Something in her voice prompted him. 'Who is he?'

'He's got lots o' names, and they are not to be spoken.' She stood now, her face set in a glowering look. 'So you can give me me money and get the hell out of 'ere!'

Matheson extracted the notes from his pocket and put them on the table. 'There's another ten pounds if you tell me about Martin and Wallingham and Alwyn Makepeace.'

He took another note from his wallet and held it in front of her. Her nose twitched.

'Why don't you ask Makepeace? 'E was the one got mixed up with Martin. He's still alive. Lives in Devon or some place.'

'We've seen him. Or rather his body. He was killed.'

'Christ!' said the woman. ''E's been done in an' you offer me a measly tenner?'

'Fifty,' said Margaret, opening her handbag. 'Fifty to tell us.'

Nelly Garton licked her lips, looking from the five ten pound notes in Margaret's hand to the tenner Matheson was holding. The prospect was too much for her. She snatched the five notes from Margaret and then the tenner from Matheson.

'Makepeace was like you. Wanted to know about Martin. I thought Wallingham was eggin' him on, only they even introduced Martin to me. First, I kind of liked him. Looked like Freddie, 'e did. Image o' my husband. But Martin was a clever bastard. Not like Freddie. I soon knew something warn't natural. He warn't what he seemed to be.'

'What was he then?' Matheson said.

'Dangerous. Tricky dangerous. I didn't want to ask, but I knew. An' the danger was comin' from somewhere else. I said Makepeace and the other character Wallingham wanted to know *who* he was. More like they should have asked *what* he was. That's what you should be askin'.'

'What is he then?'

'You should know now. An' if you don't, I ain't saying it. God, no!'

Margaret took a step forward. 'All right. Then tell us what he wants.'

Nelly Garton laughed coarsely. 'What he wants? Oh, that's easy. Everythin'. Everythin' and nothin'. Take everythin', reduce it to nothin'. Take people, reduce them to nothin'. That's what he always wants. Make nothin' out of somethin'. And' if he don't get away with it, he does what he can. Which ain't nice. What's that I read in one of the big toff's papers? "Conspicuous consumption." That's what they call it. An' it just about tells you what he wants. Always has . . . to consume everything.'

At once she shut her mouth. As if something might try and get into it. It became the thinnest of lines. When she spoke again she barely moved her lips.

'That's it all. Said enough. Say any more, could end up like Makepeace. Notice you didn't tell me how he died. I don't want to know. Reckon you've had your money's worth. So now bugger off an' leave me alone.'

This time she meant it. She threw the door wide, marched into the narrow hall and opened the front door.

They left. On the pavement, Matheson looked back. The front door was closed. There were no lights showing from anywhere in the house. As if it was deserted.

He took Margaret back to her Richmond flat. She invited him in but seemed relieved when he excused himself.

'I shall be in touch,' he said, as if dealing with another branch of the civil service. They were wary of each other now. Uncertain of their previous attraction. Seeing things in the other they did not like.

163

He went back to Chelsea. Dobson would be out, he knew, away for the night. Ostensibly staying overnight with his mother. Matheson suspected this to be untrue. There was more likely a relationship of another kind involving probably a woman. Of course, and Matheson had an aversion to thinking about this, it might be a man with whom Dobson was involved. In this respect, he could not conceal a streak of middle-class Scottish puritanism. Still, the man did his job and Matheson would try and convince himself he had no interest in Dobson's peccadillos, perverse or otherwise.

Thus he was all the more surprised, knowing of the servant's absence, to find the door to his flat ajar. Although the hall was in darkness there was a ribbon of light coming from beneath the sitting-room door. Taking a deep breath, he threw the door open.

The room was filled with light. From the ceiling a ring of small bulbs blazed down. A standard lamp and a number of side lights were all switched on. The only other possible source of light, the television set, was the only thing not switched on.

Matheson blinked in the excess of light, thinking that a house breaker would surely work in the dark. And then, as his eyes became accustomed to the glare, he saw his visitor.

Gilbert Martin, immaculate in dinner jacket and black tie, lounged rather than sat in one of Matheson's deeper armchairs. A cigarette dangled from the fingers of his right hand. A trace of a smile curled his lips. He appeared as a man at home; indeed, since he resembled Matheson, it was like seeing himself sitting relaxed in his own living room. The difference was that Martin, it would seem, was at home wherever he was. Matheson could be aware of his own awkwardness in strange surroundings.

'Good evening, Alistair,' Martin said pleasantly, making no effort to move.

'What are you doing here?' Matheson demanded tersely, irritation unconcealed.

The tone had no effect on his visitor. 'I was passing and called in to invite you to dinner tomorrow evening.'

Matheson was taken by surprise at his cordiality. 'But how did you get in? My . . . my servant is out this evening.'

'I'm afraid I will get the poor man into trouble, but your front door was open.'

'I've never known Dobson leave the front door open. He's usually very careful about things like that.'

'Ah, well, isn't it fortunate I came along? I thought I should wait since, if I left, I had no way of locking the door. You could have been burgled.'

Matheson was nonplussed. The man appeared to have done him a favour. Could he complain at that?

Martin straightened up and rose to his feet. 'In fact I'm very late for a dinner appointment but I felt I couldn't just leave with your home so vulnerable.'

'Oh, well, yes. Yes . . . very good of you to have waited.' The polite lie came awkwardly to Matheson's lips.

'And, of course, I do hope you'll manage to come to dinner at Catford tomorrow night?'

'Oh, you've had the house refurbished?'

A small frown furrowed Martin's brow. 'I wasn't aware that it needed refurbishment. Have you been there?'

The trace of a smile was still on his lips. Matheson felt himself flush. 'Oh, no. No. I . . . I merely assumed you'd recently moved in.'

'I've had the house for years. Many years. It's always kept exactly as I want it. Oh, I go abroad a great deal but I make sure the house is as always.' He glanced at his watch. 'I really must go but I shall look forward to seeing you tomorrow. Dinner at eight-thirty. Come at eight for a drink.'

'I'm not sure if I can.'

Martin had turned away. Now he swung around, his eyes fastening on Matheson.

'Oh, but you must come. I've told everyone about my new friend who is high in the civil service. They are very well-connected people. Interested in political science and the running of the country. They are very much looking forward to meeting you.'

'Of course it's very good of you . . .'

'And of course you're very welcome to bring a companion. The lady novelist you were dining with when we last met . . . now that would be another feather in my cap. Miss Mower's work is much admired. You will come?'

165

Martin's eyes bored into him. For the first time he knew the real meaning of that phrase.

'Yes, of course I'll come,' he said automatically. Then felt sure he had intended to say exactly the opposite. But there as the thought too that he wanted to see the house in Catford again. If it was as Martin said then he must somehow have gone to the wrong house. There could be no other explanation for the derelict building he had visited.

'Good.' Martin nodded. 'If the lady can come, so much the better. But you, I must have.'

He turned towards the door.

Matheson said, 'Wait!' Not knowing why.

Martin turned back, surprised. 'Yes?'

'I should offer you a drink.'

'Not necessary. I am a gatecrasher. And late for my dinner date.'

Matheson took a deep breath. For the first time since he had encountered Gilbert Martin he dared to question the man.

'Who are you, Martin?'

His visitor stared at him, the smile still hovering around his mouth.

'Come now, don't you know?'

166

Chapter Twenty

'Who are you?' Matheson repeated.

Martin relaxed, still smiling, moved back from the door. 'I shall be very late for my dinner engagement. Still and all, perhaps, I should talk a little more. Perhaps I owe you that. Who am I? you ask. Gilbert Martin is one of my names.'

'But it's not your real name.'

'Now what does that mean, Alistair? It's as real as any name. I have it on a passport. On a driving licence. On my bank account. What can be more real than that?'

'You said you had many names.'

Martin sat down, an eyebrow raised. 'When did I say that?'

The voice at the seance, coming from Nelly Garton's mouth but sounding like Martin's. How could he tell Martin that?

His visitor laughed. 'Oh, I see. The voice at the seance you've been to. Nelly Garton. Is she doing impersonations or was it really me?'

Matheson felt ice-cold. The man was reading his mind. Or had he been in touch with the Garton woman?

'Oh, I know all about your little seance,' Martin went on. 'I have my . . . connections. Don't look so alarmed. You've realised all along I am a positive fount of information.'

'You said . . . the voice said it. That you had many names.'

'Oh, I have. Many. But so do other people. I suppose I have more than most. One collects them as one goes through . . . existence. You want to know who I am? I'm . . . myself. The being in front of you. Gilbert Martin to you.'

167

Matheson stammered as spoke. He hadn't stammered for years. Not since he was a child. 'G . . . Gilbert M . . . Martin is a character in a b . . . b . . . book by James Hogg.'

'Ah, you've read the works of the Ettrick Shepherd.' Martin seemed pleased.

'N . . . no, I haven't.'

'But you've read *The Private Memoirs and Confessions of A Justified Sinner*?'

'N . . . no.'

'Of course. I should have known. The character's name is Gil-Martin. Miss Margaret Mower, was it, who told you about the book? Yes, she would have read it. Marvellous book. Great work of the imagination. Such perception. Freudian psychology a hundred and fifty years before Freud. Schizophrenia, the lot – all there. You must read it. So close to truth. But what were Hogg's dates now? 1770 to 1835, that's it. Friends of friends, Burns, Byron, Southey and others. My kind of people. Also he was responsible for the publication of the infamous *Translation from an Ancient Chaldee Manuscript*. Created a bit of devilry, so they said. Anyway, when I met you I thought I'd take a suitable Scotts name, Hogg's Gil-Martin, in your honour. Yes, I did.'

Alistair Matheson could only repeat his question for the third time, now in a whisper.

'Who are you then?'

'It worries you, Alistair, doesn't it? Am I who you think I am? Which is . . . unthinkable. But is it? You are perhaps an atheist? You weren't brought up one though. Go back to the time you believed in the Deity. A while ago but try. Please try and remember.'

'I . . . remember.'

'You see, I may restore our belief in God. Because if you believe in God, you can believe so easily in his opposite – Lucifer. The Fallen Angel. Believe in one, believe in the other.'

'No, it's nonsense! Superstitious nonsense.'

Martin's smile broadened and he stretched out his legs from the chair in which he was ensconced. Then he laughed aloud. 'Yes, isn't it? Of course. I'm just a simple adventurer with many helpful friends. And you're right, I have changed

168

my name often. And travelled great distances. A wanderer like Ahasuerus. Remember Ahasuerus, the Wandering Jew, or his alter ego, Cartaphilus? And then there's Vanderdecken, *Der Fliegende Holländer*. You see, I feel an affinity to all these characters. Have you ever heard of Fulcanelli? One of the great alchemists. Wrote a couple of fascinating books in the 1920s. I sometimes use his name. I sometimes use all their names. I suppose I sometimes believe I actually am one of them.'

'W . . . which one?'

Martin's eyes flickered. 'Depends how I feel.'

'Lord of the Flies?' Matheson suggested, cold as ice.

Martin laughed again. 'Nelly Garton will have her little joke. Lord of the Flies? That would be Beelzebub. Oh, really, Alistair! Now I really am the Devil then? That's what you believe?'

'I d . . . don't know w . . . what to believe.'

'And you a hard-headed Scot, and a civil servant to boot? Still, perhaps it's the old religious superstition coming out.'

Matheson shook his head, a dazed boxer on the ropes of his mind. 'Why choose me? Why strike up an acquaintance with me?'

'I didn't. You were the one who struck up the acquaintance. You approached me.'

'Because . . . you . . . you l . . . looked like m . . . me.'

'If I do, and not everybody thinks so, it is an accident of nature. I cannot accept responsibility.'

Matheson was searching frantically for another way verbally to assail the man. 'What about Makepeace?'

'What about Alwyn Makepeace?'

'You knew him.'

'A long time ago. A sad case. Mentally unstable.'

'He's dead.'

'It comes to us all.'

'He was murdered. Horribly.'

The smile had gone from the visitor's face. He pursed his lips. 'I'm sorry. Though I hardly knew him.'

Greatly daring now. 'You . . . you k . . . killed him.'

Martin raised his eyebrows. '*I* killed him?'

'I think so.'

'Then I suggest you telephone the police at once and tell them you have the murderer in your apartment. When was he murdered?'

'Last weekend.'

Martin laughed again. He laughed easily. Pleasantly. 'I could make a great deal of money here. I can see the headlines. "Top Civil Servant Sued for Libel Accuses Innocent Business Man of Murder." Cost you a fortune. And think of the scandal. How could I be on Dartmoor and in London at the same time? I have witnesses who can prove I was here.'

'How did you know Makepeace was killed on Dartmoor? I never mentioned Dartmoor.'

'No, you didn't. Just testing. I believe there was something in the newspapers about it. Anyway, that'll serve, won't it? As an explanation. And I really can provide an alibi.'

'And what has happened to Randall?'

'Randall? Who is he?'

'He knew about you. He . . . had you under observation.'

'Under observation! What right had he? Was he some kind of ecclesiastical witch hunter?'

'He was an intelligence officer. He told me about you and Makepeace and Wallingham.'

'I'm afraid you've lost me, Alistair.'

'Makepeace worked for the government. GCHQ. Government Communications. You befriended him as your way in to Communications. That's what Randall believed.'

'That I was a spy? How fascinating.'

'Wallingham was sent to investigate. He died. And now Makepeace is dead and Randall has disappeared.'

'And I'm responsible for all this? How clever I am. And . . . ruthless. Yes, that would be the word. I always wanted to be ruthless. But what can I say? You can't believe all this, Alistair?'

'Then where is Randall?'

'I don't know the gentleman and haven't the faintest idea what you are talking about.'

'And there's the house in Catford. Your house. It's derelict. A ruin. I went there. I saw . . .'

Martin stood up. 'I really have to go. But your last fantasy I can easily disprove. You will come to dinner tomorrow night.

170

I promise you, I will not murder you.' A wide grin here. 'Leave word at your office where you are dining and with whom. That should set your mind at rest. I shall have some friends there. *Nice* people. Such a weak inadequate word "*nice*". But it's exactly what they are. Perhaps, then, as they say in the novels, all will be revealed. And turn out to be in your fertile imagination. Now I must go. I'll see myself out. Oh, and thank you for an amusing interlude. My dear Alistair, your imagination has been working overtime. I believe you really thought I was . . . who you really thought I was.'

He went to the door and stopped again.

'One thing you are right about. I do enjoy it, but I am such a terrible liar . . . Goodnight.'

He went. Leaving Matheson staring after him. Trembling. Only God knew why.

'I am such a terrible liar.' But which were lies and which were truths And how could he have the house in Catford ready for tomorrow? Unless he'd had workers redecorating the place every minute of the last few days.

He couldn't wait until tomorrow night to find out. He could go to Catford now, tonight. Just maybe Randall was there. And if Martin really was dining out, then there would be no one at the house in Catford. Except, perhaps, for decorators working overtime.

It would be something to do. Now. Right away. Give Martin ten minutes to be clear and he would go. To number five Lower Cotton Street, Catford, for the second time.

It was nearly eleven o'clock when he arrived in Catford in the Aston Martin. Although it wasn't actually raining, a damp mist permeated the night air, swirling and drifting up from the Thames. He parked the car a street away this time and walked to Cotton Street. There seemed to be no traffic and no people. And no sound except for his own footsteps echoing against the walls of the houses.

Cotton Street looked no different from his previous visit. A number of the street lamps were dark and broken, and the few that still worked cast small pools of light here and there between the dominant darknesses.

Number five looked exactly as before. As if it was still derelict, at least from the outside. Matheson climbed the six steps and stood facing the door and the brass figure five, still tarnished. He paused for a moment, wondering whether the door might still be open as it had been the previous visit. Then he reached forward tentatively and with the flat of his hand pushed gently.

Again the door swung open and again his nostrils were assailed by the same musty smell. Dust and dampness, he'd thought before, but this time there was something else: the odour of putrefaction, of rotting animal flesh. It brought back memories of an old wash house in Edinburgh, and a dead rat decaying on the stone floor. So there was a dead rat somewhere in the darkness of the house in Cotton Street? Probably the rat he had seen on his first visit.

Or something else was dead in the house.

He felt for the light switch and pressed it down.

The same yellow light, high up towards the ceiling, flared on. The same naked bulb.

He looked around the hall.

Nothing had changed. Bare floorboards as before. No redecoration had been effected. The same torn tapestry on the wall. The same bare staircase leading upwards.

Surely this could not be the house in which Gilbert Martin, or whatever his real name was, intended to hold a dinner party tomorrow night? Unless it was some gruesome joke. Like dining in Dracula's castle, he thought, and forced himself to smile at the thought.

He went to the foot of the staircase. No point in climbing the stairs again. He'd been there before. Right to the top floor. Where he'd encountered the old man. Probably the old man was still there.

'You still there?' he called up into the darkness above. His voice seemed to echo upwards, resounding against bare walls and through deserted rooms. The domain of spiders. No, he would not climb this time. Instead, he went around the staircase towards the back of the house. At the end of the hall was a single door which should lead to the kitchens and servants' quarters.

He pushed the heavy door open, breaking a web, causing a large spider to scuttle across the door on to the wall.

Beyond he found another light switch and was surprised when he pressed it and another bare bulb above him flared into live. He was in a passageway at the end of which was a stone staircase leading downwards. Before it was another door to his right. He went forward, surprising himself by his calmness. No nerves now. Simply curiosity.

The stairway twisted around and after about twenty steps he was on a small landing overlooking the kitchen. A large old-fashioned kitchen range dominated one wall; the kind of range that had once been black-leaded daily by a kitchen skivvy. Now, in the dim light from the corridor, he could see the range was choked, clogged with dust and rubble. Above and around it, shelves stretched around the kitchen walls, empty but for the occasional battered pot or twisted pan, abandoned from better days. In the centre of the kitchen was a large wooden trestle table, once a working area, now with a cracked surface dust-clogged fissures in the wood. To his right, Matheson could make out deep sinks, at least three large, porcelain basins, the porcelain cracked, the sinks clogged with dirt and dried mud. Behind the basins, windows with cracked glass looked on to dark brick walls.

He turned away from the kitchen. It matched the rest of the house: derelict and filthy, long since abandoned. God help the diners if anyone tried to cook a meal here tomorrow. The house did not need redecoration, it needed gutting and its interior rebuilt.

He stopped at the door in the corridor. Where could this lead?

He put his hands on the door knob and pulled. The door opened towards him with a loud creaking sound, hinges protesting. In front of him steps led downwards into a thick blackness. The smell of putrefaction was even stronger here, strong enough to cause him to gag and turn his head away, breathing quickly. He wanted to turn away now, go back to the hall and the front door. Yet he felt impelled to go down to what must be the entrance to the cellars of the house.

He groped around feeling for a light switch. Nothing. And then a shelf and something round metallic. He gripped and withdrew from the unseen shelf a candleholder with some two inches of candle, dust-enshrouded but viable. He blew the dust from the receptacle and with his cigarette lighter attempted to light the wick of the candle. After a long moment it flared into life.

Holding the candle aloft, he took his first step on to the stone stairs leading downwards. The stairs here were much steeper than those that had led to the kitchen, the descent steep, almost vertical. Something flared above his head; the candle had fired a thick spider's web. As the flame died, he could see only stone walls, large slabs of stone under broken and cracked plasterwork. Again the phrase came to him: The domain of spiders.

He went down.

He tried to hold his breath against the unpleasant odour which seemed to get stronger the further down he descended.

He counted the steps. Twenty, thirty, forty . . . and then he reached bottom. The cellar floor. Not stone now but packed earth. Puddled in patches, he could see in the light from the candle. Cold too. A slight stirring of the air, a draught causing the flame of the candle to dance. Causing the shapes in front of him to dance in time to the candle's light.

Large shapes, structures as high as himself, loomed before him. He moved forward, peering ahead until the structures defined themselves. Rows and rows of open shelving, bottles on their sides here and there, necks protruding; empty spaces too where bottles had been removed.

At least, if there was a dinner here, they would drink well. He was in a wine cellar, and not a depleted one. The bottles were, as everything else, shrouded in dust but they were there and not empty. He picked one, blew the dust from it and stared at a bottle of Chablis 1932. Another he selected was a Medoc. And on yet another shelf a Burgundy '28. He replaced the bottles and moved on beyond the wine racks. And again into darkness.

The earth crunched underfoot. Dry now. He stumbled against something and lowered the candle.

He was standing against a bundle of old rags. Or so it seemed. Tentatively he prodded the bundle with his foot. And then knew it was something else.

A body.

The tramp he had seen here before. Matheson knelt. The odour of putrefaction was all around him. Phelgm rose at the back of his throat. The man must be dead but he had to be sure. He had to turn him over. He reached forward, hand trembling, nausea rising, and turned the body over.

The rags fluttered in a draught of air. A hand, mottled, thin, skeletal, fell into the light. The flesh was shrivelled, greenish patches under dirt. No need to try for a pulse. Obviously the hand of a man sometime dead. Small wounds were apparent on the fingers and around the wrists. Rat bites.

He forced himself to turn the body further. To see the face. The face of the tramp.

The head fell under the light, face upwards. He drew his hand back quickly, aware that part of the nose and one cheek had been gnawed away. By rats? Or other creatures?

He stared down at the face. The wrong face. Not the tramp's, not the face he had expected to see.

What was left of Gavin Randall's face, sightless, one eye socket empty, stared up at him. The face had two mouths. Below the normal mouth was another, longer, redder. Randall's throat had been cut.

Chapter Twenty-One

Matheson vomited.

He staggered away from the corpse before vomiting in the furthest corner of the cellar.

When he had finished he stood for some moments alternately shivering and sweating. He tried to tell himself he was not afraid but could not lie to himself. Finally, circling the corpse, he made his way towards the stairway, the hand holding the candle trembling now, the moving light causing shadows and shapes to dance in front of them. On his way towards the stairs, he stopped twice thinking he saw movement ahead of him or to his side. He was relieved when he realised it was the flame of the candle shaking that caused the shadows to appear to jump and leap within his vision.

Quickly he climbed from the cellar to the corridor above. There he stood breathless, gulping air, still shaking. And trying to think. What to do now? The body of the missing intelligence man was below in the cellar of this house which he should not even be in. The murdered rotting body of his friend, Gavin Randall. He should go at once to the police and bring them to the cellar. But how would he explain his presence there?

'I was invited here for dinner tomorrow night and I wanted to see if the house was still derelict.'

'The man who claims to own the house looks exactly like me. But there's something . . . something strange about him.'

'What kind of strange? How can I explain? What does he do? I don't know. Yes, all right I was first to speak to him because of this resemblance. Like looking in a mirror. A mirror image, yes, that's it.'

'We didn't exactly become friends . . . acquaintances, really.'

'Randall was interested in him. Why? I don't really know Something that happened years ago concerning a man called Alwyn Makepeace who was murdered on Dartmoor last weekend.'

It all sounded so crazy, so improbable. They would then ask where they could get hold of this Mr Gilbert Martin and he wouldn't be able to tell them. This was the only address he had for the man, a derelict house in Catford. The murder of Makepeace would be brought into it. On the scene of two murders, he would be an obvious suspect.

Then there would be the publicity. 'Senior Civil Servant in Defence Ministry Involved in Second Murder Case.' Headlines that would finish him. The dead man was an intelligence officer. End of career of senior civil servant. Even if it was hushed up because Randall had been in Intelligence, he, Matheson, would be forever suspect within the Service. If he was not charged with murder.

He should, but could not, go to the police.

He could go, leave this house, leave Catford and go back to his own place. As if he'd never been here. Who would know? Outside the streets were deserted. It was highly unlikely anyone would spot the parked Aston Martin. Anyway, it was a street away. Nobody knew he'd been near the house in Lower Cotton Street.

He braced himself and went into the front hall. The bare electric light bulb still illuminated the room. His first thought to put it out. Anyone passing in the street would see it, the front door was still ajar. He crossed the hall and switched out the light, leaving himself standing in the darkness at the door. He eased it open and peered out into Lower Cotton Street.

There was no one in sight, no sound of distant footsteps. He could be clear of the house and away. He stepped out and drew the door shut behind him, standing in the shadow listening and looking. Still no one in sight. He went down the six steps to the street silently and moved along the pavement. He hesitated at a darker shape against the wall that separated the basement area from the street. Nothing, he thought, shrugged and moved forward.

177

But then in the corner of his eye, the darker shape seemed to stir and move.

'You again, guv'nor. Been to view the house again, eh? Thinkin' of buyin' it? Desirable residence for City gent, eh?'

The shape moved into the dim light cast by the street lamp. It was the old man, the squatter who had been in the house on his first visit. Same tattered coat, same bearded face, mouth twisted in a crooked grin.

'Are . . . are you still squatting in that house?'

'What? Me? Never. Never squatted in there. You can't ever prove I did.'

'Who owns the house?'

'Don't you know? You're the one's been visitin'. Twice now, eh?'

Never a direct answer. Always questions answered by questions. Martin's technique too.

The old man suddenly crackled at him. 'Want to know a secret?' Said like a child.

'All right. Tell me a secret.'

'Not what it seems to be, that house.'

'I'm sure.'

'Folk go in, they don't come out. 'Cepting you, that is.'

'You saw Randall go in?'

'Don't know no names. Just saw people go in and not come out.'

'You . . . seen what happens to them?'

'How could I do that? Never been in the house.'

'You were in that house when I first saw you!'

The man leaned forward, staring up at him, ferret face scowling. 'You prove that! You just try. You got no witnesses. You can't get me to say I was ever in the house.'

Matheson scowled back at his scowl. 'You know there's a dead body in the cellar?'

'Told you, don't know nothing'. 'Specially 'bout dead bodies. Anyways, why'd you think I don't go into that house.'

Suddenly, to Matheson's surprise, the man's eyes blurred and tears carved deltas on the grime-encrusted flesh of his cheeks. 'Dead bodies, y'say. Aw, Gawd! It's him. That's what he does to them what goes in there. Murders 'em. Carves 'em, hangs 'em up like a goat, slits their throats an' lets the blood drip out of their bodies. Like one of them vampires, he is.'

178

'You've seen the body? You've seen other bodies?'

'Naw! Naw . . . naw, I ain't seen nothin'. What I'm telling you. Nothing. But I got an imagination.'

'But you say *'him'*. Who? You must have seen the man?'

'Naw. See me? Almost blind, me. Couldn't see a ten ton truck less it were under my nose. Which a ten ton truck ain't likely to be. Can't even see you there in front of me.'

Matheson said quietly, 'You're a liar, aren't you?'

'You got no right to say that. No right insultin' blokes down on their luck.' The ferret face leaned closer again. Matheson caught a whiff of stale breath and the odour of cheap wine. The face was streaked where the salt tears had carved their way through the grime. The expression under this was sly, hopeful.

'How about a few quid to get a wet an' a bed for the night?'

Matheson recoiled in disgust. He wanted to be away from this caricature of a human being, away from the house itself to which the old man seemed inextricably linked. He took his wallet from his inside pocket, felt for the crinkled shape of a five pound note and thrust it into the outstretched hand.

'Paper money, eh? A fiver. Thank you kindly. Always grateful for small mercies. An' cheap enough, 'specially if it makes you feel good, eh?' The wheezing chuckle came again from the old man.

Matheson stepped back and turned away, walking quickly. He cursed himself for stopping. The old tramp could be a witness against him when the body was found, could perhaps even describe him to the police. Still, that didn't mean they could identify Alistair Matheson, Permanent Under Secretary to the Ministry of Defence. If the old man could identify anyone at all with his claim to have failing eyesight. As he crossed the street, he heard the tramp wheeze and call out.

'That house . . . see that house? On the edge, that house is. On the edge. Go over the edge and you're in another place. An' once you're in that place you don't get back. Sure you don't.'

Matheson reached the far side of the street. The mist seemed to be getting thicker. From behind him came again the wheezing crackle of the old man. Then it stopped and it seemed another voice called out.

179

'Your good deed for the day, Mr Matheson? Positive little Samaritan, eh?' It was a different voice, a familiar voice. Sounding quite unlike the old tramp. Sounding like Gilbert Martin. He turned but could no longer see the tramp or anyone else. The mist was thick, impenetrable to the eye. A trick of the night and the mist? Or a trick of his imagination? That would be it. A voice from his imagination.

Two minutes later he was climbing into the Aston Martin with relief. Which would increase when he got back to Chelsea.

The next morning in the Ministry.

Matheson had slept badly, his mind filled with strange images from the depths of his dreams. *A house on the edge?* One of the images. On the edge of a great precipice; sheer cliffs going down and down into blackness. And from the blackness, wailing voices crying for succour; screams of agony, moans of pain. As if, below, there were souls in torment.

He'd come awake feeling heavy, almost depressed. A tired, rundown feeling. Stomach muscles aching where they had been strained the previous night when he had vomited. Mind turning away from the fast dissipating images of the dream. Yet when he finally rose, he felt better. The dream's effect was slowly draining away.

Of course Martin had been in the dream. There, unchanged, the mirror image again. And Randall too. The dead intelligence man walking upright in the dream, saying, 'I told you so.' With his throat cut and all the scars made by the hungry rats marking his dead flesh. As if staking their claim on the body.

By the time he'd reached Whitehall the memory of the dream had drained away. He could no longer remember any of the dream's details. It seemed as if the sun, now shining from a cloudless sky, had dissipated all unpleasantness. It was almost too bright, and Whitehall seemed cleaner than the rest of London, straight lines of light unblemished masonry leading towards the Palace of Westminster; even the stone ornamentations and embellishments on the older buildings appeared fresh, almost new, under this summer sun. The gates across Downing Street, gold paint sparkling, monument to a previous Prime Minister's arrogance or perhaps simple fear of terrorism, seemed less of a stupidity this morning. The summer had finally arrived.

In his office Matheson settled behind his desk, now almost exhilarated, keen to start working on the boxes and papers in front of him. As if his dream of the night before had somehow expunged the memory of the house in Catford. Had he really visited the house again or was it another part of his nightmares? He could no longer be sure. Then he remembered that this coming evening he was expected to dine there.

He smiled to himself. He would go, most surely. The house would still be derelict. He would be interested to see how Martin wriggled out of the invitation.

Then, and only then, did he remember Randall's body. Of course Martin would have disposed of it by now; he wouldn't take the chance of Matheson calling the police. If Martin did indeed know he had visited the house the night before? Had he really heard Martin's voice as he'd come away from the house?

He tried to dismiss the thought. Caused confusion. Created too many questions. Muddled his mind.

If Martin could kill Randall, he could also kill Matheson. There was another thought.

Precautions must be taken.

He called Miss Lubovious into the office.

'Sir?' She seemed nervous, pale-faced.

'Miss Lubovious, I am dining tonight with a gentleman called Martin. Gilbert Martin.'

'Yes, sir.' Curiosity overcame her nervousness as to why she was being so informed.

'The address is 5 Lower Cotton Street, Catford.'

Lubovious waited, eyes restless.

'You will remember that address?'

'5 Lower Cotton Street.'

'Catford!'

'Catford.'

'Fine.'

The woman shuffled her feet. 'Is . . . is there any particular reason why I should remember this address, sir?'

'I don't know. But I want you to remember it. Write it down,' He could hardly tell her he was afraid that he might be

181

murdered. He could hardly admit it to himself far less inform Lubovious.

'Are you perhaps expecting it may be necessary for the Ministry to contact you this evening? Has the house a telephone number? I should leave it with the duty-officer.'

'Yes, do that.' He was completely calm which surprised him. After last night, should he not be in panic and fear? Yet he could calmly leave the Catford address with Lubovious as if nothing had happened.

The phone on his desk rang.

He lifted the receiver. 'Matheson here.'

'Alistair, it's Margaret.'

Lubovious stood still, immobile, as if waiting formal dismissal.

'Oh, yes. Good morning,' he said coolly and then covered the phone with his hand. 'That will be all just now, Miss Lubovious.'

She did not move.

'Yes? What is it now?' he said.

'The Minister wants to see you in his office right away.'

'Why didn't you say so?'

'You were giving me the address in Catford.'

'I shall see the Minister immediately after this call.'

'Yes, sir. I . . . I'm sorry, sir.'

Lubovious went out. Leaving him wondering at the apology? For what? He dismissed the question and took his hand from the phone. 'Sorry. I had my secretary in the office. Look, Margaret, I'm very busy . . .'

'I had a phone call from Mr Martin this morning!' she said.

'What?'

'Yes, dear, he phoned me.'

'What did he want?'

'He invited me to dinner tonight. With you. At his house in Catford.'

He was surprised, and then crept into his mind the old fear. As if he could have rid himself of it in one summer's day.

'Will you pick me up in your car?' Margaret asked.

'I don't think you should come.'

A pause at the end of the line.

'Why not?'

182

'It could be unpleasant. Even dangerous.'

'In that case, is it wise for you to go?'

'I'm not sure if I will,' he said. It wasn't a lie. The thought had come to him just then. Why go in harm's way?

'You'll go, Alistair. Just as you went to Dartmoor,' she insisted.

'I didn't know, when we went to Dartmoor, what we would find.'

'But are we sure it was connected to Martin? He . . . he sounded so rational on the 'phone.'

'He always does. He plays with people.' It was true. Martin played his games all the time. One moment admitting a half truth, the next denying everything. Seeking to create confusion. Had he even intended Matheson to go to Catford again last night? There was another thought. The last words from the mist might so imply.

Margaret went on: 'He said he was anxious to meet me properly. Felt you might have misunderstood him in the last few days and even transferred that feeling to me.'

'He would say that!'

'He said that, after all, you had been the first to speak to him. He . . . he liked you, he said, and felt circumstances which had nothing to do with him, had somehow distorted your image of him.'

'What else could he say?'

'That I must be his guest. In order that he could clear up all these misunderstandings. Alistair, he could be right.'

'And Randall could be wrong? I don't think so.'

'You told me he had disappeared?'

He was about to tell her he had found Randall. But would it be wise to tell her of his discovery of another body? Might she not react as he felt the police would? Two bodies discovered by Alistair Matheson. Would they believe the discoveries were accidental? Would they even believe Gilbert Martin existed? And even if they did, what could link Martin to the bodies? His ownership of a derelict house in Catford where he, Matheson, had found Randall's body? And surely Martin would not be foolish enough to leave the body in the house. His head was starting to ache with question after question. His earlier elation was gone.

183

'Alistair! Alistair, are you still there?' Margaret, insistent.

'Yes, I'm still here. Margaret, you are not coming to Catford with me tonight.'

'Isn't that up to me?'

'I'm telling you, I'm not even sure I'll go. And, anyway, I'm sure there will be no dinner party at that house tonight '

'Don't be ridiculous. The man's just off the telephone inviting me.'

'Forget it, Margaret. I'm not going to take you to Catford tonight. That's definite.'

He heard the receiver slam down. He shrugged. Better she stayed angry and alive and away from the house in Catford. Better too that he should not go himself. Yet he was curious – no, more than that, fascinated – at the idea of Martin holding a dinner party in an empty ruin of a house.

The intercom on his desk buzzed impatiently.

Miss Lubovious's voice, trembling perceptibly. 'The Minister is asking where you are?'

'I'm going up now.'

The Minister was not alone. Two familiar figures, one tall, one not so tall, were standing in front of his desk as Matheson came in.

'Good morning, sir.'

'Is it, Mr Matheson? Oh, I believe you've met Chief Inspector Claypole and Inspector Burns of the Special Branch?'

Matheson felt his stomach cramp, a sudden anticipatory pain.

'Yes, of course. Have you found Gavin Randall?'

Because if you have, I found him first. And he was very horribly dead.

'This is not about Randall,' Claypole said.

'Who is Randall?' said the Minister. 'Never mind that. You were working on papers concerning defence cuts?'

'Yes, sir. You knew that.'

'You know how highly confidential these papers were?' the Minister pressed on.

'Top secret,' Claypole said.

'Of course, sir.'

184

Claypole cleared his throat. 'Then perhaps you can explain how these papers were found by a beat constable in a refuse bin outside a church in South London?'

Matheson was taken by surprise. Certainly he had been working on the papers, but he had no inkling of their disappearance.

'They were last signed out of the registry to you,' the Minister added.

'Of course they were, Minister.I was working on them. And they were to the best of knowledge returned to the registry safe the other evening. By Miss Lubovious.'

Burns, the other policeman, spoke now. 'Miss Lubovious says they were left with you the other evening.'

'Miss Lubovious said nothing to me this morning!'

'She was so instructed by us,' said Claypole.

'But it's all nonsense! I was working on them. And . . . and I'm sure . . . at least I think . . . I handed them over to Miss Lubovious. She has security clearance.'

'We're aware of that. We have questioned her, and if necessary will do so further,' Claypole again.

'Fortunately they have been recovered,' the Minister went on. 'But we cannot exclude the possibility they have been copied. Oh, I don't think they'd be of great value to any enemy agent. They are, after all, only proposals at this stage. Subject to Cabinet approval. But the Opposition could damage the government if these proposed cuts were leaked. I cannot believe you would be so careless as to remove them from the Ministry, but it does seem to rest between you and the Lubovious woman. And she is most insistent that it was not her.'

'It's ridiculous. Why should I? I don't see why Lubovious should either but . . . where were the papers found?'

'Luckily the beat policeman spotted the Ministry logo on the top document.'

Matheson persisted. 'Yes, but where?'

'South London,' said Burns. 'Outside a church in Callender Road. That's in Catford, I believe.'

Chapter Twenty-Two

The Ministry of Defence was, that day, inundated with secretive, poker-faced men in sports jackets and flannels who questioned everybody regarding the documents lost and found. They were Special Branch detectives, there was no mistaking them. After each session, the questioned were informed that if any word of this inquisition were to be whispered outside the Ministry there would be dire consequences for the whisperer. The Official Secrets Act was invoked at the end of every interrogation.

It all seemed so unnecessary to Alistair Matheson. The investigation was taking place not only after the horse had bolted the barn, but after the selfsame horse had been returned apparently unharmed.

He personally was much more concerned with the location at which the documents had been found. Catford! Everything led to Catford. Alone in his office, he consulted a London Street directory. Callender Road was only two streets away from Lower Cotton Street. Indeed it was only around the corner from where Matheson had parked the Aston Martin the previous night. Was it possible that, without realising it, he had taken documents from the Ministry and left them in a refuse basket in a Catford street? He dismissed the thought at once. There was no possibility of his having done such a thing. Was it possible the documents had been stolen and left in Catford by someone who had perhaps followed Matheson last night? Again he dismissed the thought. He had only gone to Catford after Gilbert Martin had left his flat in Chelsea and he, Matheson, had taken the decision on the spur of the moment to revisit the house in Cotton Street. Unless whoever had taken the documents had followed him around all evening hoping to find a place somewhere close to him where they could be abandoned? But how would that person have been sure the documents would be found so quickly by the police? No, he determined, there had to be an element of coincidence here.

That still did not answer the question, who had taken the documents from the Ministry?

Miss Lubovious seemed to be avoiding his eyes for the rest of the day. She flushed, eyes averted, whenever she came face to face with him. Did she consider herself some kind of Judas Iscariot, betrayer of her master to the powers that be? Or had she removed the documents and was ridden with conscience? By late-afternoon he could no longer stand any more of this attitude. How could he work with a woman who only answered him in monosyllables, whose eyes seemed fastened to her feet? He called her into his office.

'Miss Lubovious?'

'Sir?' Eyes cast downwards, face scarlet.

'This can't go on!'

'No, sir.' No change in her stance, face a deeper scarlet.

'We have to work together, you know.'

Tears suddenly coursed down her face. 'Oh, I'm so sorry, sir.'

'About what?'

'The policemen. Talking to them. Not being able to tell you I had talked to them. Not that I wanted to, but they make it difficult.'

'Miss Lubovious, it was your duty to talk to them.'

'Yes, sir, I suppose so. But when they asked me questions about you, what could I say?'

'Only the truth, Miss Lubovious, only the truth.'

'Yes, sir, but what is the truth? I thought you'd retained those papers. Then I hear that you thought I'd taken them back to the registry. So that meant you didn't believe me.'

'It also meant you didn't believe me, Miss Lubovious.'

She frowned now, a puzzled expression on her face. She looked up at him for the first time since the morning. 'Hadn't thought of it that way, sir.'

187

'Anyway, Miss Lubovious, I do not subscribe to the opinion that one of us is lying.' He wasn't actually sure of this statement. Indeed, he was probably convinced that she was, if not lying, certainly mistaken. But that did not mean she herself had appropriated the documents.

'No, sir,' she replied. 'Of course not, sir.'

'I'm convinced a mistake has been made.' Another lie. He was not so convinced. But after all, he had to work with the damned woman. And there was certainly no malice, aforethought or otherwise, in her. She was innocent of any ill intent. Almost certainly had returned the documents to the registry after he had been working on them, and forgotten doing so. Someone else had spirited the documents from the registry. Someone else? Who? Or did he even have to ask himself the question?

'Since I came to London, we've worked as a team, Lubovious. I wish us to continue doing so. I am therefore going to ask you to erase all this from your mind.'

'Oh, yes, sir!' She was pleased. Actually trying to smile.

'That does not mean that if you can help Special Branch people, or remember anything you have omitted to tell them, you should not do so.'

'Of . . . of course, sir.' Uncertain again. Examining her basic loyalties. Which inevitably were to him.

'We will therefore forget this whole matter and continue to work together as before.'

'Yes, sir. Thank you sir.'

She left the room her step lighter, her flush diminishing. Matheson looked at his watch. Four-thirty. He was determined to leave before five and get back to Chelsea with plenty of time to dress for dinner. He pressed the intercom on his desk and spoke again to Miss Lubovious.

'I'm leaving early today. There is no reason for the Minister to want me tonight. The debate in the House is on agriculture. If he or anyone else should want me I shall be at home until seven-thirty after which I shall be going to dinner at the house in Lower Cotton Street. You still have the address?'

'Yes, of course, sir. Is Cotton Street on the telephone?'

'I think it is in the phone book. Though I somehow doubt if the number will be obtainable. Anyway, I shall probably be home early.' Thinking, since it was highly unlikely there would be a dinner party in that derelict house.

As he was leaving the Ministry, briefcase in hand, he encountered Claypole in the entrance hall.

'Leaving early, Mr Matheson?'

'I have completed my various tasks of the day, Chief Inspector. And I'm sure you won't be surprised to learn that Permanent Under Secretaries do not have to clock in and out of their Ministries.'

'Hadn't thought about it, sir.'

'You see, Mr Claypole, this is my Ministry. Oh, the Minister is temporarily in charge, but the Permanent Under Secretary is really in control. Ministers come and go. We go on forever.'

'How satisfying for you. What's in the briefcase, Mr Matheson?'

'I could say, not for your eyes, Claypole.'

'You could say it, sir, but it wouldn't matter. Special Branch and, believe it or not, Customs and Excise, can go everywhere and anywhere, see anything and everything. Can go even more places than the Inland Revenue. Could you open the briefcase, sir?'

Matheson went over to the small table at which the customary serjeant-at-arms sat greeting all new arrivals.

'You think I'm smuggling out another set of papers, Mr Claypole?' he said to the policeman.

'Another set, Mr Matheson? Does that mean you took the first set?'

'No, I didn't. And you're welcome to look into the case.'

He unlocked and opened it. Claypole peered in and then, reaching inside, produced from within a copy of Punch. This was followed by Matheson's daily copies of *The Times* and the *Scotsman* (London edition).

'Nothing subversive there, Claypole. Unless you consider *Punch* so to be.'

Claypole shrugged. 'Just doing my job, Mr Matheson.'

'Well, if you don't mind, I'll be off.' Matheson replaced newspapers and magazine and shut his briefcase. 'Will we see you tomorrow?'

'We shall be around and about. Like bulldogs, us, Mr Matheson. Never let go, eh? Oh, by the way, you haven't heard from Mr Randall again, have you?'

Matheson felt sick. The vision of the body returned. He'd been very successful in keeping it out of mind all day. As if it was part of his nightmare and not reality. Could he be sure it wasn't?

'No, I haven't,' he heard himself say. 'Have your people?'

'No. I'm just beginning to think maybe he did take a long trip. to the East. Though with all this *glasnost* stuff, I don't see the point. Anyway, 'night, Mr Matheson. See you tomorrow.'

Matheson took a taxi to Chelsea. Dobson was waiting when he reached the flat.

'You're still dining out tonight, sir?'

'I'm still dining out. You can take the evening off if you wish.'

'Very good of you, sir. But I was away last night, if you remember.'

'So go to the cinema tonight. If I'm home before you I am capable of getting anything I need. You can however run a bath for me now.'

He luxuriated in the hot water. He was inevitably thinking about the coming evening. How could Martin have a dinner party in the house in Catford? He would probably, on his guests' arrival, be waiting with some excuse to take them out to a restaurant. Yes, that would be his most likely move.

If there were other guests.

Or was the man simply luring him to the empty house to deal with him as he had already dealt with Gavin Randall? In which case he should not go unarmed. Problem; he possessed no weapon. He could hardly go in a dinner jacket with a concealed kitchen knife. Not quite right, not quite the done thing. Anyway, he could not see himself stabbing anyone, even in self defence.

Then he remembered – Dobson had a gun. He was a member of some local gun club, had a licence to own a weapon, took part in competitions and practised regularly at the gun club.

From the bath, robed in a heavy towelling dressing gown, he summoned his manservant into the living room.

190

'Dobson, you own some kind of revolver, don't you?'

'I own a brace of target pistols, sir. As you know I'm a member of the Fulham Gun Club.'

'I want to borrow one of your guns.'

'They're pistols, sir.'

'Pistols then.'

Dobson frowned. 'I'm sorry, sir, but you have to be licensed to carry a pistol. You haven't a licence.'

Ruminating, Matheson stared at the carpet. 'Dobson, tonight I'm possibly going in harm's way.'

The servant's frown deepened. 'Don't you think it might be better to inform the police?'

'No, in this case, it would not.'

'How long will you need the pistol for, sir?'

'Hopefully only for this evening.'

'Will you let me show you how it is operated?'

'I'd be grateful.'

The make of the weapon meant nothing to Matheson. It held six rounds of ammunition . . . he had no idea what size . . . but Dobson loaded it expertly, put the safety catch on and showed Matheson how to put the catch off.

'Then the gun is ready to fire,' he said. 'You simply aim at the target and press the trigger. As it is primarily a target pistol, the bullets are .22 calibre, fairly lightweight, and will only wound unless they hit a vital spot. Otherwise they can do sufficient damage to disable. I hope you'll find no need to use it.'

Matheson pursed his lips. 'I subscribe to that thought, Dobson., And . . . er, how does one carry it? Do I have some sort of shoulder holster?'

'I am afraid I am hardly as well equipped as the gentlemen in gangster motion pictures. Still, I'm sure we can place it in the inside pocket of your dinner jacket or the back pocket of your trousers without creating an unsightly bulge.'

The pistol was placed in the latter position. Although he could feel it, Dobson assured him that it was not noticeable. He would however have to be careful not to sit down too quickly. Matheson duly thanked him for the advice.

'One other thing,' said Dobson. 'You've told me you intend to go "in harm's way", as you put it. Wouldn't it be better if I went with you?'

Matheson looked up at the manservant. Dobson's face was bland as ever.

'Thanks, Dobson. Won't forget it. But I may be exaggerating.' Please God, he told himself, he was indeed. 'And as it happens this dinner invitation is for me only.'

'If you're sure, sir?'

'I'm sure.'

He left the house at seven-thirty and drove directly to Catford. This time he parked in Lower Cotton Street directly across the road from number five. He climbed out, locked the car door and stared across at the house. It looked no different from the previous evening. Dark, shuttered, unlived in.

He felt cold. A numbing cold deep in the marrow of the bone. The cold inspired by fear. He wished now Dobson could have been with him. He was aware his imagination was working overtime and a companion would have alleviated the images that filled his mind. Thank God, he told himself, he had refused to take Margaret with him. There was something wrong with the time and the world at this minute and it had to be safer for anyone else if he faced it alone.

He walked across the road. There were no cars in sight, parked or otherwise.

He climbed the six steps to the door.

He felt sure everything would be as it was last night. No way could the house have been made habitable for dinner guests. Indeed for anyone. He would go into that empty, dusty hall with its solitary bare electric light bulb high on the ceiling. Would Randall's body still be in the cellar? If it was . . . if it was still there, this time he would do something. At least inform the police. What kind of story would he tell? That was the main problem. Could he tell the truth? Could he convince people like Claypole he was telling the truth? It all had to be thought out. For now, see if the body of Randall was still there. And perhaps, in going into the house, learn why Martin had invited him.

He felt for the pistol in his back pocket. It wasn't there. But he was sure he'd put it there.

He pushed the door expecting it to open as on his two previous visits. It did not do so. Tonight somebody had closed it. Not surprising with the body in the cellar. The problem now was, how to get in. He leaned against the door and pushed harder. Nothing happened.

Then he heard from the other side an unlocking of bolts, followed by a scraping sound as the handle turned.

The door opened.

To a blaze of light that caused him to blink at its intensity. And against the flood of light the black outline of a tall figure in immaculate tails.

'Mr Matheson, is it? You are expected, sir.'

Chapter Twenty-Three

The house in Lower Cotton Street *en fete*.

Matheson stepped into the hall, his eyes taking some seconds to adjust to the light. He looked up at the ceiling. Instead of the solitary light bulb he found himself staring up at an elaborate chandelier, many bulbs reflected in a multitude of crystal facets.

Lowering his eyes, he gazed around the hall. The walls were oak-panelled, polished until the wood almost reflected the room. Where the tattered tapestry had been there was now a new brilliantly colourful tapestry, a cloth diorama illustrating some medieval scene. In front of the tapestry was a small antique table and two chairs. On the other side wall of the hall, in a huge gilt frame, was a large painting, the style of which Matheson found vaguely familiar although at first he could not place it. He surveyed the floor, only last night a dirt-encrusted area of rubble. Now polished wood met his gaze, a dark, rich mahogany colour on the centre of which was an enormous Persian carpet so colourful as to appear new. Suits of armour stood sentinel against the walls, and the staircase climbing not into darkness now but into light was carpeted with a wide expensive runner. More wall lights gleamed from the first landing.

Matheson thought, there was no way this could have happened overnight. He seemed to be in the wrong house, a different hall, a different edifice. Except for the outside which was exactly as before. He could not be in the wrong house.

He turned to face the figure that had let him in – over six feet tall, in white tie and tails, hands covered in white gloves.

The long, thin aquiline features stared down at the new arrival. Almost a caricature of a butler. He stood, waiting while Matheson surveyed the room.

'Er, good evening,' Matheson said for want of anything else that might come to mind. As he spoke, his eyes went back to the large painting.

'Good evening, sir,' said the butler. 'May I take your coat?'

Matheson divested himself of his light raincoat and handed it to the man, still staring at the painting.

'Mr Martin and his other guests are in the sitting room on the first floor,' the butler said, folding Matheson's coat carefully over his arm.

'Ah, yes, of course.'

'If you will follow me, sir?'

But the painting still held Matheson's eyes. Small figures across the canvas were huddled down engaged in occupations he could not quite make out. Other figures seemed to surround them – thin sinister figures. There was snow on the ground in one part of the picture; in another steam seemed to surround the feet of the figures. The predominant colours were brown and orange. Matheson blinked. Despite the size of the painting which was considerable he could not quite make out the action, as if the lights from the chandelier dazzled. Again he thought the style was familiar.

'That painting?' he said aloud. 'I seem to know the style . . .'

'Hieronymous Bosch,' the butler replied knowingly.

'Of course. I should have known,' Matheson said, and told himself he certainly should have. He prided himself on an appreciation of painting and held certain painters as favourites. He had been introduced to Bosch and Brueghel early in life by his father. There was something in the horrors depicted in many of the paintings by these two artists that had appealed to the severity of Matheson Senior's religious beliefs.

'I thought I knew most of Bosch's work but that painting is unfamiliar to me,' Matheson said.

The butler amended his previous statement. 'If not Bosch, certainly the school of Bosch.'

'I can't quite make out . . .'

'The subject, sir, purports to be Hades. Hell intruding on everyday life, that is how Mr Martin interprets it.' The butler

195

stepped forward and with a swift motion of a white-gloved hand seemed to flick an invisible mote of dust from the frame.

'Recently hung there?' Matheson said as casually as he could.

'Oh, no, sir. It has been hanging there for a considerable time. Ever since Mr Martin bought the house some years ago.' It was said in such a matter-of-fact tone that, in view of his previous visits, Matheson could only marvel at the lie or shudder at the unbelievable statement.

He turned again to the painting, at first standing back a few feet to take in the scope of the canvas then moving closer to study the detail. Dutch peasants were depicted at work. But not quite at work. There was the milkman wrestling with a milk churn. But over his shoulder a shrouded figure loomed, and the milk was spilling upon the ground, clotting and curdling at the milkman's feet. On another part of the canvas a farmer was slaughtering a goat, cutting its throat with every sign of relish. Behind the farmer was another shrouded figure, arm around the man's waist, and as he was cutting the beast's throat so the large figure, blade in hand, was eviscerating the farmer. Only this time the shroud had slipped from one shoulder of the figure, revealing grey-whitish skin as of some kind of slug-like creature or a body long submerged in water. All that could be seen of the head was another patch of hairless skin. The effect was of something putrid. And, sure enough, on yet another part of the canvas was depicted some kind of opening in the ground, a crevice from which figures were emerging, shrouds clinging to bodies, some of them merely fragments of tattered cloth. Although they were shaped like men, torso, legs, arms, the grey white skin predominated. And in the genital area, the organs were large, twice the size of a normal man's. And throughout the painting these creatures, demons from some nether world, were there attacking a respectable woman, here assaulting a nun, in another place sodomising a young girl. Sexual depravities appeared side by side with acts of murderous violence.

Matheson turned away, feeling sick at the power of the painting and all that it depicted.

'It's quite priceless,' a familiar voice said from above him. 'Of course it's never been exhibited, never shown. A strange

196

existence for a masterpiece. Hidden away in the cellar of the rich pervert who purchased it then passed down to others until it reached its rightful home, its rightful owner, the one who commissioned it. Myself.'

It was Martin speaking from the first landing, one foot on the last step of the staircase. Elegant in dinner jacket and black tie, he was smiling down at Matheson. And of course resembled him as always. Except perhaps on this occasion Martin seemed taller, slimmer, more handsome. As if he was as Matheson might wish to see himself, the idealised version, the figure he would like to be.

'Then it's a modern painting,' he said, surprised.

'Oh, no,' Martin replied. 'No, fifteenth-century definitely. But difficult to establish its provenance. Yet isn't it unforgettable after first viewing?'

Matheson told himself he should have expected that. Part of Martin's act. The outrageous, impossible lie, his commissioning the painting, uttered and thrown away deliberately to astonish. Part of the technique. Had to be. Any other explanation was . . . unthinkable. Even if he'd thought it at other times: allowed it into his mind on Dartmoor; tolerated it when he'd spoken to the Bishop of Storford; entertained it again last night over Randall's body.

Now, contemplating it yet again, he was forced by commonsense, by everything rational in his world, to reject the end product of consideration and turn to a more logical explanation.

'But welcome, my dear Alistair,' Martin went on, smiling and bland as ever. 'Come up and meet my other guests.'

Matheson climbed the staircase thinking, I have been here before but in such different circumstances. And altered surroundings.

Martin greeted him with outstretched hand, gripping his guest's with strength and seeming enthusiasm, the flesh warm and dry in contrast to Matheson's awareness that his own hand was damp with perspiration. Nevertheless, as always, he shuddered at the feeling of shaking hands with his own mirror image.

'Delighted to see you, my dear fellow,' said Martin.

'I hope I'm not late,' Matheson replied.

197

'Not at all. My other guests always seem to make a point of being early. I don't know why.'

'You've had the house redecorated recently?'

'Not really. A few minor adjustments. I like the place to be comfortable and homely. And to show off my few art treasures to their best advantage. No point in owning a few exquisite artifacts unless one can display them to the best advantage. And I do appreciate the soothing beauty of great paintings.'

He took Matheson by the arm and led him towards the nearest door. It was the one he had entered on his first visit to the house. There should be a derelict drawing room, no lights, bare boards and a marble fireplace covered in dust. There should be, but he was sure now it would no longer be so.

Martin opened the door.

The first impression was of light again, so bright as to be almost white, the marble fireplace reflecting the brilliance of the room. On the mantelpiece some small exquisite jade ornaments. Above it a portrait which seemed to Matheson to depict himself, slim and poised, dressed in white tie and tails, the ribbon of the Légion D'Honneur around his neck, the eyes above staring straight ahead. Of course the portrait was of Martin.

Matheson turned to survey the rest of the room. An impression of shimmering gold surfaces; Louis XV furniture; a rich red curtain covering the bay window; a smaller but even more brilliant chandelier hanging from a painted ceiling; the ceiling ornate, rococo, a depiction of some scene Matheson could not make out; the whole an excess of ornamentation.

There were five people in the room.

The first couple to be introduced, the tall thin figures seeming to shimmer under the light, were instantly recognisable.

'I believe you have met Sir Herbert and Lady Gosforth?'

Gosforth inclined his head, a sardonic look on his face. 'Ah, yes, the civil servant. We met at a dinner party at Charles Groves.'

Lady Gosforth inclined her head without looking at Matheson. Her eyes were fixed on her host as if she was unable to look at anyone else.

Martin turned to another guest, another tall slim figure. 'Mynheer Van der Boek, a visitor from South Africa. Where he holds an important position in the . . . the Security Services.'

The man's face was a mass of lines, criss-crossing the cheeks, creating deep fissures where there should be none. The skin was yellow parchment, the nose long and straight under eyes sunk into the head. The eyes themselves registered no emotion.

'Sir,' said Van der Boek. 'A pleasure.' With no indication of any kind of pleasure.

'Delighted to meet you,' Matheson said, issuing the lie without effort.

The fourth guest, a fat man, excessively large in bulk, a round bald head on top of the even rounder body, rolls of fat curved over the neck of the man's dress shirt, did actually look at Matheson, staring with a twisted grin into his face, sizing him up with small round eyes that gleamed and glinted like two round silver coins, polished to excess. An exotic, almost sickly odour came from the man, some kind of body lotion or aftershave of excessively unpleasant strength.

'Charlie Beal,' said Martin. 'An old business colleague of mine. This is Alistair Matheson. I've spoken of him to you.'

'Indeed he has, Mr Matheson,' said Charles Beal, fat hand outstretched. Martin felt his own hand sink into flesh. 'Says you believe he resembles you. I suppose there is a superficial resemblance. Though I'd say you're a damn sight better looking than old Gilbert here.'

Martin smiled. 'Always trying to get one over on me is Charlie. But in the end he never quite succeeds. Knows who's in charge, eh, Charlie?'

Beal laughed, a wheezing sound, shoulders heaving.

Martin again gripped Matheson's arm and turned him towards the heavy curtain. And he saw the fifth guest.

'Of course you have met,' Martin said.

Matheson found himself facing Margaret Mower.

199

Chapter Twenty-Four

Drinks before dinner in the house on Lower Cotton Street.

Served by the butler, the same obsequious figure who had opened the door to Matheson, the guests drank dry martinis and other aperitifs. They formed themselves into groups of two, Martin flitting from one group to the next.

Charlie Beal became involved in a long conversation with Van Der Boek, the small fat man straining his neck to listen to the ponderous words of the South African. The Gosforth's seemed to prefer their own company although the host lingered with them for some time. All this permitted Matheson to move to Margaret's side. She was dressed in a shimmering eye-catching gown, the plunging neckline revealing a considerable amount of cleavage.

Matheson said under his breath, 'What are you doing here?'

'I was invited.' Margaret was staring straight ahead.

'I told you I didn't want you to come.'

'I wanted to come, so I came. I wanted a closer look at your Mr Martin.'

'He's not *my* Mr Martin!'

'No, he isn't. He's not very like you, is he?'

'You saw him in the restaurant that night . . .'

'And I thought then he wasn't very like you.'

'Still, you didn't have to see him again.'

Margaret looked up at him, grinning. 'No, I didn't. But as I've told you, I decided I wanted to come.'

Matheson dropped his voice, speaking through clenched teeth. 'For God's sake, you could be in danger here!'

'So you say. But I don't see any sign of danger.'

'You saw Makepeace's body on Dartmoor.'

'Yes, I saw it. I don't see any connection between it and Gilbert Martin.'

He was exasperated now. 'I told you!'

'Yes, you did. That was the only connection. What you told me.'

He was fighting to keep his voice low. 'You . . . you don't believe me, then?'

'Alistair, you told me this was a derelict house.'

'It was. And it was derelict last night.'

'And our host waved a wand and overnight it became this very civilised establishment? Or are you sure you didn't visit the wrong house?'

Matheson clenched and unclenched his fists. 'I didn't visit the wrong house!'

'Then either Martin has employed some superbly fast workmen or . . . or you are a liar and a fantasist.'

He opened his mouth to reply angrily when he realised Martin was approaching.

'I always find at these parties everybody sticks to the one they know,' Martin said, addressing himself to Margaret. 'So difficult at the beginning to get people to circulate.'

'I intend to do so any minute now,' Margaret replied, looking away from Matheson. 'You have a very beautiful home, Mr Martin.'

'Gilbert, please. And, with your permission, I shall call you Margaret. I'm glad you like my home. Oh, I know there are some who might consider it a touch garish. But I like bright and beautiful things around me.'

'You've had the house for long?'

'Oh, yes, for many years. More than I care to admit. I was aware, when I bought it, that Catford was not the most fashionable district in London. But then who cares about fashion? This house was so exactly what I was looking for that I snapped it up. Four storeys and ground floor, and an extensive cellar. I . . . I like space. I like being able to accommodate as many guests as I can. For as long as they care to stay.'

'You have other homes, Martin?' Alistair broke in, suppressing a feeling of irritation at Margaret's pleasant attitude

201

to the host. Not that he could think she would behave otherwise. But her manner irritated him. She was warming to the man and Martin was basking in the heat.

'Come now, you must not monopolise the most beautiful woman in the room,' said Charlie Beal materialising behind his host. He spoke quietly, perhaps out of consideration for the angular Lady Gosforth across the room.

Margaret took the compliment with evident pleasure. Beal somehow infiltrated the space between Martin and Margaret. His face was glowing with a damp film of perspiration. He was hardly a pleasing vision and yet Margaret seemed susceptible to his obvious flattery.

'You are the novelist Margaret Mower,' he went on, making a statement rather than asking a question. 'You may not believe it but I have read everything you have written. And admired it all so very much.'

Had he really read her novels, Matheson wondered, or was this the natural extension of flattery? Martin however seemed to confirm Beal's reading habits.

'It's perfectly true, Margaret. He positively inters himself in your novels. Now, while I enjoy them, oh, yes, I do, Charlie has lavishly praised you for years. When I told him, I was inviting you tonight, he went into a positive ecstasy of excitement. I'm not quite sure, even now, if I had intended to invite him . . . oh, he is an old friend certainly . . . but at times one wants to limit numbers. However he insisted and if I had not invited him, I doubt if our friendship would have survived.'

But Beal seemed impatient of all that his host was saying. He obviously wanted to talk to Margaret and not surprisingly about her work. 'Oh, yes, *The Hotel at Montpellier* is very, very good. Should have won the Booker that year. Mind you, I think it was too good. But *Summer Dead and Gone*, that is *the* book. So delicate. Like fine, fine lace. And the relationship between Angela and Paul . . . now that is so subtle. All the years of his adoration and, when the opportunity comes, he does nothing. I was very sad for him. Kept asking myself, why, why?'

It was as if he was speaking of living people and not characters in fiction. But Margaret was warming to him.

She replied, 'When I was writing it, I think, originally I intended to bring them together. But when I reached that sequence, it really wrote itself. It was obvious somehow that it was too late for Paul.'

Beal nodded, chins wobbling. 'So right, so true, and yet so regrettable.' He took Margaret by the arm now. 'You know, there is something else. You see, I read your very first book . . . I don't think it's in print any more . . . and I like to say to myself, I saw the talent . . . no, the genius, so early.'

Margaret was genuinely surprised. 'You read *Wilderness Hill?*'

'When it first came out. And told myself this is a writer.'

'I've always thought *Wilderness Hill* should be forgotten,' Margaret said. 'A young woman's attempt to do an Emily Bronte. Most unsuccessfully.'

'Ah, but the elements were all there. One can find the beginnings of your later hero, Paul, in the character of Roderick. Paul is Roderick with more strength and . . . and ruthlessness.'

'I think when I wrote it I was in love with Roderick. Not very satisfactory, being in love with one's own fictional character. Why, eventually, I tended to dismiss the book as overly romantic.'

'And went on to create reality, Miss Mower. But you are really a passionate realist . . . so much passion viewed through an icicle mind.'

'I'm not sure I like that.' Margaret was amused.

'Ah, but you should. You should revel in it. Passion is only valuable and enjoyable when it is circulated . . .'

They moved away, still talking, and left Matheson staring after them with rising irritation.

'He really is a fanatical admirer,' Martin said.

Matheson turned to face his host. He was transferring his irritation to Martin.

He said, 'Why am I here?'

Martin seemed amused. Matheson felt he was watching his own forehead crinkle questioningly.

'As my guest, my dear fellow.'

'No. No, there's something more . . .'

'Is there? I don't think so.'

'What do you want of me?'

Martin's amusement increased. 'What should I want of you?'

'This . . . this acquaintanceship you've struck up with me . . .'

'Alistair, I would remind you that you approached me. Regarding our resemblance. I was at first amused and then I rather liked you.'

'More than that!'

'Well, you were . . . you are an important fellow in your field. Senior civil servant. Very senior. Interested me. Very much.'

'Why should it interest you?'

Martin affected an air of puzzlement now. 'Why should it not? One finds oneself interested in many things in life. Especially power. Now you are near the seat of power in the country.'

'Like Alwyn Makepeace?'

'Alwyn Makepeace. What has he to do with anything?'

'He had power.'

'Oh, I doubt that. Wasn't he a very minor civil servant? Compared to you, old man.'

'He had access to GCHQ. To top secret government communications. Secrets.'

Martin was still smiling. 'Secrets? Are there so many? And I doubt Makepeace was of much importance. Paltry secrets, I would think.'

'Randall didn't think so.'

'Randall?'

God, he's a good actor, Matheson thought. Genuine puzzlement on his face. Almost believable. If it hadn't been for Randall's body lying in the cellar last night . . . Matheson decided to press on.

'He was an intelligence officer. He knew you.'

'I didn't know him.'

Not the time, Matheson told himself, too soon to talk about Randall's body. Let him get in deeper, dig his own grave. Time to change tack.

'Why me, Martin, why me?'

The amusement was there again. 'Is there any answer? What was it the mountaineer Mallory said when asked why he wanted to climb Mount Everest? "Because it was there", wasn't that what he said? Why you, Alistair? Perhaps because you were there.'

It was a small break, an admission of something. Matheson opened his mouth, to press home his questions, but before he could speak Martin waved a hand towards the door.

'Later, Alistair, later. I think my man is about to announce that dinner is served.'

He was right. The butler had re-entered and nodded across the room.

'Dinner!' Martin did the announcing. 'Come along, people. Food!'

He led the way alone.

Beal followed with Margaret on his arm. The Gosforths came next and Matheson brought up the rear with Van der Boek. they went on to the landing and through to the next room.

It was the perfect setting. The table was beautifully laid, the room lit only by candles strategically placed on the table and around the room, creating areas of light. Martin sat at the head of the table indicating that Margaret sit on his right, Matheson on his left across the table from her. On her right Beal, to his obvious delight, was seated. At Matheson's left Lady Gosforth sat, across the table from her husband now at Beal's other side. Van der Boek was at the foot of the table. As they settled around the table Matheson noted the candles were so positioned as to cast the shadows of the diners on the wall behind them where they loomed large, moving and seemingly dancing as the candles flickered.

Several conversations continued while the manservant, now aided by a maid, a middle-aged woman of unsurpassed ugliness, served the soup. Van der Boek was discussing with the Gosforths the state of South Africa in the middle of abolishing apartheid. From this conversation Matheson gathered that Van der Boek's first name was Cornelius.

'Of course,' said the Boer, 'it had to be so. Mandela has the black battalions. But there will be a reaction. I think there will be a bloody reaction.'

'Either way, bad for business, Cornelius,' Gosforth said gloomily. 'Why couldn't they leave things as they were? We were doing rather nicely trading with your government.'

'You traded with us? Despite sanctions?' Van der Boek said, smiling.

'You know I did, Cornelius. And why should I not? Thatcher was against sanctions. Bad for business. I made sure it wasn't bad for my business.'

As he spoke he noticed Matheson was listening. 'Ah, you are the civil servant. You must have known it was going on.'

'Hardly concerned my minister,' he said. 'I was at the Scottish Office and then only recently at Defence.'

'You authorised no arms sales to South Africa?'

Matheson reddened. 'If we did, it would be classified information.'

'But your friend Charlie Grove, his companies were avoiding . . . or should it be evading . . . sanctions? Grove was trading with S.A. all the time.'

Matheson nodded, feeling depressed. If it were true, then Charlie wasn't the man he'd thought he was. But then neither was the British government the government he liked to think it was. He turned away from them to face the other Charlie, Beal, who was still deep in conversation with Margaret.

'. . . a deep sign of sexual repression running through those types of novels,' Beal was saying.

Margaret was not looking happy now. 'I've never been aware of being sexually repressed.'

'Ah, I exclude you, of course. But so many others are, these days,' the fat man continued. 'There is no spirit of adventure in sex, written or practised. No . . . exploration of possibilities.'

'I'm not sure if I want to explore such possibilities,' Margaret replied almost primly.

'No, no, that's not true. You, like everyone else, have your fantasies. Even if you will not admit it, you would like to explore those fantasies. It is other people's fantasies you are afraid to explore.'

'Or simply don't wish to.'

'But that is the adventure. To carry out your own fantasies and then take one more step into the world of another. It is something you, as a novelist, must do.'

Margaret laughed. 'Are you trying to talk me into something, Mr Beal?'

206

'Of course. What else?' Beal returned the laughter and then caught Matheson's eye. 'You're not amused, Mr Matheson?'

'Not particularly. You seem to be arguing for a rather decadent life style.'

'Of course I am. You see, you're a selfish man. You would be happy if Miss Mower would indulge all your fantasies but no one else's. Now that attitude goes under many names. Possessiveness, yes. Love also. The great Western Christian excuse. Also an excuse for your personal morality. Your fantasy is the right, correct one. The decent one. Anyone else's is immoral. Oh, it is such a boring position.'

Matheson, tight-lipped, took a deep breath. 'That's an excuse for any behaviour you like. A *laissez-faire* attitude. Completely uncivilised.'

Beal grinned showing an irregular and none to clean row of upper teeth. 'Of course. The veneer of civilisation is un-natural and unhealthy.'

Martin, who had been listening in amused silence, now broke in. 'He's baiting you, Alistair. Charlie Beal loves baiting people. It is his great amusement in life. He'd good at it. Can stand any philosophical or moral argument on its head.'

'Doesn't mean I believe what I'm saying, Gilbert,' Beal replied. His eyes moved from Matheson to Margaret and finally settled on the cleavage of her low-cut gown.

The main course, a rack of lamb, was placed in front of the host who proceeded to carve it with relish. The conversation continued, Beal's interest in Margaret so ill-concealed as to be almost embarrassing. At least to Matheson. But not to Margaret who seemed to be enjoying the attention and revelling in Beal's more outrageous statements.

An hour later the dinner came to an end, to Matheson's relief. The food, he had to admit, had been excellent. The conversation, apart from Beal and Margaret's extended dis-cussion on morality, had become trivial. Gosforth and his wife were talking golf with Van der Boek. Martin occasion-ally broke in with his own rather ordinary golfing stories. Matheson felt out of it, isolated.

207

They moved back to the drawing room for coffee and liqueurs. As they left the dining room, Matheson found Martin at his side.

'I'm neglecting you,' said his host. 'And I know you want to talk. Let the others chatter, we'll talk.'

In the drawing room, Matheson refused coffee and accepted a Drambuie. Martin took his arm and drew him away from the other across the room to the curtained window.

'Now, Alistair, you have more questions?'

'Who are you?' Matheson repeated the question he had asked before dinner.

'Me? Oh, I try to be all things to all men.'

'Can't you give me a direct answer?'

'I can but I would rather you made the identification. And let me suggest, if you want direct answers, then ask more direct questions. Asking a man who he is, that's unanswerable. He is one personality to one man, another to another. And yet a third to himself. Of course, to himself he is wrong always. All he sees there is who he wants to be. Not who he is. So direct questions.'

'This house?'

'Ah, yes, we come to that. The house. What can I tell you?'

'I was here last night. The place was derelict. You couldn't have transformed it in a night to . . . to this.'

Martin's face became serious. 'You were here? You broke in?'

'The . . . the door was open.'

Martin's face relaxed. 'Of course you were here.'

'And of course you knew I was.'

'Of course.'

'But how did you transform the place in one night?'

'Did I? Of course now we are discussing the nature of reality, Alistair. Is there an absolute reality or does it simply exist in the mind?'

'Now you're playing games again.'

'Yes, of course. But you see it's all a game. But come, let me show you the nature of your reality and mine. Here? No, not at first. Come on to the landing.'

They crossed the room and went through the door on to the landing. Martin took him to the head of the stairs.

208

'Now there you are, Alistair. The hall and staircase as you see it tonight. In your mind's eye.'

'Not my mind's eye. I see it as it is.'

'Do you? Look again.'

The chandelier dazzled. Matheson blinked, screwing up his eyes. Shutting them. Then opening them again.

The chandelier was no longer there. A bare bulb hung from the ceiling. The hall was derelict again. The tattered tapestry stirred in a light breeze, casting dust into the air. The bare floorboards were inches deep in dust and debris. The hall was as it had been the previous night.

'So what is the nature of reality?' Martin said.

Was it Martin or was it the figure of the tramp he had encountered twice before?

Chapter Twenty-Five

Vision? Or reality?

Matheson closed his eyes and shook his head from side to side, as if to banish what he was seeing. When he opened his eyes again, he seemed to have succeeded. The chandelier shimmered in front of him. Below the hall was as it had been when he had arrived early. The painting of the school of Bosch was on the wall as before. From the top of the stairs its colours seemed to bring the scene strangely alive.

From his side, Martin spoke. 'So what did you see?'

Matheson, baffled, perhaps fearful, looked around. 'I . . . I saw nothing.' The lie was unconvincing.

'Really?' said his host. 'Come now, Alistair.'

'I tell you, I saw nothing. What was I supposed to see?'

'Then we shall have to illustrate the situation further.' Martin's voice was suddenly harsh, a schoolmaster with a recalcitrant pupil.

He took Matheson firmly by the arm and led him down the staircase. 'We need honesty from you. If only to illustrate my point.'

He wrested his arm from Martin's grip and stopped halfway down the staircase. 'All right. Honesty. On both sides.'

'Certainly.'

Matheson looked dubious. 'If you are who I think you purport to be, then honesty must come hard to you.'

Martin's only reply was a thin smile.

Matheson said, 'What about Randall? And please don't ask me again who he is. I find the question unconvincing.'

'Why are you concerned about Randall?'

'Because I believe I saw his dead body last night in the cellar of this house.'

'Shall we then pay a visit to the cellar?'

They went down to the foot of the stairs and Martin led the way to the cellar door.

'Of course, doubtless the body will have been removed,' Matheson said.

'If it were there in the first place.'

'Oh, it was there, Martin. I saw it. I touched it.'

Martin unlocked the cellar door.

'It wasn't locked last night,' Matheson said.

Martin smiled and stretched out his hand to open the door. He stood aside then and gestured for the civil servant to go first.

'After you,' Matheson said.

The other gave a slight shrug and stepped down into blackness. But, as he did so, he reached out, pressed down a switch and flooded the stairway with light.

'I presume you didn't notice the light switch last night?'

'If it were there last night.'

'Yes, of course. If it were there.'

At the foot of the cellar stairs Martin pressed another light switch and the cellar was illuminated.

Matheson found himself staring at a wine cellar, racks of bottles as they had been the previous night. But the earth floor was firm and swept clean, and the walls were white-washed. The area was uncluttered for some distance. Indeed, Matheson could not see the far wall. Beside the wine racks there was a trestle table and four matching wooden chairs.

'I sometimes have little wine tastings here. For a few friends,' Martin explained. 'Now where did you say you saw the body of Randall?'

'Some yards along here.'

Now Matheson led the way by the side of the trestle table and beyond. He could see nothing on the ground in front of him. But he was at once aware that the cellar was much larger than he had realised. Still he could not see the end wall.

'Something worrying you?' Martin said from behind him.

'The cellar seems much longer than it did last night. But then it was much darker.'

211

'And everything is so deceptive.'

Matheson stopped suddenly. He looked down at the earthen floor.

'Here!' he said. 'The body was here.'

'If it were there,' Martin echoed him with an expression which might be taken as a sneer. 'How can you tell?'

'I know it. I sense it.'

'It doesn't appear to be here now.'

'Of course you moved it.'

Martin smiled. 'Of course I would do that. Unless he moved himself.'

'He was dead. I know he was dead.'

'If you say so.'

Matheson suddenly felt anger rising within him. Great anger. Rage building up inside him. 'For God's sake, why is this happening to me?' Turning he brought his face close to Martin. 'You chose me, didn't you? You put yourself in my way that day on Oxford Street.'

Martin stopped smiling. He gazed evenly at his guest. 'You wish honesty? Then I did. And of course you knew it all the time.'

'Then stop playing games with me! Why did you choose me? I know. Because like Mallory and Everest, I was there. Not good enough.'

Martin took a step backwards. It was not a retreat. It was as if he could control events easier from a few feet away where he could calmly view the angry man.

'I chose you because you were so very right for the purpose. And ripe to be chosen. On the ladder of power, yet with all your weaknesses there, waiting to be used.'

'I don't understand.'

'Of course you understand. You were the upright Presbyterian Scot, the belief in your own rectitude instilled by your parents. The Elect, in their eyes. And ours. The fear of God firmly in place, again from your parents. But you must understand, the fear of God leaves you with no place to go to find love. Except that you should come to me. Tut-tut, am I paraphrasing someone else?'

'But to what purpose?'

'Isn't that my business. Collecting those . . . ready to be collected. Anything else will become apparent. But I must tell

212

you, when you recognised me as your likeness, you were already mine. In recognising me, you were recognising that part of me already in you. Oh, there's much of me in any man, but you . . . you were so . . . perfect. So vulnerable. So right to be added to my collection.'

'But I don't believe in you!'

The man who was Martin laughed. 'The Bishop of Storford doesn't believe in me. But you, when you talked to him, already believed in me.'

Matheson's anger had turned to fear now. 'So what happens next? You . . . you kill me?'

'Oh, no! That would be so pointless. People only die when they . . . put themselves in the way of death. No point in killing you. Even I abhor wastage. No, you are here to be used. To rise in power to the top of your profession. Under my patronage.'

'You really are . . .?' Matheson started the question.

'Your Miss Mower now, she could see it from the beginning. For herself. And for me. You never did follow her advice and read *The Justified Sinner*. A pity. She was giving you clues. But you couldn't see. I was leading the blind. No matter. I bring light to them.'

'But you are . . . you have a name?'

'I have a thousand names.' Martin was smiling again, showing even white teeth. 'And all fastened on me by people. What would you call me? Lord of Light? Always liked that one. And Ashmodeus has a ring to it . . . I like the sound.'

Names came into his head. So many. He forced himself to articulate. 'B . . . Beelzebub.'

'No. A small technical error. He was an aide, a helper. Also known as Beal.'

Martin looked back to the stairs and upwards. 'Yes, Charlie. A *nom de guerre*. He likes it.'

'And the others?'

'Merely as you are. Only they've moved further ahead. They have agreed to assist me. Except, of course, Margaret. Who is merely Gilbert Martin's dinner guest.'

Matheson swam through dark waters. He felt dazed, dizzy, something at the back of his mind telling him this was not happening, could not be happening. He stared at Martin,

213

hoping he would suddenly disappear; everything – the house, the cellar – would dissolve. It didn't. He was compelled to say something.

'But you did . . . kill Randall?' said with tremulous curiosity.

'He might have interfered. But come, let me show you more.' Again he took Matheson's arm. This time Matheson allowed himself to be led.

They proceeded further along the cellar passing more wine racks, whitewashed walls stretching onwards. Everything was spotless. Where was the domain of spiders? None was visible. As he walked, Matheson shook his head.

'Something bothering you, Alistair?'

'This . . . this is not real. It is not happening.'

'Your senses tell you it is.'

'My senses tell me you're a lunatic. With sick delusions.'

The Other laughed. 'Your people never believe. How should I appear to you? Black cloak? Horns? Oh, really. I have, you must remember, a distinguished lineage. The Lord of Light. Or would you rather think of me as a denizen of the dark? This place as the . . . what did you call it, in your mind? The domain of spiders. Should I then turn into a spider?'

'You . . . you crawl into my mind?' Matheson heard his own voice tremble.

'A small trick. You only have to have a small talent to do that. Even your psychiatrists can do it. Come now. I have plenty of time, but you haven't.'

The end of the cellar came unexpectedly. Around a wine rack there was an enormous burst of light. Matheson, dazzled, found his eyes trying to focus.

When they did he was facing the entire end wall. But this time it wasn't whitewashed but covered in what he at first took to be an enormous reproduction of the Bosch painting from the hall.

Only it was not a reproduction.

It was more like a window, looking out on to the canvas. Then again it wasn't a canvas.

The figures in the painting were alive and moving.

'You see,' said Martin. 'The painting in the hall was done from life. Or death.'

214

Alistair Matheson looked upon the scene. There was the milkman wrestling with his milk churn, trying to lift it. And there the shrouded figure moved behind him. There too was the farmer slaying the goat while at his back the other figure, only half covered by the shroud, was plunging its large blade into the farmer's stomach and the blood gushing out, flooding the ground at the man's feet. There were the torsos of men, there the shrouded figures, dead grey skin covering them. A man, clothes tattered, throat cut, was still screaming as one of the figures dragged him down into a crevice from which smoke and steam issued. The young girl who was being sodomised at once stopped screaming and turned her face towards Matheson, features contorted into a hideous grin. Everything was happening in front of his eyes.

Matheson remembered the line from Conrad's *Heart of Darkness*. 'The horror. The horror of it.'

'Of course it's expected of me,' his companion replied. 'Oh, the cruelty and the agony are yours. The sexual element is an innovation of your Christian church. When they decided sex was unclean, then I had to create the perverse to keep them happy. After all, the business of sex was, if you like, God given. I merely add the trimmings.'

Matheson wanted to look away but could not.

'It distresses you? But you are the people who do these things. You are really one of the shrouded ones. But you inflict the expectation of it on me. Of course I'm like the scorpion who offered to carry the ant across the stream. The ant said, "Oh, no, you will sting me to death." The scorpion assured him he would not do so, so that ant finally accepted the offer. But when they were halfway across the stream, sure enough the scorpion stung the ant. As he was dying the ant gasped, "Why?" The scorpion shrugged. "I can't help it. It's my nature." I have the same excuse. It's my nature. You people haven't even got that excuse.'

Finally Matheson was able to tear his eyes from the scene in front of him.

'So what do you want of me?'

There was a long pause.

Then Matheson answered his own question. 'Of course. What you always want. My . . . soul.'

The Other laughed.

'Dear me, no! Nothing so insubstantial. Have you ever seen a soul? Can you prove it exists? No, I want something else. And not your body, God forbid! It may be legal and as fashionable as heterosexuality but all those activities are so boring. When you're not doing it, you're thinking about it. Takes up so much time. No, no, I want . . . I want your mind.'

'My mind?'

'So few people realise that. And they're mostly politicians. Hitler did. So did Stalin. And most of your own politicians here. Without the concomitant sadism of the first two.'

Matheson's mind was swimming. 'If that's what you want, that . . . that illustration . . . and the painting . . . are those the people who rejected you? Is that a vision of hell?'

'It's what people expect. I endeavour to fulfill expectations. But then, hell is so many different things to different people.' Again Martin produced his sardonic smile. 'Whatever they want . . . or fear . . . that is what they will get. Unless of course they agree to give me their mind. To become an ally.'

'To do what?'

'In your terms, shall we call it . . . free enterprise? Join my organisation, so to speak. You will achieve wealth and power. What is the pinnacle of your profession? Head of the Home Civil Service? Cabinet Secretary? It can happen. And soon. Very soon.'

'You're insane!'

'No more than anyone else. Come now, I require an answer.'

There was silence. A long loud silence. Matheson stared at his host.

Finally Matheson spoke. 'It's ridiculous.'

'Life is ridiculous. You spend your three score and ten working, playing to keep alive, and in the end you lose. Why not assure yourself of something easier?'

Their eyes met. Matheson found himself staring into the Other's, into depths of darkness. And memories of his childhood came back to him. A drab, unhappy childhood filled with strictures and religious dogma. So it seemed. But there was something more than dogma. Words and phrases came back, all of them going to build the man he was, and perhaps was pleased to be. One memory in particular came to him.

216

'. . . the devil taketh him up into an exceeding and showeth him all the kingdoms of the world, and the glory of them.

And saith unto him, "All these things will I give thee if thou wilt fall down and worship me . . . "'

Martin broke in on the thought as if again reading his mind. 'Aren't you being presumptuous? That was supposed to be someone rather more important than Mr Alistair Matheson, senior civil servant. And this is not a high mountain but a cellar in Catford.'

'It . . . it was the example for us all to follow,' Matheson responded, suddenly sounding like his father all those years past.

'I take it you are refusing an offer to participate in my little enterprise.'

Matheson gulped in the air of the cellar which suddenly seemed filled with a swirling dust.

'It's all so ridiculous . . . so unbelievable . . . but, yes, of course I'm refusing.'

The cellar was dark now, the dust thick and choking. The only illumination came from the scene where the rear wall should have been. Now he could hear the sounds of the vision, the cries of the tormented, the screams of the sufferers, the agony of those who were beyond all hope.

Was the man called Gilbert Martin . . . Gil-Martin . . . still there? Matheson could no longer see him in the blackness that filled the main part of the cellar.

The blackness started to spin around him. He swayed and stumbled in the grip of a vertigo he had never before experienced. He tried to turn and stagger back towards the stairway and the entrance to the cellar. But he tripped and stumbled. And finally fell forward into the blackness and a negation of consciousness . . .

Chapter Twenty-Six

Then there was the dream.

He came out of blackness into a grey universe. Above him a slate-coloured sky. He stood on a vast plain that stretched as far as the eye could see. Beneath his feet there was no vegetation but only a dark sandy grit, an eternity's accumulation of dust, dirt and sand on which he could see the tiny bodies of dead beetles and other insects. Certainly none of them moved and they appeared moribund. Yet a short distance from where he stood there was movement on the surface, a slithering, sliding motion as of snakes or other living reptiles on, or just under, the surface of the sand.

He moved forward cautiously. There seemed no point in simply standing. He told himself he must move on towards some destination; if he simply stood still he would be nowhere and that, he reiterated to himself, was no place to be.

The question as he moved forward was how he had come here? Was this another illusion created by Martin? That would seem the most likely answer. Martin would, he presumed, eventually appear . . . he was never far away from his nightmare creations. Matheson turned a full three hundred and sixty degrees, eyes searching the desolate landscape. No sign of the man. No sign of anything except the line of the horizon and the grey surface, still moving slightly, a distance away from him.

Then he became aware of his clothes. He should still have been wearing his dinner jacket and so on. Hardly suitable for the terrain. But, looking down, he saw he was now clad in a long grey monk's habit, a kind of belted shroud with a cowl

218

around his head and shoulders. It seemed familiar garb, something he'd seen only recently. But where? It was at the edge of his memory but he could not quite reach it. He dismissed the thought. He would think about it later.

Something slithered away from under his feet. He looked down. He was wearing rope sandals, much of his foot bare, and something cold and sticky had slid across his flesh. A snake, he thought, but it wasn't a snake. He glimpsed the body of it, two feet in length, as it burrowed on and then into the sand as if trying to hide its own ugliness. Like nothing he knew, a reptile certainly, but slimy, ill-formed, with tentacles and protuberances around a body part-scaled, part jelly-like substance which palpitated as the creature moved. A moment later it had dug itself out of sight under the sand.

He moved on. Now he was aware of movement beneath him; more reptilian creatures, some similar to the one that had crossed his foot, others of different, even more outlandish shapes, elongations of shell and jelly, malformed carapaces, the very stuff of nightmares.

He stumbled, suddenly nauseous, and started to run. Another terror. Running, with no place to run to; no destination, aim, sense of direction. Running, he tripped over the hem of his own habit and fell among what felt like a struggling sticky mass of the creatures. He struggled to his feet, aware at once that he remembered where he had seen the garment he was wearing. The creatures in the painting, school of Bosch, the creatures that had crawled out of the earth to torment the peasants, the milkman, the tinker, the tailor, soldier, sailor, civil servant . . . all the people of the world.

And not just the painting. The actuality revealed in front of him in the cellar of the house in Catford. They were there too, the cowled torturers from hell with their grey-white dead skin. The emissaries and servants of . . .

No! Whatever he was, he was not one of those creatures!

He lifted the sleeve of the shroud and stared down at the flesh of his arm. The skin was a dead greyish colour. He was indeed one of the creatures of the shroud.

Again, nausea rose in his stomach and this time he stopped, leaned forward, and vomitted.

After a long moment of retching he raised his head, struggling to breathe, and stared ahead of him. The horizon was broken now by a tall edifice, a tower of damp reddish stone pointing to the sky some few hundred yards from him.

He moved forward, grateful for a man-made habitation. If indeed it was man-made.

But trying to move forward was like moving through a thick, glutinous liquid. It was a two steps forward, one step backwards progression. Breathing was difficult. His lungs strained painfully. It seemed to take hours to reach the arched doorway which appeared to be the only entrance to the tower. When he did reach it and felt under his hand the stone of the building, so cold as almost to burn his palm, he was able again to move freely and breath air, albeit with a strange, musty aroma, a graveyard smell of dust, decay and dead, rotting things.

He forced himself through the doorway and found himself in a vast chamber. The heat was oppressive. Huge open furnaces roared, scorching those who stoked them. By each furnace were the stokers, shrouded figures feeding the great fiery maws. From piles of something he could not make out they threw article after article into the flames.

As he entered, a figure, taller than the rest, but shrouded still, turned and beckoned to him.

'Of course we have been expecting you.' To Matheson the voice was not unlike that of the butler at Lower Cotton Street, an almost farcical thought. A sick joke of Martin's?

'No, no, this is a dream,' Matheson heard himself say. 'Martin's done this.' As he said it acrid smoke seemed to reach out and clog his throat and he started to cough.

He tried to suppress the cough and when he had succeeded, looked up as if expecting the scene in front of him to have dissolved. But it had not done so. He still faced the tall cowled figure.

'This . . . this has to be a dream. This kind of thing is . . . is only in legend. Doesn't happen . . . doesn't . . .'

Then there was a change. One change. The tower was the same, the furnaces still roared. Only the cowled figures had changed. Or rather their dress had. Matheson was now facing a figure in a black uniform, death's head badge on the black cap. The face of the tall figure was revealed. A heavy brutal face under short-cropped hair. And Matheson himself was

220

wearing the same uniform, crooked cross on the armband of the sleeve.

'It happens. You know it happens,' the tall man said, 'And you have come to join us.' The man, if he was a man, indicated the pile of fuel for the furnace.

Matheson stared at the 'fuel' and realised with what the furnaces were fed.

Corpses. Pieces of corpses. Arms, legs, heads, torsos. Male and female. And children. Fuel for the furnaces. One of the corpses looked up at him.

The tall man said, 'Your doing. Your responsibility. Your hand cutting his throat.'

Matheson recognised the body.

The dead eye of Gavin Randall stared up at him.

He screamed.

He could hear himself scream. A tormented, terrified scream.

The horror. The horror of it.

He came to consciousness. Forced himself to do so, anything to get away from the scene in the tower.

He was in his own bed, in his own room, in the flat in Chelsea.

He raised his head from the pillow, aware he was soaked in perspiration and looked around the room. His room, his bedroom, as always, early morning light at the edges of the heavy curtains. How had he come to be here? His last memory was of Martin in the cellar at the house in Lower Cotton Street. Then there had been something else. Something unpleasant. A trace of it lingered, a vast plain, a grey sky and things unpleasant underfoot. Of course that had to be a dream, the memory receding fast. In moments he would lose all recollection of it.

But how had he come to be at home? How had he come home from the house in Catford? He had no memory of travelling. Yet he did remember clearly all that had happened at Catford. The arrival, the brightly lit hall with its massive chandelier, the painting, school of Bosch. And his fellow guests, the Gosforths, the South African . . . what was his name? Van der something or other. And Beal, Charlie Beal, who had another name according to his host. Margaret was there too after he had told her he didn't want her to be.

221

He remembered the rest of it too. The visit with Martin to the cellar. Why had they gone to the cellar in the first place? Now he remembered that too, his own accusation about the dead body of Gavin Randall. There had been no body but there had been . . . what could he call it, the vision, the painting in the hall come to life. How the hell . . .? Yes, hell indeed; it had to be some kind of projection, a motion picture projected on to the whitewashed wall, that had to be the explanation. Yet it was curiously unsatisfactory.

And then there had been an offer from Martin, a kind of proposition, which he had rejected. A proposition from Ashmodeus? Ridiculous in this day and age. More than ridiculous, an unreal fantasy. The whole dinner party had been that.

Could he have dreamt the dinner party too?

Why not? He was here, lying in his own bed, with no memory of returning from Catford. Another part of the nightmare? Certainly he could remember that part in detail. The other, the later part, that he couldn't even remember now. And then there was the house in Catford, only the night before the dinner party a derelict ruin. Yes, it had to be a dream. The house could never have been cleaned and decorated in one day.

He had to have dreamt the whole thing.

The bedside telephone screamed, startling him. The new phone with its new ring so close to a shrill scream, demanding attention.

He lifted the receiver.

'Yes?'

'Darling, how are you feeling now?' Margaret assuming he would know her voice at once.

'I'm fine. Why shouldn't I be? Who is that?' Let her think he might not recognise her voice. He was still annoyed that she had gone to the dinner party. If there *had* been a dinner party. Wasn't her presence there another assurance that it had been a dream? She surely would not have gone against his wishes? Before she could reply, he changed his attitude.

'Oh, it's you, Margaret! Sorry. I was half asleep. I'm . . . all right. I think. Just tired.'

'I'm sorry I phoned so early.'

'No, it's all right. How are you?'

'I was worried about you. You weren't quite yourself on the way home.'

He shivered.

'On . . . on the way home?'

'From the dinner party. I think you drank a little too much. Haven't seen you do that before.'

'No, I didn't. I didn't drink very much. The dinner party . . .?'

'I'm sorry you were annoyed at my turning up, but I wanted to meet Gilbert Martin. Am I forgiven?'

Not a dream. Reality. He was cold now, so very cold. The hand holding the phone trembled.

She went on, 'Anyway, it's good to know we were wrong.'

'Why were we wrong?'

'About Martin. I told you on the way home, I thought he was charming. And he didn't really look very much like you. Of course, I'll never understand all that business about a derelict house. You must have gone to the wrong one . . .'

Slowly and deliberately he echoed her words. 'The wrong house?'

'Anyway, never mind all that. I hope you've thought more about Martin's offer?'

She'd been his ally, his confidante, his . . . she'd slept with him. Now she was talking as if Martin was a good friend, as if . . . he couldn't think straight now.

'What offer?' he said.

'He knows a lot of influential people. He wants to help you.'

He changed the subject. 'Did I drive home last night?'

'You can't have forgotten! I drove your car. You were a little too merry.'

I was merry, he thought. God, how could I have been merry?

'And, after a time, thoughtful. I parked your car for you, saw you into your flat, and took a taxi home.'

He was breathing heavily. 'Margaret, you remember, just after dinner, Martin took me out of the room?'

'Yes, he told me he was going to do that.'

'Told you?'

'To offer his help. You know the Cabinet Secretary is going to resign soon?'

'I didn't know that. If it were true, I would have known.'

'No,' she replied emphatically. 'Gilbert told me. It's been kept quiet.'

'Oh, I see. It's been kept quiet but Gilbert Martin knows. I find that difficult to believe.'

'But, Alistair, didn't he tell you? He's a personal friend of . . . people in high places.'

'Oh, I'm sure he is.' Said with a cutting edge of sarcasm.

'Alistair, you can be anything you want. If Martin wants it. That's what he's saying. You have to accept his help.'

'Maybe the price is too high. If I could believe it.'

Her voice changed. Became harder. Emotionless. Factual. 'You will find out. Any time now. And then you ring me back. Give me your answer.'

'Give *you* my answer?'

'I'll convey it to Gilbert. That is already understood.'

He tried to keep the astonishment from his voice. 'You and he must have become very close last night. Or have you been close for a much longer time?'

'You will phone me back,' she said.

He heard the click as she replaced the receiver.

He sat back, hand shaking. All the time she had been on the other side. If there was another side. Her conversion hadn't happened the previous night at the dinner party. The connection with Martin had been there before; had been there for a long time. But of what nature was that connection? If Martin was . . . who he said he was. Even now Matheson had difficulty using a name. The thought was insane. The thought with him from early on. But this wasn't the dark ages. It couldn't be real. All he had been through, all he had seen with his own eyes. Illusion? Illusion born of a strictly religious upbringing? He'd always been told nothing could happen to him if he followed that upbringing. Not merely been told, it had been bred into the very bone. The God-fearing Presbyterianism of his parents, that was it. The way to salvation. The other way, that was legend. A myth, an image that didn't really exist. The metaphor for Evil. Satan incarnate. Lucifer, the fallen angel. Nobody could believe in the metaphor. Evil was an abstraction.

But now he knew otherwise.

The telephone rang again.

'Alistair Matheson here.'

'Mr Matheson, Cabinet Office here. Stanley Faber.'

Faber was an assistant to the Prime Minister, a spokesman, an informed source as the papers often called him, a rumour always about to become a fact, a one-man think tank.

'Mr Faber?'

'The Prime Minister would like to see you. Midday today at Number Ten.'

'Yes, of course. May I know the subject of his request?'

'Not officially. However, I can tell you that the Cabinet Secretary is retiring.'

'Sir John has only held the job for a year.'

The reply came quietly. 'Ill health. He has cancer. An announcement will be made this morning.'

'But why should the P.M. want to see me?'

Faber laughed. His laugh was known in Whitehall. A sound without humour, a punctuation mark to an announcement. 'I've no doubt the P.M. will tell you himself. But of course you have been very busy making a reputation for yourself. The P.M. prefers merit to old notions of seniority. And you have powerful friends. See you at noon.'

The call was over. Slowly Matheson rose. He washed, shaved and dressed mechanically. All the time thinking of what Margaret Mower had said. 'He is a personal friend of people in high places.'

And it seems he knew about events before they happened. Or else Stanley Faber was in communication with the . . . man?

The phone rang yet a third time.

'Matheson here.'

'Well, Alistair, do you believe him now?' Margaret again. The same emotionless tone.

'What am I supposed to believe?'

'In Gil-Martin.'

'Oh, I believe in him. I . . . I don't know that I believe in the rest.'

'But you can accept his . . . friendship? You can see the results.'

Matheson took a long, deep breath. 'I can see I have an opportunity of progressing through my own merit. I don't want to see Martin again. I don't want to know him. Whoever and whatever he is, I want nothing more to do with him.'

Silence at the other end of the line.

'Do you hear me?' he said. 'Nothing more. And I want to know what happened to Gavin Randall.'

'I'm sorry to hear that.' Another voice now. His voice. The voice of a man who looked like him. 'I had great hopes of you, Matheson. All, alas, sadly dashed. By you.'

'Are they? Are you sure? I've to meet the P.M. at midday. The offer will be made then.'

Martin's voice again. Cold now, humourless, emotionless. 'Oh, yes, the appointment's made. But will you keep it? Goodbye, Alistair Matheson. One way or another, you come to me. You had no choice the minute you saw we appeared to resemble each other.'

The call ended with a click as the receiver went down again.

Later, before breakfast, a silent obsequious Dobson served him coffee. Matheson still felt cold. He couldn't shake off the icicle feeling that had been with him since the last call.

'The coffee's cold, Dobson.'

'I'm sorry, sir. I'll make fresh right away.'

'The damn' room's like ice too.'

'The central heating's been on since six. I do find it quite warm myself, sir.'

The doorbell rang. Dobson went out to answer it. He returned a moment later.

'Two gentlemen to see you, sir.'

'Before breakfast!'

'Police officers, sir.'

'What the devil do they want? I'm in a hurry to get to the Ministry . . .'

But the two visitors had already entered.

'Mr Matheson,' said Chief Inspector Claypole. 'We have to request you accompany us to New Scotland Yard.'

'That's impossible. I . . . I haven't had my breakfast yet. And I have a great deal of work at the Ministry and an important appointment at midday.'

'I'm afraid we must insist, sir.'

'What on earth for?'

Inspector Burns replied this time. 'We believe you may be able to assist us in an investigation into the murder of Gavin Randall.'

Chapter Twenty-Seven

Matheson in custody.

Rooms with dull green walls. People coming and going carrying papers. And questions. Outside the rumble of traffic in Victoria Street.

'Mr Matheson, what did you discuss with Mr Randall the last time you saw him?'

'I don't remember.' A half truth. What had they talked about? Martin, certainly. But in what context, he couldn't remember. It occurred to him there was so much he couldn't remember where Martin was concerned. It seemed now every encounter with the man had a dreamlike quality and much of what was said vanished from memory as if in a dream.

He asked his own question then. 'Why am I here?'

'You are assisting us in our enquiries.'

'Into what?'

'The death of Mr Randall.'

Then an interlude. Tea was brought in a thick mug, official issue.

'I am expected at the Ministry of Defence.'

'They have been informed.'

'Of what?'

'The circumstances.'

More comings and goings. Claypole talking. Then Burns. Then he was left alone for a time. Then through corridors to other rooms which were identical. More people passing through these rooms. An authoritative-looking official came in, stared at him and left without speaking.

Time passing. Now it was well into the morning.

'I have had no breakfast,' Matheson informed a uniformed policeman. This important remark was passed on to a higher authority. A plainclothes man came in and said, 'Would you like some sandwiches from the canteen?'

'I don't eat sandwiches,' Matheson said with a kind of pompous defiance.

The plainclothes man left. After a time, another came. 'Would you like bacon and eggs?'

'And kidneys. And tea and toast.'

The man looked puzzled. 'I'll see what can be done. We have to pay for breakfasts like that.'

'Then pay for it. I didn't ask to be brought here.'

Later the breakfast was brought to him. After he had eaten, he asked to go to the lavatory. No one paid attention. He became uncomfortable.

More time passed.

Claypole returned accompanied by another man, a grey-faced, grey-suited man.

Claypole said, 'Would you care to answer some further questions?'

'After I've been to the lavatory. Or is it policy to hold people in physical discomfort?'

He was taken to the lavatory by a constable who watched him all the time. Could they be afraid he would attempt to drown himself in the urinal? When he had finished he was taken back to the interview room.

'You will now answer some questions.'

'I thought that's what I'd been doing.'

'Quite so. Have you any knowledge of a house in Lower Cotton Street, Catford.'

'Number five?'

'Number five.'

'Yes, I have been there. I was there for dinner last night.

Claypole looked with raised eyebrows at the grey man who shrugged.

'Dinner last night?' Claypole echoed.

'I said so.'

'Uh-huh. We'll come back to that.'

'Why should we do that?'

Claypole ignored the question. 'We want to know about Gavin Randall.'

'So you said. And I have told you all I know.'

'You know he's dead.'

Matheson hesitated. If he told them he knew Randall was dead, they'd want to know when and how. Instead, after a moment, he said, 'You told me so this morning. You told me he had been murdered.'

Claypole flushed. 'Yes, that is so.'

Again he looked across at the grey man. The man gave an imperceptible nod. Claypole opened his mouth to speak but Matheson interrupted.

'I know who you are, Mr Claypole, but I don't know this gentleman.'

Claypole coughed, his face reddening. The grey man shrugged and stepped forward. 'My name is Ames. Frederick Ames. I am Cabinet liaison on security matters.'

'So my Minister and the Cabinet know I am here?'

'That is so.'

Matheson sat down on an upright chair in front of a small table. He did this slowly, with every appearance of being relaxed.

'I think you must know I am a senior civil servant,' he said, taking his time. 'And probably outrank you, Mr Ames.'

Ames' complexion now rivalled Claypole's in colour. 'I appreciate that, sir. But this *is* a police matter.'

'Mr Ames, Claypole here is in Special Branch. It is therefore much more than an ordinary police matter.'

'That is so.'

'Therefore would it not be more sensible to take me, as a senior civil servant, into your confidence in this matter and we could therefore openly discuss it? That way I might return to my own work the quicker.'

'I . . . I will talk with Mr Claypole.'

Again they withdrew from the room, leaving Matheson with only a uniformed officer in attendance. He sat drumming his fingers on the table top. He should, he told himself, be thinking about the death of Randall and his own knowledge of the matter.

He sat for twenty minutes and then Claypole came back into the room followed by Burns and a uniformed sergeant carrying a heavy book like a ledger. They placed the book on the table and opened it. Meanwhile Claypole cleared his throat. But it was Burns who spoke first.

'Will you please stand up.'

Matheson stood, surprised.

Then it was Claypole's turn to speak. 'Alistair Matheson?'

'You know who I am?'

'I have to inform you that you are being charged with the murder of Gavin Roscommer Randall. You do not have to say anything but if you do I also have to warn you that any statement you make will be taken down and may be used in evidence. You may of course see a solicitor.'

Matheson was too shocked to reply at once. He stood, mouth open, astonished at the charge.

'Do you wish to make a statement?' The second half of the double act, Burns, asked him.

Matheson, breathing heavily, managed to say, 'I am innocent.' And then, suddenly embarrassed at the simplicity of his statement, he added 'This is ridiculous.'

The six words were duly written down in the large book by the large sergeant. Otherwise his protestation was ignored.

'I asked if you wished to make a statement?' Burns repeated himself.

Matheson made up his mind. 'I . . . I would like to make a statement.' The old maxim came to him: When in doubt, tell the truth.

Claypole seemed to relax. 'I'm very glad, Matheson.' He dismissed the sergeant and his ledger. 'Now if you'll just sit down, Inspector Burns will take down your confession and I will listen.'

Matheson frowned. The word was wrong. *Confession*.

'I said I would like to make a statement. Not a confession. I have nothing to confess to. In the matter of Gavin Randall.' Had he anything to confess to? he asked himself. The venial sins of a lifetime? Mortal sins? But he was not a Catholic, far from it. He didn't believe in confession of that kind. He said, 'I still maintain I am innocent.'

Claypole looked disappointed. Burns said, 'Be easier if you made a confession.'

'Burns once thought of becoming a priest,' Claypole said. 'He likes to hear confessions.'

231

'Do you wish me to make a statement or not?' Matheson said impatiently marvelling at the incompetence of junior civil servants. Which was, after all, what he considered the police to be.

'We'll take your statement, Matheson,' Burns sighed. He noted that since he had been officially charged he had become simply Matheson. The 'mister' had been discarded.

He proceeded to tell the story from the beginning, from the day of the sighting in Oxford Street. He told them of the dinner party at Charlie Grove's, the first meeting with Margaret Mower, his account of his meeting in Oxford Street. He went on, omitting nothing. This was not he told himself, the time to hold back. Once the charge was withdrawn, as he was sure it would be, he could get back to his work. There must still be time to inform the Prime Minister why he could not keep his appointment at Downing Street? He'd almost forgotten about something which might be the most important single career factor in his life.

He interrupted his story . . . he had reached the trip to Dartmoor . . . to ask if he could telephone Stanley Faber at Downing Street.

'No need,' said Claypole. 'The P.M.'s secretariat appreciate the situation. As Mr Ames told you.'

'Yes, but this was a vitally important appointment. When you release me . . .'

Burns said, 'Then no doubt it will be rescheduled. *If* we release you. Please continue with your statement.'

Shifting uncomfortably in his seat, Matheson continued to relate his story to two seemingly impassive faces. The expression on the faces only changed when he described discovering Randall's body in the derelict house. They looked surprised.

'You didn't tell us this when we called on you the other day.' Claypole said. 'Why not?'

He was aware his reply sounded inadequate. 'I wasn't sure whether I'd seen . . . what I had seen.'

'Why didn't you inform the police the moment you found the body?' Burns asked.

'I . . . don't . . . know. I think I wanted to find out more about Martin. And the rest is true. I wasn't sure the next day whether or not I had dreamt all that had happened.'

232

'Go on.'

The faces were again expressionless until he described the overnight transformation of number five Lower Cotton Street. Claypole and Burns looked at each other in what was obviously disbelief. But this time they did not interrupt him. He went on to describe the dinner party.

'You say Miss Mower was there?' Claypole finally cut in.

'I told her I didn't want her to go. But she went anyway.'

'Go on.'

He described the house and the other guests.

Burns said, 'A man called Charles Beal was there?'

'Yes, I said so. What about him?'

'Never mind. Go on.'

He was aware that, when he described leaving the rest of the guests and accompanying Martin through the hall and down into the cellar, he was in difficulties.

'I'm telling you what I saw. The best way I can. I know it sounds unbelievable. But then, it seemed so to me at the time.'

He told them all that he had seen in the cellar. When he had finished there was a long silence. Then Claypole spoke.

'And after you fainted in the cellar, you woke up in your own bed this morning?'

'Yes. I . . . I thought it was part of a dream I'd had. But then Margaret Mower phoned and . . . and she had been at the dinner party.'

'Of course she wouldn't see what you saw in the cellar?'

'How could she? She wasn't in the cellar.'

Claypole nodded, face bland. 'I see. Of course. How could she?'

Burns said, 'That is your statement?' He'd finished writing and was staring at Matheson.

'Yes. That's how it all happened.'

'And of course you didn't kill Randall?'

'I told you I didn't kill him.'

'Then who do you think did?' Claypole asked.

'Martin. Who else? And . . . and he must have killed Makepeace on Dartmoor, of course.'

'Of course,' said Burns. 'You have nothing to add?'

'I've told you everything.'

233

Burns rose, Claypole following.

'Mr Burns will have this typed and you will sign it?'

'Yes, of course.'

'You will want to see you brief . . . your solicitor?'

'Is there any need? I've told you everything. Perhaps I was foolish not to have done so before, but it's done now.'

'I think it would be better for you if you saw a solicitor.'

'The only solicitor I know is Mr Travis of Travis, Lee and Pemberton. They did the conveyancing on my flat.'

'I'll contact Mr Travis.'

They went to the door. They were talking in undertones. Matheson could only make out fragments of sentences.

'. . . what to make of it . . .'

'. . . setting himself up for an insanity plea . . .'

'. . . may be that he *is* insane . . .'

'. . . God's sake, he's a top civil servant!'

'. . . proves the point . . . all mad anyway, our masters.'

'. . . leave it to the brief.'

They went out. He was left alone.

For a long time.

More cups of tea were brought. The door opened several times and people looked in.

Matheson waited. At first impatiently. Then, as time went by, he became more relaxed. He had told them everything. It was a weight from his shoulders.

They took him to another room, a cell-like room. Cell-like because it was a cell. He dozed off, at ease for the first time in weeks. Nothing to worry about. Margaret would back his story, they would search for Martin. As Randall had been searching.

They would find Martin, he felt sure.

Chapter Twenty-Eight

More interview rooms. Or was it the same room? The rooms all looked alike.

Mr Travis came to see him. It must have been the next day. Matheson was aware he had slept fitfully but without dreaming. Travis seemed upset and out of place. Which he confessed.

'I'm very upset, Mr Matheson.'

'We have that in common, Mr Travis.'

'Not our usual kind of business, Mr Matheson. We're not a criminal practice.'

'I'm not a criminal, Mr Travis.'

'No. No, of course not. But I shall arrange for someone to see you who is more accustomed to this . . . this kind of case. A Mr Amboy. He will instruct a Q.C. But in the meanwhile, if I were you, I should say nothing more to the police.'

'Why not? I have nothing to hide.'

'Still, I should say nothing. I will instruct Mr Amboy to visit you as soon as possible.'

Travis left. Matheson decided to ignore his advice about not speaking to the police. He was innocent. They would help him.

Claypole came to see him again. In another room. Or was it the same room? Later that day. The man called Ames was with him. And Inspector Burns in the background.

Claypole did the talking. The other two were obviously there to listen.

'Regarding Miss Mower . . .'

'Yes?'

'She confirms she went to Dartmoor with you.'

'She could hardly do otherwise.'

'And was with you when you found Makepeace.'

'Of course.'

'She says that she thought you were unwell. Had . . . strange ideas about a man called Martin.'

'She met him.'

'She did! In a restaurant with me. And then, of course, in the house in Catford.'

'She insists she never met Martin. And was never at a dinner party at Catford.'

For Matheson the room went round. The figures came and went. Vertigo. Dizziness. And nausea. What was Margaret saying? She'd never met Martin, never been at Catford? Some kind of mistake. It had to be. Perhaps she thought she was protecting him?

'We visited the house in Catford,' Claypole went on.

'Well, then . . .' Trying to collect his thought.

'It was derelict.'

'Until the other night. I told you . . .'

'It was no place to hold a dinner party. Almost a ruin.'

'That's . . . that's Martin! I don't know how he did it. Or I suppose I do. Although I find it hard to believe myself. I mean to believe in . . . in him. And who he says he is.'

'Who does he say he is?'

'I told you. In the statement.'

'You did. Speaking metaphorically, I presumed. You say he owned the house in Catford?'

'Yes.' The room was settling again. He forced himself to take deep breaths.

'Would it surprise you if I told you the house in Catford is owned by a Mr Charles Beal?'

'Charlie Beal! He was at the dinner . . .'

'You described him as a small fat man?'

'Yes. That's him.'

'Mr Charles Beal lives near Naples. The Villa Avernus. He is ninety-three years old and unable to travel. He's a sick man. Oh, yes, he owns the house in Catford and has been for years intending to have it redecorated. But illness prevented this. And when he dies, which will probably be soon, the house will doubtless pass to his heirs. What do you say to that?'

236

'Can't be true. He wasn't more than late-fifties, small, fat and definitely in London.'

'We have, with the help of the Italian police, verified all I have said.'

'Of course he was with Martin! One of his people. I told you that. In my statement. Yes, I did. He was one of them . . .'

Claypole shrugged and looked over at Ames who shrugged back. They shrugged a lot, these people, Matheson told himself.

Claypole said, 'We can find no trace of your Mr Gilbert Martin.'

'Randall knew of him.'

'There's nothing in Randall's files.'

'He told me he was investigating Martin. He told me about Makepeace and Monty Wallingham.'

'And they're both dead. Convenient for you. Certainly Randall was involved years ago in an investigation with Wallingham and Makepeace. No mention of anyone called Martin. The whole affair is long since over and done with. Except for one thing.'

'What . . . what's that?'

'The Exeter police want to talk to you again.'

Matheson shook his head. It was all too much. He was feeling very, very tired. 'I already made a statement to them.'

'In view of all that's happened here, they want another statement.'

'What's happened here?' He felt puzzled again.

Claypole coughed. 'Something else, Matheson. You were seen at the house in Catford before the night of your supposed dinner party.'

'I told you. I went there twice. When I saw the place it was completely derelict.'

The Chief Inspector consulted his notebook.

'You were seen there more than twice. And on a previous occasion . . . the night Randall disappeared . . . you were seen unloading a heavy trunk at the house. We have two neighbours as witnesses and a passer-by who helped you lift this trunk into the house.'

'No, not me.'

'We found the trunk in the house. Inside was Randall's body. With his throat cut.'

Matheson was silent for a moment, embraced again by nausea and icy sweat. Again he concentrated on breathing heavily. It dispelled the nausea that kept rising within him.

Finally, he said, 'I'm glad you've found Randall.'

'Then you admit you took his body to Catford?'

'No. That wasn't me – Martin. It would be Martin. I told you, he looks very like me. At . . . at times exactly like me. It's why I was fascinated by him in the first place.'

This time it was Claypole who took his time to speak. 'Wouldn't it be easier if you admitted you killed Randall? You'd feel easier. We'd understand if it was an accident.'

'How do you cut somebody's throat accidentally? Don't be stupid, Mr Claypole.'

'But you did cut his throat?'

'I did not! I told you in my statement, I didn't. I simply found the body. Not in a trunk. On the cellar floor.'

'With his throat cut?'

'I said so.'

'And despite the witnesses, you say you did not take Randall's body to the house?'

'I told you, that would be Martin. There are times, you can hardly tell him from me. He . . . he's like a . . . a fetch.'

'A what?'

'A Fetch. The double of a living person. The wraith of that person.'

'You believe this?'

Matheson pursued his lips. 'Would I say it if I didn't believe it?'

'You might. You're saying many strange things. You know we have found traces of blood in the bathroom of your Chelsea flat? Same blood group as Randall's.'

Matheson blinked and was conscious he was blinking. This was something new. So much he was hearing was new. Like being identified as bringing Randall's body to Catford. Like Margaret Mower denying she was ever at the dinner party at Catford. Like Beal being ninety-three and never having left Italy. Oh, that could be got over. It might be a different Charlie Beal . . . even a relative. But then what was it Martin said about Beal? He couldn't quite remember . . . but there were many things he couldn't quite remember now. Like

238

dreams. It was as if the whole thing was slowly melding into one great mass of memory and it was difficult to be selective.

He was taken back to his cell. Later he was taken to another room, this time definitely a different room . . . he thought . . . and then wasn't sure. Here he met a small, dark man call Amboy, who was, so Amboy informed him, to be his solicitor. Matheson told his story again. Amboy listened and said nothing. After a time he left, only to return later with a tall, distinguished-looking man in dark jacket and striped trousers. Amboy introduced the man as Sir Aidan Mansell, Q.C., who was to be Matheson's barrister. Again Matheson told his story. He expected the barrister to ask him questions. Yes, he was prepared for searching questions. None came. Mansell listened and then left.

Then, it seemed, days passed.

He was shown in and out of other rooms. Green-walled rooms and grey-walled rooms. He was taken in a van to another place. Here all the rooms had grey walls. Here too Claypole came to visit again.

'You mention Sir Herbert Gosforth and his wife as being at this dinner party?'

'Yes, they were.'

They tell me they've never been in any house in Catford at any dinner party. They did meet you at a dinner party at Charles Groves' home.'

'Yes, but that was a few weeks ago.'

'They haven't seen you since.'

'They're lying.'

'And Miss Mower is lying too?'

'I don't . . . don't know why but, yes, she's lying if you say so.'

'And a man called Van der Boek? We've located him. He's a South African businessman.'

'Yes.'

'He's been in Cape Town for the past six months. He doesn't know anybody called Gilbert Martin. Neither do the Gosforths.'

'But they were all there,' Matheson insisted loudly, and then became quiet. What was the use? They were denying everything. Even Margaret was denying everything. He

239

looked down at his hands. They were dripping with sweat. He was opening and closing them over and over again.

Claypole left.

A man called Harris came to see him in another grey room.

'Max Harris. Will you talk with me, Mr Matheson?'

'I don't know you.'

'Nevertheless.'

'I'll talk to you. Nice to see a new face.'

'Good. Also I have some tests I'd like you to take.'

'Tests? What kind of tests?'

'Oh, they're quite simple. First I want you to tell me your story.'

Matheson did so, for it seemed the umpteenth time. Max Harris listened but made no comment. Later he opened a briefcase and took out some sheaves of paper.

'I want to show you some shapes and you must tell me what they remind you of.'

'The Rorshach test. Inkblots. Stupid. You're a psychiatrist?'

'Yes.'

'I've told you the truth. All that has happened. You think I'm crazy?'

'The term is meaningless. I just want to study your state of mind.'

'My state of mind? That term also is meaningless.'

Harris sighed. 'Please co-operate, Mr Matheson.'

'I'm co-operating. I told you everything that happened. Why did you not start off by telling me you're a psychiatrist?'

Harris tried to look him straight in the eye but couldn't sustain the direct approach. Man's got a conscience, Matheson told himself.

'All right, I'm a psychiatrist. The police asked me to talk to you.'

'I've told them the truth.'

'They find your truth . . . difficult. Wouldn't you, Mr Matheson, if you had heard your story?'

Matheson took his time replying. Had he not undergone what he had, he would very probably have agreed with the police. Perhaps if he had gone through it all on his own, again he might have agreed with the police. But Margaret Mower

had been involved, Gavin Randall had known about Martin
. . . all right, so Gavin was dead, but he, Matheson, had no
motive for killing him. And above all he knew what he had
experienced, it had left his mark on him. Yet this man Harris
was talking sense. It *was* an incredible story.

'Yes,' he finally agreed with Harris.

'Unbelievable,' the psychiatrist added.

'But it happened. To me. God, why me? It happened. And
nobody believes me. Isn't that true? Nobody believes it
happened.'

Harris assumed his sympathetic look. It usually worked. 'I
believe you believe it.'

Matheson thought, That's something.

'I want to help,' Harris went on. 'Your believing it is
important. Now they will all want to help. You see, Alistair
. . . I may call you Alistair? . . . until now they have wanted
to put you on trial for murder.'

'I haven't murdered anybody.'

'They'll be relieved. While they wanted to try you for
murder, on the other hand they didn't want all the fuss and
publicity. You're an important civil servant.'

'That's what I told Claypole. I am a senior civil servant. I
. . . I believe I'm in line for Permanent Secretary to the
Cabinet.'

'But you've been ill, Alistair. You appreciate that? You
understand?'

Matheson sounded grudging now. 'I suppose it has taken a
lot out of me. I've been worried, that's true. Concerned.
Very. Perhaps I should have gone to the P.M. Perhaps I
should still go . . .'

'Not necessary. The P.M. has been kept informed. But you
must agree you need treatment? A rest, perhaps?'

'Yes, I need a rest.'

'I think it can be arranged. You see, they . . . Claypole,
Ames, and the others . . . they don't feel a trial of senior civil
servant would be in the public interest.'

Matheson agreed vigorously. 'Of course not. And what
could they charge me with? It would be a deal of publicity and
all over an innocent man.'

'It can be put like that to your Q.C. I think he would only
agree.'

241

Matheson was beginning to like Harris. He was a reasonable man. He obviously understood what Matheson had been through.

Later, sometime after Harris had gone, Claypole visited him. The Chief Inspector did not seem happy.

'You think you're going to get away with it.'

'What?' asked Matheson who was now half asleep.

'The murder of Gavin Randall. I knew him, you know. We worked with him on occasion. Special Branch and M.I.5. Now I know you killed him . . .'

'No!'

'That was the non-existent Martin, I suppose? Anyway, they don't want it all in the public domain.'

'Who?'

'The powers that be. So you evade a trial. And you're taken care of. Well, I'm demanding one thing from them. You're to be taken care of for the rest of your natural!'

'I don't understand.'

'You will, you fucking lunatic!'

Matheson winced. He didn't like that kind of language. Not to be tolerated in the ranks of the Service. He would have told Claypole only the Special Branch man had simply walked away from him, out of the door which was at once locked from the outside.

All doors seemed to be locked from the outside now, Matheson thought.

Some days later he was taken to another room in another place. This room was different. Oak-panelled walls. High-backed chairs. A man behind a desk, an old man in striped trousers and dark jacket. Formal informality. The old man might have been a judge. Indeed it transpired that he was a judge. Aidan Mansell was there too beside Matheson. And Claypole, looking annoyed, and the little man, Ames. Max Harris was also there. And others.

After much talk, most of which Matheson couldn't make out, and much nodding, Harris spent a long time talking to the judge. There was much talk about schizophrenic personalities, paranoia, psychosis, and other words of which of course Matheson knew the meaning but could not hear the context. Finally some kind of agreement was reached, there was much shaking of hands and Matheson was led into a small side room. Aiden Mansell joined him.

'It's for the best, Mr Matheson.'

'Yes? What is?'

'You'll be looked after. There will be treatment, Max Harris has assured us of that. If it is successful, who knows . . . might not be for too long.'

Matheson nodded. 'Might not be too long,' he echoed. But he was puzzled. He would be puzzled for a long time.

He was in another place now.

Grey walls, grey building. In the countryside. Pleasant corridors but bars on the windows. A bright room of his own, no longer a cell but a room. Still with bars on the windows though. Others there too, in a large room with deep leather armchairs, old but comfortable. A large television set in a corner, dominating, a window on the world.

Of the people, most were quite friendly, although a few said nothing and stared straight ahead.

One man, in a sports jacket and flannels with a scarf around his neck, said, 'Not to worry. Quite good here. Only a few of them think they're Napoleon or a teapot or whatever. All a bit *Alice in Wonderland*. I'm Pritchard. You might have heard of me? The Canongate business. These girls had no right to bother me. They didn't afterwards. What's your name?'

'Matheson.'

'Oh, yes. I expected you.'

'How did you . . .?'

'Martin told me you were coming.'

Pritchard walked away, leaving Matheson sick and shivering.

After he had been there two months he had a visitor. It was Margaret.

'How are you Alistair?'

'I'm quite comfortable but I'd rather be at work in the Ministry.'

'It was your own choice.'

'Was it?'

'You turned down His offer.'

243

'You told lies.'

She gave a small secretive smile. 'Of course. It was expected of me.'

She went on to tell him she was awaiting publication of her latest novel and would send him a copy. She also brought him fruit. And then rose to leave.

'I won't be coming again.' she said.

'Oh, no?'

'I may go to America. Be well soon, Alistair. Although He can't help you now. You are no longer of any use to Him. Pity.' She took a deep breath. 'Goodbye.'

The days wore on, each much the same. They were still grey days despite the more colourful surroundings. And bars predominated. Pritchard was affable as were others but Matheson felt, despite the affability, despite some amiable discourse, they were each and every one an isolated island unto themselves.

Then, in the dark of night, he had an unexpected visitor. One of the attendants, a gruff character in a white coat, Rampion by name, came into his room and wakened him from another dreamless sleep.

'How are you, Alistair?'

At first it looked like Rampion but then the light, or lack of it, played tricks and it was no longer Rampion but Matheson found himself looking up again at his own mirror image.

'Martin?' he said uncertainly.

'It is. You look well. I'm sorry you hate this place.'

'I didn't say that.'

'But I know you do. You made the wrong choice. Should have let me help you.'

'I'd be in hell.'

'Where are you now?'

'Where am I now?'

'In a criminal lunatic asylum. There's hell for you. And it goes on for a long time. Probably forever. Even when they die, they stay here.'

Matheson shook his head violently. 'No, there's something else.' He remembered a phrase his father had used. 'There's God's infinite mercy.'

244

'Perhaps. If He can be bothered. If you come to His notice. But there are so many and He has so little time. Infinity is really quite small from my perspective. And God's. And He's always so angry.'

'But what have I done?'

'Does it matter? Nothing. Everything. There's always some reason we can find, He and I. I must go now. So busy these days. Gets better all the time. Or worse, depending on your viewpoint. Anyway, keep the faith, as they say.'

He was Rampion again as he left the room. But a fraction of a second before Martin became Rampion, Matheson saw something. A glimpse a fleeting glance of something that wasn't a man, wasn't human, but a shape that towered above him, a shape that belonged in lino-cuts of old manuscripts, perhaps in ancient illuminated books; so he convinced himself later. The shape was taller than a man, as tall as the room, as grotesque as a nightmare. It was a demon-shape, a horned devil, a giant bestial creature. A shape conventional in the hell of a man's imagination. Then again he was Rampion and out of the room.

The brief image was something Matheson had to try and forget, had to cast from memory. Must not, he told himself, allow nursery terrors to haunt a normal adult.

Except for Max Harris, who was hardly a visitor, and gave a few people like Matheson some kind of treatment, mostly conversation, no one else came to the place to visit. Except once when Sir Aidan Mansell came. Decent of him, he had no need to do so. Matheson told him he felt he was aware he was becoming part of the place, part of the recreation rooms, part of his own room, part of corridors and bars and brick and mortar and despair. And the waiting. It was the truth.

Always the waiting. For what?

There was the thought. That he might be waiting for nothing.

245

Epilogue

You travel the world, you hear strange stories, David Sutherland told himself, as he strolled back to the Hyde Park Hotel that night. Clement had offered him a lift in an ancient, rather grand Bentley but it was a pleasant balmy night and he felt like walking.

He'd been staying at the Hyde Park since his return from America, waiting for the flat he had purchased in the Barbican to be redecorated.

As he walked, he remembered Matheson. A very efficient civil servant with the kind of dedication you often found in the austere, puritanical Scot. The puritanical element must have got the better of the man and the result . . . crack up!

Of course Sutherland took the story with a large pinch of salt. St John Clement was an embroiderer of gossip, an old woman on a dull day with nothing better to do. Still it was an odd tale and there must be some basis of truth in it, no matter how much embroidery Clement had adorned it with.

Sutherland made a mental note to ask about Matheson. He had a number of acquaintances in the higher ranks of the Civil Service who would tell him the true story. And of course politicians like the Minister of Defence would know.

He could perhaps even visit Matheson? Not that he liked the idea of visiting that kind of institution. But he was a compassionate man and could tell himself, There but for the grace of God and all that . . .

Arriving at the hotel, he at once went to bed. He dreamt about Matheson, the tall barely remembered figure facing him as if trying to say something, convey the story of his

246

plight. But in the morning, beyond that image, he could recall nothing more of the dream.

Sutherland's next weeks were spent between Number 10 and Number 11 Downing Street, closeted with either the P.M. or the Chancellor of the Exchequer or both. It seemed to him that the country was in its usual chaotic economic state, disaster being always imminent. Of course the country would survive; not through any advice of his but because despite hardship and depression, the pendulum would swing back. It was at these times that he wondered why he had ever bothered to study economics. It was like studying the oceans of the world: one could learn about the great tides and streams, the depths and the shallows, but could do nothing to alter them.

Then Parliament went into recess and the Ministers with whom he was dealing departed on their various vacations. Sutherland now found time finally to supervise the redecoration of the Barbican apartment and shop for various items of antique furniture, a hobby in which he had normally little time to indulge.

The story Clement had told him of Alistair Matheson had been banished to somewhere at the back of his mind.

It was a Saturday. Sutherland had been visiting an antique shop on Hampstead High Street but had found nothing to interest him. He was walking up the High Street wondering whether he should take a stroll on Hampstead Heath, something he hadn't done since he was a child, when he saw what appeared to be a familiar figure on the opposite side of the street, walking in the opposite direction.

He made to cross the road, trying to remember who the figure might be. But at the kerb he stopped. The figure had half turned, smiling, to face him.

He found himself staring at the mirror image of himself!

The thought came to mind, This is how Matheson must have felt, this must have been the beginning for Matheson.

And now, for himself.

247

You have been reading a novel published by Piatkus Books. We hope you have enjoyed it and that you would like to read more of our titles. Please ask for them in your local library or bookshop.

If you would like to be put on our mailing list to receive details of new publications, please send a large stamped addressed envelope (UK only) to:

Piatkus Books: 5 Windmill Street
London W1P 1HF

PIATKUS

The sign of a good book